AINSLIE HOGARTH

MOTHERTHING

Ainslie Hogarth is the author of *The Lonely* and *The Boy Meets Girl Massacre (Annotated)*. She lives in Canada with her husband, kids, and little dog.

MOTHERTHING

MOTHERTHING

Ainslie Hogarth

VINTAGE BOOKS

A DIVISION OF PENGUIN RANDOM HOUSE LLC

NEW YORK

A VINTAGE BOOKS ORIGINAL 2022

Library of Congress Cataloging-in-Publication Data
Names: Hogarth, Ainslie, author.
Title: Motherthing / Ainslie Hogarth.
Description: First Vintage Books edition. |
New York : Vintage Books, 2022.
Identifiers: LCCN 2022002957 (print) | LCCN 2022002958 (ebook) |
ISBN 9780593467022 (trade paperback) | ISBN 9780593467039 (ebook)
Subjects: LCGFT: Domestic fiction. | Horror fiction.
Classification: LCC PR9199.4.H6433 M68 2022 (print) |
LCC PR9199.4.H6433 (ebook) | DDC 813/.6—dc23/eng/20220216
LC record available at https://lccn.loc.gov/2022002957
LC ebook record available at https://lccn.loc.gov/2022002958

Vintage Books Trade Paperback ISBN: 978-0-593-46702-2
eBook ISBN: 978-0-593-46703-9

Book design by Nicholas Alguire

vintagebooks.com

Printed in the United States of America
10 9 8 7 6

For Pauly

MOTHERTHING

1

THE NIGHT RALPH'S MOTHER flayed her forearms, a woman in a red dress handed him a business card. I know how *woman in a red dress* sounds because I thought the same thing at first. When I got back to the ICU waiting room with our sodas, I said, what do you mean *woman in a red dress,* a Jessica Rabbit type came va-va-vooming down the hall, pendulum hips pounding sound waves into the souls of dicks?

Christ, said Ralph. No. He cracked his soda and took half of it down. The dress was floor-length, thick cotton, a chaste cream turtleneck underneath. She would bring ambrosia salad to a church potluck, you know what I mean? Secretly hates her nephews, never swims in public. Would definitely take in and gaslight a feeble sister.

I frowned. What do *you* know about ambrosia salad?

I know it's got marshmallows. Isn't that enough? Then he paused, still hitched to the red-dressed woman's memory: nice hair, he said, more to himself than to me. Very—he searched for the right word—*muscly* braid, hanging in front of her shoulder all the way down to her waist. White-blond, but not fine. Fuzzy around her face. And those *eyes*.

What about her eyes?

He started with how the woman had glided up to him, gently, as though he might spook. And he might have, absorbed the way he was: elbows on his knees, fingertips together, mesmerized by the slow jellyfish motion he made with his hands. The card appeared in front of his face, and with a whispered spell, *Thank you, sir,* it was in his hand. He looked up, seized so completely by her bottomless brown eyes that the waiting room's relentless torments—flickering fluorescents, tacky surfaces, cast of swollen-eyed kin—evaporated completely.

Then I arrived with the sodas.

Soda because if either of us has more coffee, our colons are going to disintegrate. But we need caffeine, have to stay awake. Poor Ralph isn't leaving this hospital until he knows for sure whether his mother is going to make it. There would be no *go home and get some rest* for Ralph; no *we'll call you when we have more information.* Ralph just wasn't that kind of son.

"Bottomless brown eyes," I repeat, wincing as I open my can, a mysterious habit with an origin I've buried for good reason I'm sure.

"They were strange. Almost *frothing.*"

I sip my soda, slurp the rim. "Brown hot tubs."

He frowns. "You're thinking about diarrhea."

"Well, obviously, Ralph. You're thinking about diarrhea too."

"Only because I know that you are."

"Perfect body temperature, thick enough to hold you. Might actually be better than water."

He admits with a shrug that it *would* be nice to sag nearly suspended, perfectly warm, in a pool of slack shit. "It would have to be ethically sourced, of course."

"Of *course*. Completely voluntary."

"Naturally. Oh, except . . . well, I don't know." He sinks in his seat, starts to bring his hand to his chin, then thinks better of it, reminded by the conversation, perhaps, of all the bodily fluids that've passed through these rooms. A sensible instinct that I'll now try to keep in mind for myself.

"What?"

"I mean, do we want to lounge in the feces of someone who's old enough to consent to it?"

I shift into the soothing articulation of mutinous AI: "Ethically extracted from exclusively breastfed infants, ORGANICA baths are available in three therapeutic densities, and—" I stop, struck with the realization that hot tubs are essentially artificial wombs: our bootleg attempt to revisit that safest, most perfect, capital-*H* Home, and therefore the worst imaginable thing to be describing to someone whose mother is currently dying. I set my soda down on the side table, drag my hands down my face.

"You really shouldn't do that in here," Ralph warns.

And of course he's right, I've forgotten already. I rub my hands on my thighs instead, cleansing them against the exfoliating grain of the denim.

"Maybe we should get a hot tub," I suggest, a gently used surrogate with deep, jetted seats and a marbled liner.

"I don't know. Seems like a whole *culture*." He whispers the word *culture*.

"*Culture*," I mimic him.

"*Pervert culture.*"

"Plus they're expensive. And where would we find all that human shit?"

He smiles, blows a little laugh from his nose, then glances warily at the mechanized double doors, which would, sooner or later, wheeze open with information about his mother. His genuine love for her is evident in his expression right now, the muscles of his mouth and forehead clenched, anticipating the loss already, all the luster leeched from his skin.

Her depression had become, it sounds awful to say, just so *grating* in the days leading up to this: *cloying* and *relentless,* with no end in sight as far as she was concerned, having refused all forms of medication and therapy, but now that she was quiet, now that she might be gone, Ralph was being pummeled by the full typhoon of his love for her, one of life's cruelest tricks, that the extent of this love waits to reveal itself.

I burrow beneath his arm and he pulls me into him, my length along his, ear against his chest, the top of my head grazing his jaw. I draw his hand to my mouth, take a nip of his skin between my teeth, try to suck the sadness from his pores like venom. He shakes it free as he always does when he's not in the mood for my biting and drinks more of his soda.

Humans like to put their mouths on the things they love. I remember seeing two mothers on the subway once, babies wrapped snug to their chests with their sleep-soft mouths gaping skyward. "Have you chewed on her feet yet?" one mother asked the other. "Oh, *God,* yes," the other mother replied.

I imagine the gentle pressure I'll apply to my own baby's foot one day, practice longingly on my bottom lip, the bounce of her new flesh between my teeth. And how she'll look at me without recoiling, letting me because she doesn't know any better. She won't even realize that we're not the same person, not for a while.

I'll encourage Ralph to have a bite, and he'll be just delighted. Though he likes their necks best, protected by the pressed flesh of cheek and chest. He likes their translucent fingernails too; the indents of their knuckles and knees; how quickly their profound suspicion becomes puzzled amusement becomes wriggling joy.

I'd chew on Ralph's feet if he'd let me; if it'd soften the razor-sharp edges of what he'd just seen: his own mother, still as seaweed, washed up on the basement carpet, which was so saturated in blood that it squished beneath his feet and wrung pale around his knees when he slid to her side. *No, no, no, no,* he muttered, fumbling for a pulse, relieved to find the gentlest vein still whimpering in her throat.

He screamed, *CALL AN AMBULANCE!* So I did, right away, without asking, without thinking. They said, *Nine one one, what is your emergency?* And I said, *I don't know!* I hollered down to Ralph, *Ralph, what happened?* And he shouted back, *Mom's had an accident, there's blood everywhere,* so that's what I told them: *My mother-in-law's had an accident. There's blood everywhere!* Maybe Ralph didn't realize at first what'd happened, thought she'd *accidentally* snapped her veins against that kitchen knife's cold blade.

A short while later a team of paramedics marched in and, with the orderly calm of ants, strapped her to a gurney and pulled her up the stairs. The ceaseless squeal of their bloody boots against the hardwood, the hymnal repetition of their internal communications, Ralph and I helpless as ghosts. We followed them out the front door, watched them slide her into the back of the ambulance. "We're right behind you, Laura!" I shouted, and one of the paramedics nodded at me, as if to let me know that'd been the right thing to say.

And Ralph's reactions to everything up until this point had been predictable because they were always predictable. Ralph Lamb had never contained a single surprise in his whole life. He was grief-stricken on the way to the hospital, as anyone would be, anxious while they worked on her in emergency, as I was—all the understandable and expected behaviors of a devastated anyone.

But then the doctors finally emerge to tell us that they haven't managed to save her. They tell us that we need to make arrangements with a funeral home. That they're very sorry and they did all they could, and do we want the clothes she was brought in? And Ralph, again quite predictably, nods, yes, please, and accepts a clear plastic bag containing her bloody housecoat and nightgown the way a child handles a goldfish won from a carnival, steeled by the magnitude of what's been passed to him. He brings the bag to his face, evaluating its contents: fabric dense and red and wrinkled as placenta. And that's when he, quite unpredictably, hands me the business card from the woman in the red dress. "Can you drive me here?" he asks.

I look down at the card. I don't understand what he's talking about at first. Cheap white stock, black writing you can feel beneath your thumb: *Find out why.*

I stretch my lungs with a gulp of overprocessed hospital air, hold it till I can figure out what to say, but nothing comes.

"Turn it over," he says.

I exhale with emphasis. There's an address on the back, not far from the hospital, along with a picture of a single, lashless eye: almond shaped with a circle and a dot in the middle. I realize that the woman in the red dress with the bottomless browns and the ambrosia salad recipe is a seer—a medium or a psychic or whatever they prefer to be called. I assume they must have a preference, in which case that should really be on the card too. What if we call her the wrong thing and she takes offense and blinds us both with a spell?

I blink at the card for a moment until a man coughs and I remember that it's late, and there are other people in this ICU waiting room: swollen-eyed kin with their feet out, pinching blankets beneath their chins, trying to make their cumbersome bodies comfortable but also polite, aware that if they're lucky, in a little while they'll lose consciousness, sink, spread, off-gas like great snoring molds, beyond reproach.

Everyone is horizontal-ish except for one woman, maybe a hundred years old, peering so deep into nothing that it has to be something. Some *thing*. Every flap of the woman's flesh—lips, ears, nostrils, eyelids—curls inward. One of her unblinking eyes is as cloudy as Ralph's mother's engagement ring, an oval opal, set in four diamond prongs and an elegant gold band, thin as a hair. She'd promised to give it to Ralph one day when he was ready to propose to someone, but when I came along, and he was ready to propose, she didn't want to anymore, didn't think it suited me and maybe Ralph should check out Kay Jewelers in the mall because Irena had told her they were having a pretty significant sale.

She'd been wearing it tonight when she died. I noticed a plump of blood had parted around it, connecting again at her cuticle, restored, dripped whole from her fingertip. The ring was still shimmering despite the mess, commanding the respect of so much blood.

Ralph and I, we were going to have a baby soon. Soon,

soon, soon. Maybe a girl, who'd be proud to inherit her grand-mother's ring, or a boy, who might love someone so much one day that he'll want to claim them with an heirloom. *Selfish not to, Abby, think of the children, Abby.* And an impulse, raw and manic as lightning, screamed through my nerves, sidled the ring up off Laura's bloody finger, and thumbed it deep down into my pocket while Ralph continued to pace, to mutter *no, no, no, no, no, no, no*s, behind stiff hands, blinders, pressed against his temples.

Right away hot, frantic guilt snatched my chest. The impulse cackled, climaxed and drowsy, distracted enough for me to quickly pull the ring back out of my pocket, start to force it back onto Laura's uncooperative hand. But then the front door banged open, the paramedics thundered down, Ralph stopped muttering and turned to me so I had to hide it again, first in my palm then back into my pocket, the mischievous impulse satisfied, cackling harder as it fluttered away.

Back in the ICU waiting room old Opal-eye blinks, turns her head, fixes her gaze on me, like she knows what I did, what's hiding in my pocket, and a cruel thought violates the folds of my mind, residue left over from the evil impulse: *I got the ring anyway, Laura, it's mine now, isn't it, now that you're dead.* I press my pocket, feel the ring's undeniable *there-ness*. I need to close myself off to mischievous impulses and bad thoughts. But it's hard because no one ever taught me how.

"Can you drive me?" Ralph repeats. I'm still transfixed by the card. *Find out why. Find out why. No,* I think, *no, I can't drive you to this quack who's going to take all the cash in your wallet, lie to your face, and play with your pain.* And in his right mind, Ralph wouldn't want me to either. In his right mind, he wouldn't have given this card a second thought; he'd have taken it to be nice of course, because that's the kind of person he is, but then he'd have thrown it away or, more likely, slipped it into his wallet and forgotten about it until it was time to get a new wallet, find it again one day when he was emptying this one and feel low, drift back to this terrible night in the fluorescent ICU and into the bottomless browns of the woman who'd given it to him. I'd ask him what was wrong and he'd tell me what he'd found. I'd make him his favorite dinner from *Secrets of a Famous Chef*—chicken à la king—and give him a nice, enthusiastic blow job before bed.

"Oh, Ralphie," I say, and pull him close and hold him and start to cry, my poor baby, feeling every bit a thirty-one-year-old orphan. But he's not crying with me. He's assumed the posture of a human cannonball: arms stiff and straight down his sides, chin tucked in like a braced nut sack.

I let go and look him over, sniff the sobs back into my head as though saving them for later. "Okay, listen, I just have to say for the *record*." I look around at whatever invisible entity stirs to attention when somebody says that, careful, though, to avoid the old woman's knowing opal eye, which may or may not still be fixed on me. "I don't think this is a great idea. You have no idea who this woman is, Ralph, you have no idea what's waiting for you here." He stares at me, wide eyes battered, exhausted, definitely about to ask me again in the exact same way, *I know, but can you drive me?* And I can't bear to hear it, honestly, if he asks me that way one more time, I'll scream, I really will, scream and startle all the melting, gaseous molds in this waiting room so they sit up and blink at me and shake their heads. "But if this is what you want to do right now, then, yes, I can drive you."

"Thank you." He stands up, chugs the dregs of his soda, and

heads for the exit. I quickly gather our things—jackets, garbage, Laura's bloody clothes—and follow him, retracing our steps from earlier till we finally find the frosted revolving door we came in through.

We both shatter in the freezing cold, confused and isolated as Martians, just landed and groping for truth. I'd felt the same way once before, leaving the casino with Ralph's mother in a daze, short an entire precious night and an upsetting amount of money. On the drive home she wrangled my wheezing anxiety by promising to just let me handle it, swearing on her good-luck charms not to say a word to Ralph, then as soon as we walked through the door, she plopped her plastic bag of troll dolls on the counter and told Ralph just how much I'd lost, *a decent bite out of your savings, the poor thing,* and halfheartedly begged him not to be mad at me: *Go easy on her, Ralph, she's so ashamed.*

I'd never been to a casino before in my life and I haven't been back since. I just got so carried away with the lights and the bells and everything so dreadful and cold and eternal. Ralph's mother loved the slots. She loved her rituals and her charms and I was hoping that I would go with her and she'd win lots of money and she'd love me as much as one of her grinning, big-bellied troll dolls.

"Ralph." He's marching ahead of me, warm huffs caught and held by the cold. Winter never lets you forget you're alive. Maybe that's why it makes people sad. "Ralph!" Louder this time. "Slow down!"

He spins around. "Sorry. I just want to get away from there."

"It's okay." I catch up to him, pass him his coat. "Do you have cash? We're going to need cash I think."

"Oh, good point." Feeding his arms through the sleeves,

ousting the hat I'd shoved there hours ago. He picks it up, smacks the snow from it. Keeps walking toward the car. "How much?" he yells over his shoulder.

"I don't know." I punch my arms through my own coat sleeves, catch my neck with my scarf. "But it can't be cheap, can it? I mean if a massage is a hundred dollars, then surely talking to the dead is going to be more."

"I know you're making fun of me, but that makes sense."

"I'm actually not even making fun of you, I think it makes sense too." I dig my hand into my coat pocket, press the lock button on the car keys a few times. "There." I point in the direction of the honks.

Ralph changes course accordingly. "Okay, so let's just take out, I don't know, two hundred bucks? Does that seem reasonable?"

"Sure." I nod, ducking into the driver's seat. Ralph ducks in after me. "Two hundred, just in case."

Inside Ralph's mother's car it always smells like a refrigerator drawer. Another good-luck charm, a pair of fuzzy pink dice, sways from the rearview mirror. Ralph is nervous, hands clasped and pulsing between his knees, curly hair peeking from beneath his hat in boyish hooks that break my heart.

I drive us to the all-night ATM drive-through, which is new to the area, and usually very busy, but not at 1:30 a.m. on a Thursday night. The big yellow poles meant to guide your car along the side of the building are wrapped in garlands of plastic pine needles, a few in silver-and-red wrapping paper. Happy holidays from the bank, because why not? Though a full month into the new year it seems they should have taken all of this down by now. The charm of holidays preserved only by the fact of their passing, and the bank should know better than to toy with people's emotions this way. Usually institutions are very respectful of these types of rules, and it gives the lingering garlands an ominous feel.

It'd been Ralph's last Christmas with his mother. My first. "I'm sorry I couldn't get out and get you anything," she'd said on Christmas morning, rubbing her knees through her housecoat, every word a great, quivering labor.

"Oh, Mom, that's okay." Ralph reached over, squeezed her hand.

"It's not okay, I should have gotten you something, even something little, everything you've done for me already, moving in here to take care of me and I can't even be bothered to get you a card? I'm just so selfish, just so unbelievably selfish. It makes me sick. I make myself sick."

I stood listening in the kitchen, sipping coffee and Baileys. So far Ralph had been good about not taking the bait, using the various methods he'd cultivated since moving out a decade ago to steel himself against her influence. It took Ralph a long time to become his own person, or at least something resembling his own person, freed from the responsibility of keeping his mother alive. She was always trying to extract compliments from him, forgiveness, reassurance that she was a good person, a good mother. It used to be that Ralph *had* to participate, had to rise to her needling, otherwise she might just go ahead and kill herself. I'd told him she'd never, ever do that—that it was a method, a manipulation, a lie.

"We're going to have a great Christmas," I'd heard Ralph say, but she'd been weeping too heavily to reply.

I spent the morning on Baileys, Bloody Marys in the afternoon, small amounts of controlled, intentional poisoning. "I'm facing my darkest period head-on," Laura said when she'd wandered into the kitchen for her cigarettes, "no drugs, no alcohol." At that point I was deep into the wine coolers, mashing cream cheese and mayonnaise and sharp cheddar together to form a cheese ball, which I ate half of all by myself, then couldn't shit till New Year's.

The ATM machine is beeping, it wants things from me: my approval, my particulars. It rewards my obedience with money, fresh and hot from the oven.

I put the money in my wallet, slide it into my back pocket. Its folded heat emanating into my butt cheek. "God," I say, squirming into the heat a little. "No wonder this place is so busy all the time."

The address on the card is just a few blocks away now. I try to drive as quietly as I can, crunching slow over delicate snow in this middle-of-the-night dark. Some houses are still done up with lights and wreaths and grinning reindeer, and some are not; all of them quiet and sleeping and trusting the world not to fuck with them. Long icicles drool from the snarling grills of parked cars, just in case.

We pull up to a Laundromat in a small brick plaza, unexpected on an otherwise residential street. It's flanked by a dreamily lit florist on one side and an intimidatingly laid-back take-out restaurant on the other, offering only full hot chickens and radioactive slaw.

"This is it," I whisper.

Ralph nods, careful not to make noise. It's unwise to stand out from quiet, middle-of-the-night dark. Like how your body has to imitate water to stay alive in it, arms and legs undulating with the waves to keep your head up and breathing. This quiet, middle-of-the-night dark could drown you if you didn't conform to it completely. Especially here, now, parked in front of this strange Laundromat in the hour after Laura's death. If we're too loud or bright, her spirit, sore and confused, might spot us, smash the car windows, pull us screaming and clawing into a glowing red crack in the pavement.

Then I notice it, wedged in the corner of the Laundromat's big frosty window: the small, lashless eye from the business card. Red. Winking neon.

"Look," I say.

"I see."

We stare at it, huffing steam into the air together.

"So, what now?" I ask.

Ralph stares at it in silence for a long time until he finally closes his eyes, drops his head. "Let's go home."

I squeeze his hand. "Okay."

And I start to drive.

Back to Ralph's childhood home, where he first lived with a mother and a father, then just a mother, then a mother and a wife, and now just a wife.

The house is in a neighborhood of tall, proper homes that'd been erected tight as matches within walking distance of what had been an extremely successful gin distillery. Similar, but not identical, appointed with enough thoughtful detail to harvest boundless loyalty in the employees for whom they'd originally been built.

Now the century-old distillery is a popular event venue. Mostly weddings. On Sunday mornings Ralph's mother would sniff around the alley for discarded centerpieces and flower arrangements, accompanied from time to time by Irena from

next door, and Irena's dog, Cud, a fourteen-year-old Pomera-
nian, which hung from her hip like a colostomy bag and always
had a look on his face like you'd forgotten to wish him a happy
birthday.

Ralph and I would roll our eyes at each other when Laura
elbowed her way through the back door, arms in full bloom,
obscuring her face like the poor disguise of a very inept spy.

"I know you think it's crazy," she'd say, "I can feel your
looks"—slamming the vase on the table for emphasis, actually
mad, not a joke—"but what's crazy is letting a hundred-dollar
centerpiece go to waste!" To Laura, collecting these centerpieces simply made good sense, consistent with the meticulous
penny-pinching she'd employed without shame to buy this
house, and feed her son, and put him through school.

This steady supply of $100 centerpieces, rotting through wed-
ding season, gave the house a damp, jungle-ripe quality you
could taste. I could taste it now, that same humid influence,
but different. Like a river of gore had rerouted itself through
the house on its way out of hell.

I'd half expected the house to absorb the blood, suck it into
its bones and hold on to Laura forever. A little loyalty to its
longtime master, not this sprawling, indifferent mess.

Ralph is staring at the paramedics' bloody boot prints, fingers straight against his temples again, rubbing, as though trying to work an explanation from the chaos of dragged heels
and clipped treads. It was one of the curses of Ralph's brain, to
always be looking for answers, Brain insisting that they existed,
of course, they just had to be figured out, and then everything
would be fine.

"Ralph." I grab his arm, pull him from his trance. "Go to

bed. When you wake up, all of this will be gone, okay? You're not allowed to say no, you have to go."

"Abby, it's two in the morning. You're exhausted."

"You're exhausted. Go upstairs or I'll beat you up." I make a fist and graze it against his chin, then quickly kiss where I've touched him, like, don't make me hit you, baby, because I love you, but I will.

He smiles and hugs me. I seep through his arms like Play-Doh. There's no greater feeling than being squished to death by Ralph. "Good night, my love," I croak, lungs at half capacity. "You're gonna feel better tomorrow."

I feel him nod into my shoulder, then he releases me and goes up to bed.

I open the pantry, all of her cleaning products on the bottom shelf so they didn't leak into anything else and poison us. Laura told me a story about that, a family who kept a leaky drain-clog remover above their potatoes and onions under the sink, slowly poisoned to death by it, the whole family, incremental symptoms like a plague: diarrhea, then vomiting, then motor function decay. Cleaning products are serious chemicals. If you drink them, you die.

I feel angry with Laura that she didn't just quietly gulp some of these neon poisons: a few bundles of froth to clean from around her mouth, maybe, *maybe* some diarrhea, a nice lady-size amount, sub-spa-grade ORGANICA gracefully contained by her pants. A Virginia Slims suicide: Laura wearing a coral button-up shirt and white ankle-length chinos, sprawled peacefully on a spotless kitchen floor, limbs lean, bent ladylike, an empty tumbler glazed in electric blue rolling from her lifeless hand.

I fill a bucket with lemon-scented, biodegradable suds and kneel at the craze of bloody prints. Run my fingers along the stubborn ridges of her dried blood, let my sponge inhale a few rounds of soapy water, then empty it over the mess. The prints liquefy, invade one another before disappearing. Quickly they're almost gone. Maybe with them, their memory: in the morning Ralph will have forgotten about his mother completely, forgot he ever even had a mother. Tomorrow Ralph will be a man born spontaneously, a miracle, appearing with a pop and falling sparkle next to a stream; a wayward water-lily boy, deep in one of the last magical forests on earth: glowing fresh skin speckled with sun, gummy mouth wide and crying from the shock of suddenly being alive, jerking his tight fists in the novel way babies do, curiously protective of their palms. Tomorrow Ralph will be a man raised by the wildflowers and critters of the forest, which will be alive forever as long as we buy biodegradable soap.

When the water in the bucket pinks to red, I empty it, refill the water, feed it more glugs of biodegradable soap. It works everywhere but in the basement, where I discover it's worthless against so much blood-steeped carpet. I scrub and scrub and make everything worse.

One last thing to do before I go to sleep: put the opal ring in my tiny Kay Jewelers box, put that tiny box into a resealable plastic bag, boil a pot of water, and pour it slowly over a concentrated patch of frozen ground in the backyard. This way I'm able to penetrate the soil with a spade, dig a decent enough hole, bury the ring in the trembling shadow of a bare, brain-shaped bush where Ralph will never, ever, find it.

It's nearly morning by the time I wash up and snuggle in

next to Ralph, whose snore skips a beat to squeeze me in his sleep, then resumes as though nothing had happened. I fall asleep in an instant, knowing that downstairs the house is clean, the ring is hidden, and when Ralph wakes up, he'll be a wayward water-lily boy, born from the earth, and Laura will never have existed at all.

2

IN THE BEDROOM that Ralph grew up in, there's a galaxy of glow-in-the-dark stars on the ceiling. There are chips of paint where he'd replaced posters of superheroes with posters of bands and beautiful women, all gone now, rolled up and bundled together and leaning in one of the house's many closets and crannies.

When we first moved in, we talked about peeling up the stars, softening the corners with vinegar, scraping them up with the edge of an old credit card. We use something similar at the Northern Star Seniors' Complex, where I work, to free medical tape from the natural cling of formless flesh, a special tool that only works half as well as a credit card would. We staff commonly complain about all the special tools we don't need but have to use, mock the imaginary men in suits testing things on overripe peaches and unfloured dough, and maybe they've got lots of money in their pockets, but we know that they're morons who have no idea what they're talking about.

Ralph and I also talked a lot about when we'd be moving out: *right away, as soon as possible, the minute she's well again.* Because even though he'd been strong when we'd moved in, strong enough *to* move in—equipped with resources he'd downloaded from a website called the Borderline Parent, and a swear-on-your-life promise from me that I could handle this temporary uprooting—being near her stirred rotten, dangerous things inside him. And this house too, where her health and happiness had been his sole responsibility, where she'd only showed affection when he was sad, only gave attention to his tragedies; it soon began to feel again as though that were all that mattered.

But Ralph was quick and good about consulting his coping materials, practicing his mindfulness, deep breathing, and calming visualizations, reminding himself that he was a whole and separate person from her with a whole and separate life, and that he could love her and support her without turning to dust.

And now she's dead. And the house, though ours, feels as rotten and dangerous as the things she triggered in Ralph. Crumbling tendons of tightly wound wires in the walls, some living, most dead. Sodden cupboards and feathery centipedes and malignant fissures in the foundation. Never loyal, never good, built to indenture servitude to a monstrous brick idol, poorly ventilated, belching effluent into the water supply, weakening resistance with flats of free gin.

Ralph is still asleep: even breathing, steady as a metronome, not even a flinch as I slide, limb by limb from the bed.

I pull my copy of *Secrets of a Famous Chef* from his beaten old bookshelf. My favorite and only cookbook. It's from the year 1930, and everyone you see who's covered in wrinkles and hunched over walkers and lipping bits of soup from a spoon ate stuff from that book and I want us both to be old like that.

I ease the door shut behind me and stand in the hallway, arms crossed over the book against my chest, confronted by Ralph's mother's closed bedroom door. She could still be sleeping in there. The way she could sleep all day long, emerging in the dead of night, her existence evidenced only by blooming ashtrays and vanishing produce and misplaced remote controls, the mischief of a miserable ghost.

I consider opening her bedroom door, a signal to the house that a new era is upon it, but I hate the idea of her empty room being the first thing Ralph sees this morning so instead I tiptoe down the stairs, avoid the creaks, drop my cookbook off in the kitchen, then head all the way to the basement. I dig a retractable knife from a toolbox Laura kept in the laundry room, kneel next to the bloodiest section of basement carpet, and begin to slice, layer after layer, inhaling the carpet's death rattle spew of dust and hair and skin cells, until finally I feel the scrape of concrete vibrate up through my arm and into my teeth. Then the next side, then the next side, until that darkest, most destroyed square of carpet is free. Sweating, I yank it up with both hands, roll it, lean it against the wall. I'll take it upstairs with me, take it right outside to the garbage.

Now there's a gaping hole in the floor, a little pond of exposed concrete, which could maybe be nice if we pulled up the whole carpet and polished it, glazed, so it's natural and shiny. *Modern* is what our Realtor will call it, fingers crossed. But for now I'll just reorganize the furniture, drag Ralph's mother's old corduroy couch overtop to hide it.

I still need coffee and food and to brush my teeth but instead I fall onto the couch, head back, eyes closed, stroke its softness like a pet.

Corduroy couches must have been a big deal back when our moms were buying furniture because my mother had a couch just like this one. I called her Couchy. She was pushed up against a set of windows in our old den that looked out into the backyard. It was winter when we moved into that place, and whoever we rented it from had a set of patio furniture back there all covered in ice and snow. Sugarcoated. A sugarcoated table. Two lines scraped into the sugar snow from a sugar-coated chair on its side, dragged and slammed to the ground.

What happened was Mom's latest boyfriend had got so angry with her he didn't know what to do but scream and slam a chair over onto its side. He must not have been good with his words. None of them ever were, not my dad either, I'm sure. Grown men with no way to communicate anger but scream-ing and punching walls and capsizing chairs and it would have made you feel the slightest bit bad for them if you didn't also hate their guts. I guess that's what rage is: the point where your words fail the power of your emotions. Maybe there can be happiness rage and sadness rage. I am in love rage with Ralph and sometimes it hurts so bad I could knock a patio chair over like that *sloppy, gaping fuckhole, that rotten fucking fuck-ass boy-friend* did.

I remember it was nearly an ice storm out there, everything peaceful and tinkling like a lullaby, as though the furniture were actually nice, not used a thousand times over by decades of poor shitbags like us who'd rented this cold, dripping one-story where even the roaches, quite rightly, had no respect for humans. Wandering unafraid onto the counters, squeezing and selecting butter smears and toast leavings like produce at the grocery store, nodding neighborly to one another as they pass. I'd lift my feet, bullied, watching from the corduroy couch, stroking it like a pet, *Good girl, good girl, good little Couchy.* Cheek against her corduroy skin, eyes closed, dreamy dark, so soft it seemed I could slice through her velvet ridges, scatter gently into another universe.

When a lab monkey doesn't have a mother, a cigarette-smoking man in a white coat and horn-rimmed glasses will give the monkey a rolled-up pair of socks and the socks become their mother. Or, more accurately, the monkey needs a mother so badly that it can project enough mother things onto the socks that they do the trick. Become a Motherthing. *The socks become a Motherthing,* scribbles the cigarette-smoking lab coat man, who tastes his pen and continues writing: *They can hug it and stroke it and put their cheek against it and it calms them down, really calms them down. The way a mother would. A real remarkable effect. The baby monkey's heart rate decreases, blood pressure lowers, all the magic medicine a mother is.*

So that's what I do. The same instinct as that little monkey. Find the soft couch, stroke the soft couch, nuzzle it, let it absorb my whispers, absorb my tears, dilute my squishy rhythmic sadness.

Does the couch resent having to do all this mothering when there's a perfectly good mother storming around the five small rooms of this sugarcoated, roach-infested rental, gathering armfuls of clothes, tossing them one by one out the front door hissing, spit-spraying fury: *Why her? Why her? Why her and not me, what more could I have possibly done? I mean it you sloppy, gaping fuckhole, you rotten fucking fuck ass, you tell me what I should have done, what I could have done to keep you faithful, you goddamn lowlife, you goddamn scumbag. Let you into my life, into my* daughter's *life, and this is what you do.* Useful to her this way. Her *child* for God's sake: sweet, uncorrupted creature he was turning into collateral damage. Maybe the couch does resent having to do this mothering, but it doesn't let on, because it's a better Motherthing than this real mother could ever be.

The boyfriend, he's yelling back: *Aw, fuck you, man, aw, fuck you. Aw, come on, man, don't, don't do that, I said I was fucking sorry, all right? And you know I told you, I told you I wasn't looking for anything serious, all right? I told you that.*

Couchy Motherthing warms, opens, fills my ears with her calmest, brownest warmth. Tries to be the rolled-up socks for me, more mother than couch, because this woman storming from room to room in her peach T-shirt and ripped jeans and overprocessed blondness rubbed to cotton at the temples, she really isn't perfectly good. She's able-bodied. She's not technically or traditionally sick. But there's nothing perfect or good about her.

Yeah, right, then you're here every night, I'm making you dinner and covering your phone bill, your drinks at Chuck's, and you're fucking me like it's serious, asking me—you know what you asked me—you know what you asked me to do and I guess she did it for you, didn't she? I guess she was "open-minded." Leeching off me like I don't have a kid I've gotta take care of. Why don't you come in, why don't you tell her what you did, huh? Tell her who you really are. Abby? Abby, come over here, okay, sweetie? Randy or Ralph or Reggie, *he's got something he needs to tell you, come here, right now.* Long nails, clawing the air, tap-tap-tapping against her thumb. *Come on, come over here,* tap-tap-tap, massive eyes, red rimmed, bulging and delicate like blisters, mascara packed, collected in the corners, foam lapping lakeshore.

She looks so much like a person hurt beyond belief, with her rubbed-to-fuzz hair and her screaming and her blistered eyes. Nothing else matters but her pain, the biggest, loudest thing in the world, unimaginable, a way that people only ever expect to feel maybe once in their life, if ever at all, and maybe never even really recover from. She gets this way all the time. Ripped to shreds when a relationship ends. Is this real? Could this possibly be real? Can real grief even happen this many times to a single human body?

The fuckhole boyfriend outside is freezing cold because the ground is coated in snow, not sugar, and icy air is blasting inside the house and his words are wrought with shivers, *((Come)) ((on)) ((Dani)) ((come)) ((on)) ((don't)) ((bring)) ((her)) ((into)) ((this)) ((maaaaaan))*, just stroke the couch, stroke Mama, eyes closed, breathing the couch in: cold salt, grease, cells, dust, heart rate slowing and slowing and slowing till hopefully it stops. *((At)) ((least)) ((give)) ((me)) ((my)) ((goddamn)) ((coat)) ((Dani)). ((Can)) ((you)) ((toss)) ((me)) ((my)) ((goddamn)) ((coat)) ((please)).* Chattering man, turning blue, waiting for his coat, *needing* his coat, *freezing to death.* Shhhhhhh.

The real mother, not Couchy Motherthing, not the rolled-up socks, but the real mother, she would have loved to see this man die. She would, that's the thing. It's not a joke, it's not an exaggeration, she would have loved for him to drop dead on the lawn and watch the sugar coat him, preserve him hidden till summer. Tell the police that he deserved it because he'd broken a heart that'd already been through more than any human heart should ever have to go through. She'd tell the cops about all the men who'd hurt her; what they'd done and how they'd left her: chest rotted through, flesh fallen from ribs left bare and perfect as a temple, a decomposing monument to her epic loneliness. But what about your daughter? they'd ask. Well, all alone except for Abby of course.

Ralph's mother's couch isn't Couchy though. No Couchy Motherthing, that's for sure. Ralph's mother's couch is just Ralph's mother's couch and I don't get any kind of good feeling from it the way that I used to get from Couchy, so I stop stroking it. Grind my eyes into their sockets with four straightened fingers like a mortar and pestle so they become a fine dust, which I shake down my cheeks, and everything's a little brighter now.

I head up to the kitchen to make coffee, and maybe something restorative from *Secrets of a Famous Chef*. Ralph's mother wouldn't let me keep *Secrets of a Famous Chef* in the kitchen because I made the mistake of telling her where I'd found it: next to a donation bin when I was eighteen, sharing a moldy box with a stuffed rabbit, three well-handled juggling balls, and two teacups stacked saucer cup saucer cup. "Oh, so it's garbage," she'd said, as though that should have been obvious. "We try not to keep strange garbage in the kitchen." And I almost said, *What about your centerpieces?* But I didn't, because at that point I still thought I could get her to love me.

Now that she's gone I can bring it anywhere I want. I set it right on the counter, open it up to the first page:

> As the years roll by and each new generation overtakes the last like a wave, there is one person, immovable, standing foremost as "THE" most Famous Chef in all this world, no matter what circumstance—be it "Prince or Peasant," be it "Palace or

a Thatched Cottage"—wherein we may reside, no famous cook has been able to take her place. Who is this most wonderful cook? This great authority on wholesome cookery?

"OUR MOTHER."

This tested Canadian Cookbook contains only favorite recipes of someone's Mother, every recipe throughout was signed by someone's Mother, the publishers of this book kept this foremost in their minds when having it compiled; not highly seasoned indigestible dishes, but Canadian Home Cooking that some Canadian boy or girl has enjoyed in their Canadian Home.

When she had boyfriends, my mother cooked wholesome, delicious meals, guided by nips from a tarnished teaspoon, the taste of her instincts unmistakable to me. It got to be so I craved her having a boyfriend in the same way I craved her panfried pork chops: hot, juicy slices leaking into homemade applesauce; the crunchy peaks of her shepherd's pie; the ooze of her flawless eggs. The way she could nourish me sometimes, like *OUR MOTHERS* from The Book. Runoff nourishment, really, intended first and foremost for the men; I'd happily lap scraps from the floor around their feet, lick globs from their plates, pick crumbs from their beards. Thriving. Each relationship was like a rhinoceros, and I was the little bird picking moss and bugs from between its cracks.

It's not just recipes in here either. The Book teaches you everything: what to feed a sick person, a baby, an invalid; how to butcher a goat, etch good meat from greedy sinew, find its heartiest parts, the highest quality and calorie, the most succulent and dangerous organ meat. Not that Ralph or I ever used that stuff, what with living in the city, no room to slaughter livestock or need to devour their organs, but it's certainly interesting to read about. And it assures me that this is a cookbook for the mothers of good, happy, wholesome families, with lots of mouths to feed. And that's the kind of mother I am too, even if I'm not yet.

I hear the creak of Ralph's weight upstairs. The gush of the toilet, water slapping the sink. I close The Book, lift both heels to slip it into the cupboard above the stove. It's taller than Laura's cookbooks. Slimmer.

"Hey."

I twist to find Ralph over my shoulder: puffy, sleep poisoned, dangling from his own spine like an impaled king. "Hi, Ralph."

"Thank you for cleaning."

"Of course." I pull out a kitchen chair and pour him a cup of coffee.

"You didn't have to." He sits down, rests his head in his hands.

Didn't have to. Of course I had to. Obviously we weren't going to wake up to a house splattered in his mother's blood. He's thanking me as though I were just another polished representative of the death industry, a cleaning woman who specializes in bloodstains. Black Light Blood Cleaning Services: *That better not be semen!*

Besides his small offering of cool gratitude, Ralph is quiet. Sealed. He can't get comfortable in the kitchen chair so he brings his coffee to the living room, where the seating is equally inhospitable.

I follow him upstairs. He stands at the threshold of his mother's room, door wide open now, runs his thumb along the side of his face and stares unblinking into its quiet gloom, picturing her maybe, how her touch kept him in line like a horse.

Strategic gropes, his shoulders, his arm; conservative embraces; fingers roughed through his hair, kept him believing that she could be well one day, that he could be good enough to save her.

I want to hold him now. Startle him with my arms, press myself into his back. But the way he's stroking himself, thumb along cheek, rhythmic, unfocused, imagining her, how she made him a hero when she needed him that way, helpless when that was better, and instead of rebelling the way some sons might have, Ralph leaned into whatever she needed, knowing she needed it, knowing that if he didn't, her mood might turn. It would be wrong, I realize, to hold him now. As though I were taking advantage of him to make myself feel better. I'm ashamed. Definitely not a good time to bring up moving out. Much better to bring up a baby. Our pure love baby. Imagine I could give him our pure love baby right now.

ABBY: Ralph?

RALPH: *[Leaning against the doorway without turning around.]* Hmm?

ABBY: I wasn't going to say anything quite yet, just to be sure, but . . .

[He knows what she's going to say, he turns around, his smile about to crack his face in half.]

ABBY: Yeah. *[Nodding, smiling.]* I'm pregnant.

[Flinging his sadness off like a heavy coat, he heaves her up and spins in a circle, lets her slide down and kisses her long and slow

and she feels his tears against her cheeks and they're mixing with her tears and life is starting now, life can start now, Laura tried to ruin it but she couldn't because life was happening inside her and it was stronger than Laura ever was or ever could be.]

RALPH: *[Whispering in her ear.]* If it's a girl, can we call her Laura?

ABBY: *[Startled, pulling out of his hug, needing space to find the right thing to say.]* I—um—

RALPH: *[Pulling her back in again.]* I'm kidding.

It would make everything better. I could say it and it would make everything better, Ralph suddenly the happiest man in the world. I could say it and for a little while it could just be true. Because it's not *really* a lie, is it? Not *really*. It's only a matter of time before I actually am pregnant, so what difference would it make if I just tell him now, a little advance on some good news. And worst-case scenario, I don't get pregnant for a while, I have to fake a miscarriage, but by that point he'll be over the worst of his grief, and we'll know that I *can* get pregnant, which is heartening, because it means that I can get pregnant again. And this one will take because it'll be real and soon we'll have a little family of our own and everything will be perfect. I watch him in the doorway, biting my lip, words taking shape in my throat: I'm pregnant, Ralph, *I'm pregnant*. But I can't. I can't do it. It's not right. And also what if it somehow jinxes us, like saying the words out loud will cause my fallopian tubes to fiddlehead and die.

So I say nothing. Watch him sway in the doorway, step

toward the bed, splash into her unwashed sheets, and draw the scent she's left behind into and out of his lungs noisily. I lean against the hallway wall, then slide to sit and listen as he breathes and whimpers and groans and snores all afternoon and well into the night.

3

THE NEXT MORNING, as soon as I wake up, I'm seized by a powerful vision: I haven't taken the ring. It's still with Laura now, nestled on her finger, opal diffracting the cold fluorescent lights that run along the funeral home's low ceilings. Full of hope, gratitude, relief, I bounce to the window that overlooks the backyard, convinced that the dirt beneath the brain-shaped bush will be uniformly frosty and undisturbed. But of course I'm immediately confronted by that horrible patch of meddled soil, shocked that my brain could betray me so cruelly.

I distract myself by going to the store and getting what I need for fried-egg sandwiches. I buy a tin of baked beans, the kind Ralph likes with the wretched nodule of pork fat on top. I buy crunchy Cheetos and BBQ chips and gummy bears and lay them out on our dining room table like a fantasy. Ralph loves food like this but I always give him dirty looks when he eats it.

It's one of my jobs to fret about his arteries, one of the many personal responsibilities that men subconsciously off-load onto their wives, not because they're all jerks but because that's just part of the labor agreement. Unmarried men, it's true, die fatter, younger, filthier, sadder, than their married friends, if they even have friends, because that's another thing a wife is responsible for, friends, except I'm a bust in that department, which is why I have to go extra hard on his arteries. I never even think about my own arteries—I may as well not even have them. Only Ralph's. Thick with plaque. Oxygenated blood falsetto through the tiniest pinprick. Haunting my anointed ear. In a good way, of course!

"Oh my," says Ralph when he wakes up and discovers what I've done. He sits at the table. "So many nasty treasures. You must feel extremely bad for me."

"Oh, I do. I really do."

Ralph smiles, still exhausted, hand hooked heavy to the back of his neck, rotating his head from side to side against it.

"How was your sleep?" I hand him a coffee, which he huffs deeply, then puts down without drinking.

"Eh. Not great."

"You look tired." I hand him a plate with a fried-egg sandwich, a spread of baked beans, which he parts a path through with his fork, then watches fill back up again. "Look at Moses over here," I say, and he looks up from his beans and lays his fork down next to his plate. "Don't let me stop you from performing miracles." I pop a gummy bear into my mouth, and he reaches in too, digs one out of the bag, presses it gently between his forefinger and thumb. I lean across the table, squeeze his forearm. "They say the bears don't feel a thing."

He closes his eyes, wincing like something hurts, then drops the gummy bear, slides his forearm from beneath my fingers and back into his lap. "Sorry."

"What for?" I ask.

"I don't know." He lets his head fall forward, mounted from his chest, a vanquished stag, then shifts in his chair, bones settling wrong, catching, knock-locked at the hinges like a broken toy. "I shouldn't have been so hard on her."

"*Hard* on her? How—"

"I don't know. I knew what she wanted from me. Would it have killed me to have just played along till she felt better?"

"This isn't your fault, Ralph."

He looks up at me, nodding, placating me, I can tell, because what he's thinking is that I don't understand. How could I ever understand? Growing up with the specter of suicide, his every behavior sculpted by its looming threat. His true mother, really, the motherthreat that guided him to be good and fair and capable. And Laura had only made it as long as she had because of him, because of his connection to her, his ability to inhabit her moods and control them from the inside. How dare I, an interloper who recites the textbook *It wasn't your fault*s and *I'm here for you*s, suggest he wasn't responsible, that he hadn't been in control this whole time. This suicide was his fault, he was insisting on that, and any attempt to tell him otherwise would be to undermine the driving force of his whole life up until now. So I won't say that again. I'll let him mourn this loss the way that he needs to for now, as a failure on his part to protect a person he loved very much.

Suddenly Ralph growls, a foreign sound from somewhere deep in his chest, a thing awakened, triggered by Laura's death;

he opens his mouth as wide as it will go, then, furious with his body, how it won't sit right anywhere, attempts to reset his spine by flexing back then snapping all the way forward like a strip of steel. I've never seen him do anything so physically extreme in my life, hair in front of his face, veins retreating into the darkness of his body like some sentient vine.

"Ralph, come on! Take it easy!"

"I should be celebrating!" he shouts. "*We* should be celebrating! Pop a bottle, it's over, I'm free." He stares into the moaning pores of his perfect sandwich, crust softened on one side by encroaching beans.

We're free, I think, *we're free. Let's get out of here, let's fucking go.*

"Nothing feels right. I can't breathe deep enough."

"Here." I nudge a glass of water toward him, but he ignores it.

"It feels like I'm trapped in a jar."

"You're probably gonna feel like jarred Ralph for a while."

He smiles joylessly. "Jarred Ralph."

"I would buy jarred Ralph."

"We appreciate your business." He lifts his fork and puts it back down again. It's as if his body wants to be fed but something in his mind won't let it follow through, stopping just short of the dump and chew and swallow of it. "Is jarred Ralph a cracker spread or a toast spread?"

"Are you kidding me? A toast spread."

"Why's that?"

"Because toast spreads are all classics—butter, jam, Marmite—there aren't many of them. Not really. Cracker spreads are all flashes in the pan. In fact the whole cracker world is trash. A bunch of get-rich-quick schemes."

"What about cheese? Cheese is timeless."

"Cheese isn't a spread though, is it?"

"Cream cheese spreads."

"That's a goddamn lie."

Ralph pokes again at his sandwich.

"Don't feel bad if you don't want the sandwich by the way, you don't have to eat it."

"I should probably eat it."

I shrug and pinch another gummy bear from the bag, a white one this time. Ralph looks out the window, right into Irena's kitchen, where she sits in a chair at her table, bare leg elevated, parting the faux-fur trim of her curiously decadent robe. With one hand she's applying oil of oregano to the mysterious rash that rolls across her legs every winter, a fury of welts, desperate to leave their hard little monuments behind. With her other hand she's blocking a frantic Cud, lunging tongue-first at her legs. Her cell phone lights up, jitters along the table, dangerously close to the edge. Irena rolls her eyes, uses the unoiled knuckle of her pinkie to answer it, then quickly hangs up again. She did that a lot when you were talking to her, answered the phone just to say, "Please stop calling me," then hung up as though nothing had happened.

Ralph, staring at Irena through the window, asks, "Do we write an obituary?" I know what he's thinking. He's thinking he doesn't want to have to go next door and tell Irena to her face that Laura's done the horrible inevitable. He'd rather she read it in the paper, deposit a bouquet of stolen flowers and a sympathy card on the porch.

"Sure. But we don't have to do it today."

"Would a person who didn't want a funeral want an obituary?"

"It might be nice. Just something small."

"We told them to send her to Families First Funeral Home, but that's not the one where the hearse driver flipped her off, is it?"

"No, I think that was Turner and Smythe. But we mustn't forget—she did cut off a funeral procession."

He shoots something like a laugh from his nose, shakes his head, rubs his hands together, anxious and exhausted at once. "Quite a lady."

I nod, hook a sad smile into my cheek. "Ralph?"

"Hmm."

"Let's leave."

"What?" His demeanor congeals. Hard now. Spoiled.

"It's just, well . . ." I can tell by his face that there's no going back, I've said a wrong thing and there's nothing I can do to fix it. "It's just, that was the plan, wasn't it?"

"Sure, at first. But obviously things have changed."

"Have they though?" I drag my chair around the table, closer to him, and he bristles at the sound. "Ralph, I don't want to make anything harder for you, I really don't. You know that. But I don't think it's good for us here. I think we should leave."

"How can you bring this up now—" He presses his palms into his forehead, looking like his body might suddenly jerk again.

"Ralph, how can we *stay*? After what happened, I—"

"I'm not leaving," he snaps, then softens. "Not yet. I'm sorry." He very deliberately lifts his chair, stands, and heads back up the stairs before I can respond.

"Okay," I say to no one, and I sit at the table eating gummy bears alone for what feels like a very long time, one after the other, then two at a time. "He'll be better tomorrow," I murmur to myself, peeling his bean-soaked sandwich from the plate, taking a bite. "These first days are going to be hard. Sleeping through them is actually probably the best course of action." Then scooping up beans, shoveling them into my mouth, "Healthy," fingering crunchy Cheetos past my teeth, dust billowing like from a wood chipper, "Mmm, very delicious," more Cheetos, "God, so good," more everything. I eat until I feel sick, mash the empty Cheetos bag into a hard little knot, rinse Ralph's plate, everything wiped and in its right place.

I dig a pen and a piece of paper out of the junk drawer, set the paper directly in the morning light coming in from the kitchen window, and begin to write.

Lamb, Laura. Survived by son Ralph Lamb (Abigail) and no one else. No other soul in the world had tethered itself to hers by choice, and that should tell you something. She won't really be missed by her strange, scabby neighbor, or the inanimate objects she carted to the casino and worshipped like little gods. She might have been missed by her daughter-in-law, who was ready to love her like a mother, who could have loved a rolled-up pair of socks if she had to, who did *love a fucking couch, for Christ sake. But Laura didn't want that. Despite her faults, Laura Lamb managed to raise the most genuinely good person in the entire world, and for that Abby will always love her, even though the woman was honestly a horrible fucking bitch.*

I quickly tear the paper into strips, tear those strips into squares, crumple the whole thing up in my palm, and bury it in the garbage, catching my reflection in the window, wings of orange from the corners of my mouth. Cheetos. Oh my God. Disgusting.

I cover my ears with my hands. I feel hate for her now. Real hate. I hate her for putting us through this. I hate her for not being able to take care of herself. I hate her for forcing us to move in, then making Ralph feel like he failed her. Punishing him. For daring to be well. For leaving her behind in the dark. For replacing her, with me. And now he's got exactly what he wanted, don't you Ralph, *This is what you've always wanted, isn't it?*

Later I learn a nice thing about Laura—that she was generous with her organs.

"Even her eyes are up for grabs," said the funeral director over the phone, crudely, but only to me. I must subconsciously have communicated that Laura's wasn't a death I was *mourning* exactly, his radar particularly sensitive to those he could drop his exhausting funeral director's decorum with. Director. Because funerals are sort of like little movies, with costumes and makeup and choreography and performances.

FUNERAL DIRECTOR: *[Pleasantly.]* Is there any special clothing you'd like her cremated in?

ABBY: Oh, I'm not sure.

FUNERAL DIRECTOR: *[Pleasantly.]* Is there anything you'd like to say?

ABBY: Oh, I'm not sure.

FUNERAL DIRECTOR: *[Pleasantly.]* Would you like to see the body again before she's cremated?

ABBY: Oh, I'm not sure.

FUNERAL DIRECTOR: *[Pleasantly.]* Would you like to return the ring you stole from her dying body?

ABBY: Oh, thank God. Yes. Please.

4

I FIND RALPH ASLEEP in Laura's room, surrounded by tissues as though he's either passed out crying or passed out masturbating or maybe a little bit of both.

I crawl into her bed beside him, close my eyes, try to breathe his dream into me, in and out and in and out and *in and out and back at the hospital, only this time he's looking at a baby, our baby. Our clean, fresh, brand-new family, all ours and we won't fuck it up, I promise we won't fuck it up if you'll just please give us a family. We bring the baby home with us, to this house, which is still jungle-warm and filled with Laura's blood, a real river of gore coursing through the main floor. We build a wall of baby gates around the river and seem to trigger an infestation. Demons. Hidden before. They slowly breach the surface. Walls of clenched teeth, grouted red in the cracks, staring at us with ice-blue eyes and all-black eyes and milky opal eyes like the woman in the waiting room, waiting, waiting for us to knock over the gate one day so one of them can reach out, grab our baby, tuck her under its arm, dive beneath the gore water and back to hell again. An offering for Satan, he'd eat our baby, crack a limb from her torso, wrap his whole mouth around it, then pull out a clean, fleshless bone, again and again and again till she's just rump and belly, the best for last. Burping up bits of innocent soul for a couple of hours, then nap and dream, smiling, of our pain.*

Ralph's eyes. I don't know when he woke up. He pulls me close to him, kisses me in a very precise and deliberate way, like he's nipping crumbs from my lips and cheeks. It's different, everything muted like he really is in a jar. His sleep-warm hands find their way between my legs, which I spread to accommodate, turn around, tuck in closer to him so I can feel him getting harder, and I press up against it, his wonderful penis, my absolute pet, and I'm so relieved and so happy. She's happening. I can feel her already, her shape inside me, aching to fill with cells and growth and pudge. Ralph pulls my pajamas down and he pulls his down and glides himself inside me from behind and slowly, slowly in-outs until he comes and kisses the back of my neck and rolls out and immediately falls asleep. I know that tonight I'm an elaborate sedative, but that's okay, because it also means that he's not mad at me anymore for wanting to leave.

I hold his stuff inside me as long as I can, like maybe semen works like mouthwash, hold it and swish it around, gargle with it, then finally when I feel like its potency must be spent, I let it ooze into a tissue from a box next to the bed.

Pray for Cal, please, Cal, please, Cal, find a nice, squishy, comfortable place to root, fuck me up in there if you have to, tear me to pieces if it helps you find your nest. Cal. Cal if it's a boy or a girl. Cal is a perfect name because you can't make it any shorter, and when your name has an easy short form, that puts you at a disadvantage.

For example, my name is Abigail and people call me Abby very easily and it does this thing to me where I like them right away. Makes me feel like I know them already and that they like me already. That we're close and I can trust them. Like, even if I were speaking to some prisoner through thick glass, a giant villain with a million face tattoos and a big scar from the corner of his mouth to his ear, if he called me Abby, I might smuggle something in my vagina for him next time I visited, keep him liking me because now that I've got him liking me, he's not so bad. Now that I've got him liking me, I need it to live. So Cal will just be Cal and he or she will always know for sure just how much they should trust someone.

5

RALPH WAKES UP FEELING BAD. Worse than yesterday, more quiet, more exhausted, leaving clouds of misery in his wake thick enough to chew on.

We're going to the funeral parlor today.

He pours himself a coffee and sets it on the kitchen table, asks me if I can just write the obituary, something short and simple:

Lamb, Laura
June 1, 1964—January 23, 2019
Beloved mother of Ralph Lamb (Abigail). The family would like to sincerely thank the nurses and staff at St. Joseph's Hospital who worked very hard to save her life. Arrangements will be handled by Families First Funeral Home.

Ralph looks it over and hands it back to me, approved, then shuffles to the living room, where he descends, knees, then trunk, then head, onto the bit of rug between the coffee table and the armchair. He turns his head, closes his eyes, lays a hand over his face. His socked feet are all I can see from the kitchen table, toes touching, fallen apart at the heels.

Depression becomes this house, where it's thrived in one form or another for at least thirty years: dark, claustrophobic rooms where bad thoughts collect like tide pools, slimy, brackish hazards, impossible to avoid.

And everything sealed. As though this miserable darkness were some precious vapor that Laura didn't want to lose to a cracked window or an open door. I caught Ralph doing it this morning, what she used to do, in the living room—pinching the curtains together down the middle tight as piecrust. My chest knotting as he pinched up and down the curtains with both hands, milking them, knuckles white around fistfuls of fabric.

He's doing it now, up from the floor, still too much light getting in.

"Ralph."

He turns to look at me, big, anxious lemur eyes, begging me to pretend with him that this is a completely harmless thing to be doing all the time. I feel caught, trapped by his begging eyes, so instead of pulling his hands off the curtains, I smile like nothing's happening. After all, it's part of a wife's job, in the labor agreement, to pretend to herself and the world that her husband is perfectly sane.

He lowers his head, scurries up the stairs to get dressed.

I stare at the curtains, murky down the center. Too much human touching will change a thing. In fact, my mother once told me that the reason penises are a slightly different color from the body is because of how much men touch them. Normally it would make me laugh to think about, but it's hard for me to laugh right now, with Ralph despairing the way he is. Craving dark like her.

He's not like her. He's not like his mother. He's not like his mother because he has me, and I will save him. We're special, Ralph and I. Put together by good forces in the world and being in love like this is our real and actual job in life, everything else just maintenance. This love makes it okay to be stuck here on earth; makes it okay that these routines and aches and obligations are life and that's just it; makes you open your eyes and see every little bliss a moment has to offer: Ralph and Ralph and Ralph and Ralph. In a moment. Is a moment.

I can cure Ralph. Because it's what I was born to do. *Remember that, Abby, vanquishing this depression is your true calling as a wife.* Just like every woman in a television commercial has a true calling—kill the bacteria and save your family; buy the healthy snacks and save your family; use the perfume and save your family. Just like those women, I have a calling, and I am listening for it, and I'll try out new things every day: make perfect fried-egg sandwiches and save your family; clean up the blood with biodegradable soaps and save your family; tear up the carpet and bury the ring and put him to sleep with your body.

I take a murky living room curtain in each hand and fling them apart. Light impales the room. I open the front-hallway curtain, then the shade over the kitchen sink, spears of winter bright. We're critters in a crudely perforated shoebox. This is how we'll survive. Because the dark isn't good for anyone. It wasn't good for Ralph's mother, that's for sure. Not good for

Ralph. And it's not even good for me, who's perfectly healthy in the mind.

"What was that?" Ralph hollers from upstairs.

I've got my coat on, sitting with a boot between my knees, digging up the laces. "Huh?"

"I didn't hear what you said!"

"That's because I didn't say anything!"

Ralph appears at the top of the stairs, ready to go, a dress draped over his arm. "Really?"

"Really. Except I will say now that we've gotta be at the funeral parlor in fifteen minutes." I don't mean to sound annoyed, but I'm hot in my coat and there are papers to sign and checks to drop off and obituaries to hand over.

Ralph makes his way down the steps slowly, puzzled. "I was positive I heard you upstairs."

He's done this a few times since our first night here alone, shouting to me from some other floor, asking me to repeat what I've just said. He's unnerved by it, I can tell, spends the few seconds postcorrection wandering the memory in his mind.

"That's the one?" I nod at the dress, knocking him out of it.

"Oh." He lifts it, limp over his arm like an injured wing. "Yeah. You think it's too late to put her in it?"

I run my fingers down the fabric and smell cigarettes. Her blue dress, the one she used to shuffle around the house in all the time. "I don't think so." I take it from him while he puts on his coat and boots.

The funeral parlor is a little far, but traffic is cooperative and we make it in time. We pull into the driveway. It's a large house, somehow both tall and sprawling, with tidy siding and fine details around the windows. It's the kind of house that might belong to a family of attractive, upper-class sociopaths: a brilliant son who throws dark, bacchanalian parties; an impossibly gorgeous and perverted daughter; a whole neighborhood of sinewy mothers and cruel fathers.

A blanket of fresh snow, better snow than what falls in our neighborhood, whiter and softer and thicker, like something you want to leave your teeth marks in. A perfect square rolled out over the lawn and the roof, strips of it along the bolt-like branches of a birch tree. The driveway and walk are clean and dry, enchanted somehow, existing in a different season.

"It's nice," I say, and slam the driver's-side door shut. Ralph is already out. He dips his foot into the square of puffed snow on the lawn, pulls a defiant dusting of it back onto the perfect driveway. "Ralph," I scold. He twists his mouth in a wicked, reckless way.

We walk to the front porch, where a very tall, wind-whipped blonde is just stubbing out a cigarette with the rubber end of her wooden crutch. Her foot is encased in a plastic boot, exposed toes blue-bare and wiggling. Despite her compromised mobility, she opens the front door for us, waves us off when we try to help or thank her.

She follows us into the hushed foyer, warm and thick and beige, baked carpet, baked light, Baked Lay's, for indulgent ladies, so good you'll think they're bad. But then she disappears, and I can honestly say I have no idea where or how she managed it so quickly with that boot.

A small man who seems to wear his flesh, hoisting and adjusting it like a child in his father's suit jacket, is standing behind a chest-height desk. He comes around and greets us. "You must be the Lambs." He extends his hand, shaking it free of its flesh sleeve, connecting first with Ralph, then with me. The top of his head barely comes to my chin, but he's practiced a way to make it seem like he's not looking up at you. "How are you both?"

"We're hanging in there, hey, Ralph?"

Ralph nods, smiles, takes off his hat with one hand and with the other shakes his hair back to its pre-hat shape like time travel. "We brought this." He presents his arm, lifeless folds of blue dress draped over it as if the woman he'd been lugging around this way has suddenly disappeared.

"For Laura," I add. "Obviously."

"Very good," says the small man, whose name, like that of so many serial killers, is Wayne. He takes the dress from Ralph, hangs it on a rack behind him, jots a number down on a Post-it, and sticks it to the sleeve. I can't help but imagine the mortician forcing her crudely stitched arms through the long journeys of these sleeves, fabric catching on sharp blue surgical suture a source of acute annoyance.

"There should have been a piece of jewelry too," says Ralph, already antsy about the ring's whereabouts, missing obviously, from the bag of bloody hospital clothes. "An opal ring?"

Cal's cells eddy inside me. Nausea. Is this nausea? *Real* nausea like real pregnant women get? Another flurry from Cal. The ring, of course. She knows it's for her. And Ralph will understand when the time comes. At the very least he'll buy the eventual story I concoct of having found it in the house somewhere. And at that point all this rawness will be long since scabbed over, healed-ish. We'll have a child by then, our little Cal, and Ralph will love her so much he'll be happy for her to have it, maybe even thankful that it'd been misplaced so long ago because now everything has worked out for the best. I'll say a silly sort of thing he's come to expect from me, I'll say, *Maybe Laura left it behind for her.* I'll feel sick to have said it, but Ralph will smile and, back to his consummately realistic self, roll his eyes, and I'll know he's happy to be considering the possibility, however absurd, that his mother had been aware in some way of our little Cal.

Wayne furrows his brow, draws his bottom lip over the top. "An opal ring." He hurries back behind the desk, shuffles through Laura's file. "Opal ring, opal ring." He finds the paper he'd been looking for, scans it as he speaks. "We didn't receive a ring from the hospital."

"There has to be a ring," says Ralph, both hands on the desk, his voice winding up higher, tighter. "She never took it off."

"Don't worry," Wayne hums, glancing at Ralph's hands on his desk. Wayne is a man deeply familiar and innately responsive to the sounds and energies of someone about to cry. "I'll reach out to the hospital. Things like this, little things, they often get lost in the fray. Usually they end up in the laundry." He chuckles.

I wonder now if we're supposed to tip him, or if Wayne just always seems like a man expecting a tip. Wayne. He isn't built like a Wayne. I realize I've never before met a person whose name doesn't suit them.

"If we're able to retrieve it, would you like her cremated with it?"

"If?" Ralph's whole body darts forward at once like a school of fish. "No, no, no, it has to be there."

"When. *When.* Don't worry, we'll find it. Would you like her cremated with it?"

"Yes, please."

"Wait, are you sure, Ralph?" I interject, trying to feel out how he might respond if I just came clean now: *Are you sure, Ralph, because actually I pried it from her cold, stiff finger the night she died, so if you want it, it's all yours. You're welcome!* "Might be nice for you to hold on to."

"I'm sure." Ralph pulls his hands back and into his pockets, bites his lips together. "Honestly I can't stand the idea of her without it."

I nod. Fuck. Fucking fuck. I wanted to put it back, I tried to put it back, despite wanting it so badly, I was going to put it back, even though I deserve it, it's my ring, she promised it to Ralph and me and Cal, in a way. I try very hard to clip the network of irrational connections proliferating inside my brain: *He doesn't want you to have it either, he agrees with her that it shouldn't be yours, that it's too good for you, that you're more of a Kay Jewelers type than a vintage-family-heirloom type. He still loves you, of course, he's still happy with you, but that's what he thinks of you, he chooses her over you, he chooses her over Cal.* But, Jesus Christ, Abby, that's not what this is. It's her ring, it belongs to her, she feels naked without it. Like a security blanket. Ralph doesn't want to glide her into that great, fiery oven without her security blanket. It's his *mother* for God's sake. His *mother*. And that means something to people.

"It won't burn," says Wayne to me, the asshole who dares to care about a piece of jewelry at a time like this. "It might need some TLC, of course, but it won't burn. You'll collect it along with her ashes when the time comes. I understand what you're saying, Ralph, you want her"—Wayne looks up, eyes tracking the word as though it were actively trying to evade him—"you want her *whole*"—he smiles—"for this unpleasant necessity. A lot of people feel that way. That's why I asked. So often we find closure in the symbolic. The *rituals*."

Ralph nods. "Exactly," he says. "The *rituals*."

And I nod, a show of understanding. But what I'm actually understanding is that I would have ended up with the fucking ring anyway. I've done nothing but create unnecessary pain for my sweet Ralph. I wish it were me gliding into the oven instead.

"We'll find it," says Wayne with so much conviction even I believe him.

Ralph is ever so slightly lifted by this, I can tell. "Can I see her?" he asks, which surprises me in a way that's hard to pinpoint. It's not as though he's squeamish, or so staunchly rational that he wouldn't want to say goodbye to her earthly vessel before it's gone for good—though he might make some self-deprecating joke about it on the car ride home. More so it felt like his asking to see her violated a fundamental tenet of Ralph's moral code: thou shalt not ogle a person's body without their consent.

"Of course! I mean, we won't be giving her the full viewing treatment, unless of course you'd like to upgrade." Wayne winks at me, the whore. "But she looks very peaceful."

Ralph turns to me, sensing what I'd noticed, that this request was out of character for him somehow. "I think I just need a minute with her."

"Of course." I squeeze his arm. "Good luck."

Ralph braces his whole body, starting with his face, then follows the boy-in-a-man-suit down the Baked Lay's hallway, through a door at the very end.

Alone in the lobby. Trusted by everyone even though I'm

a thief. It's too warm in here. Dry. Overbaked. I take my coat off, hang it over my arm. Ride the long, crestless wave of crown molding, down into the carpet's dense pile. Funeral parlor, beauty parlor, a place where divine transformation occurs. The same could be said for ice cream parlors: *For the divine transformation of your mood, try pleasuring your mouth hole with two sacred scoops. I scream, you scream, we all scream for the Good Lord's cream.* Tips appreciated. Thx 4 tipping. Feelin' tipsy? Tipping is hot. Tip your funeral director (not your canoe!).

Cal will know to never take ice cream from a priest, I think to myself solemnly, pressing a hand to the little mass of Cal cells making itself known in my uterus.

I nudge through a set of double doors to my left, wander into a big room with lots of wooden chairs folded up and leaned against a wall, a few pulled open, one of them occupied by the woman with the broken foot. She's got one crutch lying on the floor, the other turned upside down between her knees, and she's working the grime and ash of her cigarettes out from the rubber pad with a toothpick, scraping what she retrieves onto a tissue laid over her thigh. There's something unsettling about her. A bad omen. You wouldn't want to catch her steady eye in the boisterous crowd celebrating a ship's maiden voyage. There'd be some well-known limerick about her already, except I can't think of anything good that rhymes with *orthopedic boot*. The best I can do is *orthopedic boot, sailor take note*, except for the rhyme you pronounce *note* as *noot*. It's very bad. I'm ashamed of it.

Ralph is marching back already, Wayne struggling to keep up, flesh bustled in front like a bride. The woman hears them coming, turns around, startled. She hadn't been expecting to find a person standing behind her. For a split second she has an opal eye, like the woman in the ICU waiting room, like Ralph's mother's ring, then she doesn't. She has blue eyes, light and striking, but not cloudy, not opals.

She turns her attention back to her crutch before I can apologize.

Ralph is in the lobby, framed by the double doors I'd wandered through. He's teary, searching for me. "Abby," he exhales, grabs my arms, and pulls me into his quietest whispering range. "That wasn't her," he says just barely.

My stomach becomes lead. "What?"

"It wasn't *her,*" he hisses deep into my ear.

"Are you *serious*? Wayne?"

Wayne has planted himself behind his desk again, walking through a stack of papers with his fingers. "I know, one minute." He pulls a paper out—"Here you go, Ralph"—slides it toward us. "I realize how jarring it can be, how different our loved ones look at this stage, especially without our patented skin rejuvenation treatment and full body-viewing package, it can be a bit of a . . . a *fright.*"

I lead Ralph toward Wayne, to the paper, Laura's death certificate—the correct date, time, location of death, completed and signed by the very doctor who delivered the bad news. "I'm sorry," says Wayne.

Ralph shakes his head, face set in hard, hostile denial. "I don't care what it says," he hisses. Regular, rational Ralph would have been mortified. "That's not her. She didn't look like that. And she wore a *ring,* all right? She never took it off, there's no way it would just *fall off,* it was practically fused to her skin."

That's true. It *had* been difficult to pull up, left a deep red indent around her finger, which living flesh might have filled by now, but Laura's flesh, a bit preoccupied in those last few hectic hours, would have held the shape like clay.

"I promise you, Mr. Lamb, I'm going to do everything I can with the hospital to find it. In the meantime, why don't you check at home? Maybe it could be in her things, or maybe she took it off before—"

"Listen, do you want me to take a look at her?" I ask Ralph.

"Could you? I just . . . she doesn't look like herself, and she's not wearing the ring. Some kind of mistake has been made. This doesn't feel right."

"I'll go look." I nod at Wayne to lead the way. We leave Ralph wringing his hands in the waiting room, pass several white doors until we stop at one. Wayne gestures at the knob and steps aside. When I open it, I'm assaulted by a gust of cold, embryo-scrambling chemicals that somehow Laura seems personally responsible for, lying there on the metal examination table, covered from the collarbone down by the kind of drop cloth you'd use to protect your furniture from paint, or from dust in an old castle where certain wings are off-limits for strange and mysterious reasons.

Your own grandchild, I think, *you'd poison your own grandchild with embalming chemicals.*

Naturally, she doesn't respond.

The room is clean and blue, with a pair of long fluorescent bulbs flickering across the ceiling. There's a cluttered tray of instruments next to Laura, metal prods and tubes, scissorlike tools with unexpected ends—blunt, curved, toothed, a few very sharp. Scraps of shaped plastic and snipped foam fill a metal dish. What she must have been through since we last saw her.

And then I think, *Fuck. Fuck, fuck, fuck.* I should have brought the fucking ring; alone with her now, I could have shoved the fucking thing right back on her finger, and this whole thing would be over, motherfucking *fuck.* Instead, here I am, watching an almost unbelievably perfect moment to right a catastrophic wrong just float by. And here's Laura, not giving a fuck about her ring anyway, what with being poked and drained and shaped with foam, and definitely Laura, so obviously, undeniably Laura, Ralph in some sort of seriously profound denial to have looked at this body and thought that it *wasn't* Laura. Her hands, despite their ringlessness, were especially recognizable, fingers long and elegant; it had actually been a pleasure to watch her smoke, tamp ash, obliterate the thicker clouds with a cupped palm. I run my finger along her knuckles, along the pale groove left by her ring, realizing that I will miss her, maybe not the way she was, but the great potential we might have had, the way I'd imagined things before I got to know her. A second chance for a real mother, a grandmother for Cal, someone who would love her as much as Ralph and I do. She would have come around, I know she would have. Things would finally have been good between us all once Cal was born. *If you could have just waited, Laura, nine months, nine measly months, everything would have been better.*

Wayne clears his throat from the doorway and I can't help but think that a premium package would have bought me a little more time. "It's not uncommon," he says quietly. "It's a hard thing for people to accept, but he'll be all right."

Back in the lobby Ralph is anxious, fidgeting.

"It's her," I say.

He slumps and nods, my word more than enough, and signs the necessary paperwork in silence. I hand Wayne his check, and the obituary, keeping my eyes peeled for the woman with her crutch, but she never reappears.

In the car again, Ralph and I make our way through the traffic in dashes. I try to distract him. "She did look weird though." I turn my head, but keep my eyes on the road. "I can definitely see why you thought it might not be her. Honestly."

"It's fine." He turns to the window, pulls his hat down over his face so I can hear him struggling to breathe through it the whole way home.

6

WE'VE HAD SEVEN DAYS to cram our grief into. Bereavement days, then back to work. It's nearly impossible to organize grief at all, let alone so it fits nicely into seven twenty-four-hour units. Especially when you're Ralph, raised by a difficult single mother like Laura and you need the first few twenty-four-hour units to understand why you're so sad at all and the remaining twenty-four-hour units to tear the house apart searching for an opal ring that you'll never, ever find, calling the hospital, screaming for justice, hurling likely baseless legal threats at whoever answers the phone, then collapsing onto the living room couch, grief-weary, defeated, and definitely not ready to go back to work tomorrow.

They cremated her without the ring of course, and I felt so stupid and guilty that I nearly chewed my tongue off. I wish I could give him my bereavement days but unfortunately it doesn't work that way, like so many things earned but not yours.

On our last bereavement day I make shepherd's pie for dinner. Once Laura claimed to have no idea what shepherd's pie was, and Ralph, shocked, explained it to her in great detail, emphasizing every ingredient with the edge of his hand against the table, *potatoes, ground beef, carrots,* reminded her *incredulously* of a particular occasion in which he was certain, *certain,* she'd even *made* it. I frowned, as skeptically as I could get away with, knowing that this was all an act, a trick she performed, feigning ignorance of something common so she could be the focus of his great, stunned attention. Gently corroding his confidence in her ability to survive without him.

I lift a strikingly perfect cube of pie from the dish and slide it onto Ralph's plate: meat strata dense and rich and dark; carrots chopped painstakingly to the exact dimensions of the peas; potatoes whipped so thoroughly, peaked so uniformly, I feel a sudden pang of sadness that robots will never get to experience this kind of pride in their work.

I step back, shoulders tense, waiting for the relief of his praise. Instead of being impressed by the near-mechanical perfection of my pie, or charmed by my goofy, hopeful affect, he's filled with shame. Because he's not hungry at all and is now disgusted with himself for not being able to just *say* so instead of letting me go to all the trouble of making this extraordinary pie.

"Oh, Ralph"—I ignore the spasm of revulsion he tries to hide when I squeeze his arm—"it's fine." I pull my hand away, wipe my repulsiveness off on my shirt. "I don't mind at all!"

Soon. Soon, soon, soon, he'll sit down at the table and I'll walk toward him with a cool plate in my hand, lay it down in front of him, and there, across the center, a positive pregnancy test. He'll look up at me with tears in his eyes. *Really?* And I'll nod vigorously, smiling. And he's not sad anymore. He's a greedy mass of sentient joy, sucking me helplessly into his joy, spraying the house in bright, sparkling joy, transforming it into a place that's not so bad to live after all.

I drag his plate toward me, eat both perfect pieces of shepherd's pie, hoping that the sound of my fork scraping against the plate reminds him that despite this meticulously executed pie, I am not a robot.

Before bed I let my fingers dance under the running tap, an attempt to conjure enough heat to wash my face. The sink is plugged and filling. The shepherd's pie sits in me like a planet, every organ addled by its great, fiery mass.

I have a memory from a summer I barely saw my mother. The same summer she made me a house key and taught me how to use the microwave. For the first few weeks I played alone, nervous to encounter the kind of adult who might ask who I belonged to. But over time I realize that no one cares. I let myself be absorbed by games of tag at the park. I accept a Band-Aid from a strange mother when I fall from the monkey bars and report the injury to no one when I get home that night. I join a crowd of toasted children to slurp hot water from a hose in an unattended yard. Joints scuffed and round as tennis balls, kneeling in the grass, everyone waiting their turn. A few weeks later, another crowd. Almost exactly the same except instead of waiting our turn to nurse from the glugging end of a hose, we're staring at a dog, clipped by a speeding car, sputtering blood, and waiting for someone to come and kill him with love.

"What's that?" Ralph shouts from behind his mother's closed door.

The sink is almost overflowing. I turn off the tap, open my

mouth to respond, *I didn't say anything, Ralph, for fuck's sake!* But instead I plunge my face into the now uncomfortably warm sink, feel my brain tingling, begging for oxygen while I think of the water we craved and the dog we found and the crowds they both drew that exhilaratingly lonely summer.

7

WE FIND OUR OLD MORNING ROUTINE waiting for us on the other side of Bereavement Week. I wake a little earlier because I leave a little earlier. I'm finished with the bathroom and the toaster and the cream and sugar before Ralph is even out of bed. I hear him from downstairs—Laura's wincing bed frame, floorboards, the toilet and the sink and the whisper of their pipes—before I head out the door, catch the subway, which deposits me just a few blocks from work.

Ralph has a very good job. He manages software that tracks and organizes patient files. Over six thousand hospitals, clinics, health centers, and old age homes (old age parlors?) across the country use it. We even use it at the Northern Star, where everyone knows it's run by my Ralph and so keep quiet around me on the rare occasions it gives us trouble. He's in charge of a small team of people who fix bugs and plan updates, and together they make the software better and better all the time. It's like a living, breathing thing, this software, a superhuman athlete that a bunch of rich people have invested in, and Ralph and his team all work together to keep it in peak physical condition.

And Ralph is such a good boss. The team gets him nice Christmas gifts, and there's always lots of inside jokes in the card. They confide in him about their lives and careers and he remembers their partners' names and buys whatever confectionery their kids sell to raise money for soccer uniforms and chronic disease.

They sent over a gift basket when they heard about Laura, an expensive one with obscure cheeses and crackers so irregularly shaped only a few fit in the box; hard cookies; savory jams; the type of bitter chocolate that scandalizes unsuspecting children—all exploding from a knuckle-knit wicker basket that in itself was a treasure. Laura would have been absolutely floored by this basket, nothing in the world would have made her feel prouder of her son than the quality of this basket—the amount of *money* his employees spent on him (and her indirectly), the thoughtfulness, the superiority, the *class*. That her son led the exquisite tier of people this basket represented, it actually made me feel a bit sad she wasn't around to see it. I thought of putting it in the basement maybe, a little monument to her, the way people memorialize the nasty corners and cement medians and telephone poles that unlucky cyclists and drivers have lost their lives to.

Ralph was the first person in his family to go to college. Laura helped him pay for it, clipping coupons and patching crotches and saving every penny from her job as a 911 dispatcher, where she collected horrible stories for every occasion: the man who tripped and fell into his open dishwasher, blinding himself on the utensils; the little girl whose birthday candles gobbled up her pigtails, injuring both her and a little brother who got caught and trapped in her panic. Laura didn't mean to collect these stories. She couldn't help it. It was her brain, ravenous for the peace they brought, because to know them, to remember them, to pass them on, would prevent them from ever happening to her or Ralph. Her tender amygdala, battered by the stories, held captive by the steady paycheck; her poor son, battered by the stories, held captive by his tormented mother.

Everyone is especially nice to me when I go into work this morning. Linda from the front desk even gets up and gives me a hug. As usual, her face is laced on with an impossibly snug French braid, a seam down the back of her head so flawless it implies that someone else must have done it for her, a mother who she lives with, sitting behind her, thighs peeled apart, Linda leaning back into them, holding her neck straight against the familiar tug. I feel both jealous of Linda and embarrassed for her, a woman her age with a braid like that.

She lets go, makes her way back behind the desk, settles back down to her bagel. "Mrs. Bondy's been missing you."

"Oh, that's nice. I've been missing her too." I smile. "Is she up?"

"No. Rough night last night. Carol had to give her a sedative."

"That's too bad."

Linda's face pinches with sympathy. She collects a few nonexistent crumbs from the desk with the grease of her pinkie—this is meant to indicate that she's out of things to say, which is fine because so am I.

Poor Mrs. Bondy. She's worse when I'm not here. If not physically worse, then fussier, more difficult, only wanting me to help dress her and feed her and wipe her clean, showing me her smile, all those shabby little teeth her very own and rare as pearls around here. In my head I call her my baby.

I've been tending to my baby's moods and fluids for about a year so far. Since around the same time we moved in with Ralph's mother.

It was a hard transition, leaving our easy, comfortable apartment, shuttering ourselves in with Laura's shadowy clutter. But Laura was Ralph's mother and she needed help, and I am a loyal, loving wife. In an old-timey saloon, the men would call me *a good woman,* watch me from a distance as I scrub tables, patched with flush, blowing wayward curls to smithereens with my precise and perfect mouth.

It was Mrs. Bondy's daughter I'd met first, Janet, who wheeled her into her new room and immediately started complaining: the thoughtless layout, the tiny bathroom, the temperature, humidity, smell, reacting to the air around her with disgust. *What is that rattling, is the heater broken? I assume you'll provide a dehumidifier to manage this moisture. I won't be paying extra to make the* air *adequate, you understand? Good air is a given, I would expect, good air shouldn't cost extra for God's sake.* Mrs. Bondy's face assumed a deep, apologetic frown, which I acknowledged with a smile.

When Janet finally left, Mrs. Bondy was nervous. She rubbed her knuckles, chewed at her thumbs. I sat and talked with her forever, learning about how she wanted her room set up, where she'd lived before, how Janet was her only daughter, always a handful but she meant well, recently divorced, poor Janet, really a nice man but Janet had had problems with a daughter from his first marriage, a difficult girl since the divorce, and Mrs. Bondy knew all about difficult girls.

Her voice was low. Notched. It made you think of a bread

knife working its way through some stale loaf. The result of a certain type of throat cancer, in remission now, thankfully, but the damage was done: her vocal cords would likely deteriorate over the next few years and she was scared of the day no one would understand her anymore. I told her that we could develop some communication techniques, hand gestures for *help, hungry, thirsty, pain, cold, hot.* And some funny ones for *shut up* and *this food sucks* and *bring my car around, Jeeves.*

Mrs. Bondy set up a mirror next to her bed so that first thing in the morning she could pull a brush through her hair and apply makeup. It was incredible the way her trembling hands found the stillness they needed for liquid liner, a catch finding its groove and gliding into place. Every six weeks I helped her disguise her roots, the same darkest red as the rest of her hair, then I'd comb hot walnut oil through to her ravaged tips. I know that this particular kind of touching, grooming, is the best medicine of all, a key to longevity that the wisest, most perceptive women have preserved from our monkey ancestors.

She often talked, when she was able to, about the beauty parlor she'd owned for most of her life: a monthly subscription she had to receive cardboard cutouts of the latest hairstyles, clients sifting through them on the waiting room table, fighting for mirror space to try them out; a woman who'd had her molars removed in order to draw out her cheekbones; another woman who'd rubbed depilatory cream into her cheating husband's eyebrows as he slept—he'd woken up screaming, fanning two oozing, eyebrow-shaped sores.

She asked funny things too, like why all the men here wore pants with runny crotches, and whether Jerri, the activities coordinator, had maybe been exposed to pesticides in utero. She also helped me understand why Laura couldn't love me, not the way I wanted her to, because no one could love Laura's son the way that Laura did. *But I do love him that way,* I insisted, *I love him more than I love myself!*

That's the problem though, isn't it, Mrs. Bondy had explained, *you're doing too good a job and she's not ready to retire, you're changing all his definitions of home and leaving her out in the cold.*

I'd whispered Laura's diagnosis to Mrs. Bondy, what Ralph secretly speculated but never uttered, never confirmed. *Borderline personality disorder,* I said. *Untreatable.*

Mrs. Bondy had shrugged. *It is what it is.*

Before I can think about it much longer, Carol pokes her pouting head out from one of the resident's rooms. "Hiiiiiiii, sweetie," she says, even though she's two years younger than me. "How are you? How's Ralph?"

"Oh, you know"—I pull my coat over a hanger—"bereaved."

"Right. Of course. May I?" She opens her arms. I nod and fall into them. I guess everyone here must like to touch people because otherwise why would you get into this line of work? I love to touch people. I really do. I sometimes can't believe the way no one touches each other; how crazy it is that strangers have no idea what each other feels like. How the only strangers who ever touch you are paid to do it, like me here at work, but somehow it still feels so generous to be touched that you need to thank the person touching you over and over again, apologize for having a body that needs touching at all, how Mrs. Bondy did at first when I offered her relief with my hands: rubbed cream into her sores, pulled the pain from her knuckles. *Oh, thank you, Abby, you're so good to me.*

Maybe touching someone is the kindest thing you can do; making a person feel like it's okay to touch them, that they're touchable and not disgusting, is the easiest and best way to make a person feel good in the world.

Carol, an actual nurse, is one of the people that we page when a patient starts convulsing or vomiting or won't wake up. Even though I wear the same scrubs as her, I'm not technically a nurse. I'm a support worker, which means I do just about everything else.

Carol is thin and she has a long neck. She's the kind of woman who could look at a bouquet of flowers and know whether they were expensive. Once she had all of us girls over to her house. I brought a six-pack of coolers and she put them in the fridge and made me the most delicious drink I've ever had in my life, called a Moscow mule, then at the end of the night she gave me my coolers back, which at the time seemed nice, like, you know, you brought these and we didn't drink them and you like them, so take them home, but right now as I'm remembering, I'm wondering if she just thought they were too garish to have in her fridge, bright colors and busy branding that didn't match the rest of her high-end groceries: small jars with simple labels; fresh, colorful produce in baskets. Like she's too good for coolers, and maybe she is, because look at the things she spends her money on. But I like Carol. I liked hugging her. She'll make a good Motherthing one day.

I hope Ralph's coworkers are touching him too, hugging him and patting him on the back. I hope that when I get home tonight, he's been so thoroughly touched that he eats an enormous dinner and announces at the end that it's time to sell the house and start a family of our own.

8

I FEEL GOOD AFTER BEING AT WORK, more like myself. I stop at the grocery store and fill two reusable shopping bags with everything I need for a very hilarious dinner. I believe we should all use reusable shopping bags. So does Ralph. His mother has a collection of plastic bags that date back to when plastic was invented. They're pressed into a drawer in the pantry, a nearly solid brick of them. Sometimes when you pull one out, the rest of them crackle together for longer than you'd expect, like a ritual: when one is pulled, they must all sing the crackling songs of their ancestors.

I stick my key in the door, look up at the house, see a second-floor curtain shudder, surprised that Ralph is home already. Up there, in his mother's room, pinching the curtains shut, even though it's dark outside.

I want to sell the house right now, use the money to escape the city, move into a cottage way up north and fill it with squealing, jabbering babies. Babies everywhere: hiding in cupboards and cookie jars and under my skirt, sleeping, limbs limp and dangling over the crooked arms of a tree; floating faceup in the lake, shooting grand archways of water from their mouths for the other babies to paddle through.

I look down into my shopping bags. I know that I have to start cooking this hilarious dinner now, right now, otherwise we'll be eating later than either of us likes to. I say either of us, but I also know that Ralph won't care if we eat dinner at all.

Hilarious dinner: jellied salmon with crackers.

What you do is you soak gelatin in cold water, then you heat it up till the gelatin is all dissolved, then you add canned salmon and salad dressing. I'm going to use ranch because I think it has the right flavor for fish, the closest to tartar sauce. You mix it all together and you pour it into a mold. I have a mold that's shaped like a fish, which I think is funny and I hope that Ralph thinks it's funny too.

I toss my keys onto the table. They slide into Ralph's wallet and phone. I shake off my bag and coat and boots, lean against the banister, holler up to the second floor, "Ralph?"

He doesn't answer me, so I go up, tap on his mother's bedroom door. "Ralph?" I crack it open, just a bit, lean across the threshold. "Ralph?"

It's empty. Totally undisturbed from this morning. Magazines and tissues and water glasses all in the same place they'd been before. Ralph's impression in the sheets, somehow bathed in winter moonlight through wide-open curtains, which is impossible because they'd been closed just a minute ago, I watched him myself from the front porch, squeezing them shut the way his mother did. Exactly the way his mother did.

No, no, no.

I march over and shut the curtains tight, pinch them down

the middle the way that Ralph and Laura do, and I'm surprised to find it offers a kind of unwholesome relief that I have to shake out of my arms like pins and needles.

It's too dark in here now, my eyes too wide, achieving nothing. I pull the curtains open again, illuminate Laura's row of lucky charms, troll dolls watching me from the dresser, faces creased with the same ancient wisdom that's trapped inside newborn babies, destroyed by language, and in the slip of one second to the next my flesh seizes with goose bumps—they know I hate her.

I leave right away, make sure the door is shut behind me.

"He must be up here *some*where," I mutter out loud, casually, as though a strange thing hasn't happened, and it works because the things you say out loud like that are powerful. The semi-constant mutterings a wife makes about a husband become the truth: *Nothing strange about those curtains being open* and *Perfectly healthy to sleep all day long!*

I check our bedroom and the spare room and the bathroom. They're all empty too.

I head back down the stairs and along the front hall, lit halfway through by the foyer light but dark at the end where the basement door is. "Ralph?"

I hear whispering. Ralph whispering. From the basement. It's the sort of scratchy, desperate whispering you'd do if you ever got kidnapped and were trying to secretly get help from a stranger. I can't make out the words. I try. It's silent for a minute like he's letting someone else speak but I can't hear them.

I place my hand on the table where I tossed my keys, confirm that his phone is here. His phone is here but he's whispering down there. Whispering now hot and secret again. I want to turn on the lights and say his name, I don't want to sneak up on him and try to hear more because that's not what a healthy marriage is all about, but the way he's whispering, the way that he stopped and then started again, it's not right.

I follow the sound of his voice, toward the basement door, step around all the creaky spots in the floor. Ralph taught me where they were when we moved in—*here's the bathroom, here's our bedroom, here's the kitchen, and here are all the spots in the floor that will make her cry if you step on them.* I imagined him as a baby, taking his first steps, wobbling as best he could around the groans and creaks that would alter her mood.

I mimic his tender step, groping along the wall, hear my name jumbled up in his hot whispering. *Abigail* though, not *Abby*. I pause, close to the basement door now, hold my breath, waiting for whatever is going to happen next. "*Stop,*" I hear him hiss, followed by heavy silence, about to burst with something. *Awareness*. He knows I'm home.

"Abby?" he says. Loud. *Abby* this time. *Abby* to me, but not to whoever he was whispering to.

"Oh, yeah! Yep! Hi! I just got in!" I hop back toward the door, planting my feet too hard in all the creakiest spots on the floor, which, after years of fearing their sound, alter Ralph's mood too. I groan—*Stupid, careless*—and turn on the light, pick up my grocery bags in a hasty attempt to make it seem as though I'd just gotten home. Ralph's making his way up the steps. He's been crying. "Oh, Ralphie." I step toward him.

He flinches. Not because I'm close, but to let me know not to come any closer. "I'm okay." He smiles but his eyes are glazed cherries and his face is a yanked rag hanging spent from a hook. He heaves what remains of his tears back in through a single nostril, rubs his face from top to bottom with one hand. He's got the other hand behind his back. Which maybe isn't a big deal, but I can't think of him ever looking this way before. Legs spread, not quite blocking the basement door, but sort of. His hand quite conspicuously hidden.

He notices the grocery bags in my hands. "What's for dinner?" He steps out, closes the basement door behind him with one of his feet. Stands there. Guarding it. I move back a little bit. I'm not scared exactly. Not scared of *Ralph,* for God's sake.

"Were you upstairs just now?"

He glances up. "Nope." He nods toward the basement door. "That there is the basement door."

"Ha, ha. I thought I saw you up there a few minutes ago. From the porch. You were closing the curtains."

He gives me a confused look and changes the subject. "You got dinner?"

"Oh yes!" I raise the bags. "I got, well, actually what I got is a lot of work now that I think about it."

"Well, fuck it then. Do you want to go out?"

"Oh yes, let's do that. I just have to put these away." I lift the bags and start toward the kitchen. With his hand behind his back he presses himself against the wall to let me by, careful, I can tell, not to touch me.

It's weird. And the whispering is weird. And how he's hiding his hand. But I'm going to ignore it right now, which is easier than it should be, and the musty sleep smell I catch as I pass him, the off-gas of pajamas becoming skin after too many days and nights unchanged, the truth it reveals, that he didn't go into work today, I'm going to ignore that too. Because Cal is rooting, aren't you, Cal? Cal is becoming real and she won't become real in a place where Ralph is dark.

He's still pressed against the wall when I return. "Where should we go?"

"Aunt Tony's?" I suggest. It's actually called Anthony's, but this one time I called it Aunt Tony's and Ralph laughed. I thought maybe it would make him laugh again, but it did not.

He just says, "Oh yeah, I could eat there." He slides along the wall, away from me, toward the front door. He digs one foot into a boot, then the other, struggling a bit without his hand, which is in front of him now, because he's still hiding it from me.

I don't want to pry. I won't pry. A healthy marriage is a trusting marriage. A man's hand is his own business after all, and I trust him with his own hand business. It's good to have secrets. Maybe his hand has secretly become a tentacle and that's *fine,* I don't need to know *everything* for God's sake, I'm not that kind of wife.

But I should point out that he's still in his pajamas.

"Ralph."

He stops and turns around, moves his hand behind his back again.

"Do you want to change?"

He looks at me and kinks an eyebrow, puzzled, then looks down, contemplating his clothes for a long time. Too long. Like he's trying to understand why I see pajamas and he sees a three-piece suit.

"Yeaaaaaah," he says slowly. "I should, shouldn't I."

I want to smile but can't quite make it happen because even though I'm trying to be positive, I really, *really* am, the combination of his pajamas and his hidden hand and his secret whispering is giving me that mounting, dreadful feeling that builds when you're alone in the dark.

"I didn't go to work today." He's still looking down.

"Oh. Well, that's okay. You called in sick?"

"No."

"You just didn't go in."

He nods.

"Are you feeling okay?"

"Not really." He looks up and his eyes are all watery again and his hand is at his side now, hung open for me to see that it's bleeding. A slice across his palm so blood follows the seams, becomes quivering rubies that hang from his fingertips.

"Oh, fuck, what happened to your hand?" I step forward, but he steps back again, looks down.

"I hurt it."

"I'll say. How?"

"Let me go change." He presses his hand against his pajama pants. It's a lot of blood. It's going to leave a huge stain where he's pressed it against his pants. Not that I care about the stain, more so I care that *he* doesn't care about the stain. It's a stain of the tormented, those who really don't give a fuck anymore, Rorschachs of grease and shit and blood. I see these stains at the old age parlor, materializing despite every effort, pox-like, on a resident soon to die.

"Are you sure you want to go out? I can make that, that—" I gesture at the kitchen. Jellied salmon, Jesus Christ. It's morbid and bizarre, something left to rot at a dinner party where everyone has dropped dead at the exact same time. I don't even know who I was when I thought it might actually *cheer him up*.

"I'm sure. Let's get out of the house."

And then I hear a sound. The tiniest thud. Soft but weighted. Like something boiled. Or jellied. A hunk of my dank salmon, dropping from the height of a table to the floor. It came from the basement. I can't tell if it's just a regular sound that basements make, the house's groaning, harmless guts, or if it's something else, something down there. I look up at Ralph and he's staring at the basement door with those round lemur eyes, his hands at his sides now, both of them fists, and a little bit of blood squeezes out, splats silently onto the floor. He rubs his sock over it and moves past me, up the stairs to get changed.

I turn and stare at the closed basement door again. I want to go down there. I want to see what he was doing, why he was whispering. It's most likely nothing. It's definitely nothing. This house is always making thuds and creaks and yawns; all those layers of paint and wallpaper, the sticky grime of human fingers and human heat, have made it unstable.

I step toward the basement.

"Don't go down there."

I spin around. Ralph's watching me from the top of the stairs, injured hand held cuplike to hold the blood pooling in his palm.

"Okay," I say, because I don't know what else to say. He stares at me until he's sure I won't move toward the basement again, and I won't, because it's nothing anyway. There's nothing down there. And I've gotta be on tonight, I've got to be as much like myself as I can be. Pretend everything is fine and save your family. Normal Abby, normal, normal, like a lighthouse of normalness so that normal Ralph can see it and steer back toward it. Come closer to me, Ralphie, because right now you're not all the way well. You're halfway in the dark, seeing the light but not able to reach it, and it's my job to bring you back.

9

I LOVE TO THINK ABOUT our first night together, back at his place after the bar. His apartment was small and clean and organized and easy to be in. We sat, leaned in close to each other at his kitchen table, drinking coolers we bought along the way home, then beer when we ran out, then liquor after that, the ancient bottles, always rum, dug triumphantly from a cabinet's deepest, darkest corners.

Ralph pretended to massage one of these recovered bottles, rubbing the dust from its shoulders, dragging his thumb up and down its neck, asking it how its day was—"No one ever asks how the *rum* is doing, do they"—and he did it for so long, pouting, "Aww," never breaking character, "Mmm-hmm, mmm-hmm," and I laughed till I cried and all my mascara came off on my fingers. Ralph reacted quickly, yanking a length of paper towel deftly from the roll, running it under cool water and rubbing black flecks from my cheeks, then from my eyes, then up along my eyebrows and forehead. The way a mother would. The way a mother *should*, drawing the connection between pleasure and hygiene for her daughter so she can become effortlessly not disgusting, the way that women like Carol are: *loving* a bath, *desperate* for her next pedicure. The pursuit of cleanness, smoothness, hairlessness, her delightful *escape*.

Ralph was like this too, I could tell. Normal in this way. Enjoying to be clean.

After several horrible rums, the gears of my brain began grinding suspiciously, pulling my eyebrows together, cinching my lips over my teeth. In one of my last lucid memories from the night, like a whorl of crystal fighting through dense gray rock, I asked him, "Why can't you tell I'm disgusting?"

Ralph laughed. The question clearly preposterous to him. He set his glass down, reached beneath the table, and lifted my leg to rest on his knee.

"What are you doing?" I asked, still wary, still provoked by the rum. And angry now too that he'd laughed at me.

Ralph smiled, lifted my bare foot to his face, and suddenly splayed my toes against his nose, inhaled so deeply that one toe plugged his nostril with a thump I would have died laughing at had I not been mortified instead: hours of snow-damp stockings in cheap, airless boots, my feet withered, dank, smelly, and corpse cold. Absolute panic. As though my foot were being not sniffed by a handsome man, but pulverized by a meat grinder. Then, as quickly as the panic overwhelmed me, it disappeared again. I pressed my foot harder into Ralph's nose, then down into his mouth, which he welcomed, biting down, like I was his baby. I didn't tamp the wild, joyful scream in my chest. I let it out. Ralph joined me, foot-muffled but just as loud.

I took my foot out of his mouth so he could scream better.

He pulled my chair closer to him and he kissed me.

I tried to see if I could taste my feet in his mouth but I couldn't.

After kissing for a while, we talked more.

We talked about living in the city. How living so close to so many people, surrounded by them, actually made you good and patient, not angry and apathetic the way that it seems on TV.

Ralph showed me how to open a bottle with the side of the table and I shrieked, thrilled by the slam and rattle of it.

I told him about my mother, her boyfriends and her suffering and my suffering because of her. He told me that suffering makes a person special, fills a soul with angular gems of transcendent knowledge, so many perspectives contained within each one. I asked him how I could find those gems and use them, and he said he didn't know. I asked him why me and he said he didn't know that either. I pointed out that some people who suffer turn into Charles Manson, and he said that Charles Manson's problem wasn't suffering, but that no one loved him, not even his mother, Ralph had seen a show about it on TV. And that even though my mother was selfish, it sounded like she still loved me.

"All a person really needs is to feel unconditionally loved," he said. "It's built into our programming, a biological necessity, the species couldn't survive without it. If it weren't built-in, we'd all be monsters, filled with pain and trying to inflict it on everyone else."

Then I couldn't breathe. "Aren't we like that though?" I asked him, wanting to cry, thinking of my most private, shameful thoughts. "Aren't we all monsters filled with pain?"

"Naaaaaaaah." He shook his head. "Not really."

And the way he said it, "Naaaaaaaah," like I'd asked him if swallowing my gum could kill me, if ghosts could see me in the bathroom, if bedroom closets were portals to another dimension, it made me feel better about the whole world and the way it felt to live in it. I dropped my head in my hands and cried, surrendered all my pain to Ralph. And he surrendered his to me too.

He told me that night about his darkness: *depression*. How he got sometimes, how it was physical: waves of pain drowning him, or not him exactly, but the thing inside him that made him him, and all he could think about was destroying the vessel, the sinews, muscles, pulses, that kept him tethered to the pain, bisecting the vessel's veins like a vanilla bean, burrowing a bullet into his brain. I stared at him, mouth open, drunk eyes unfocused, trembling over him like beams from a flashlight. How could the man I was looking at, the man who believed so much in the power of love, ever get so low he couldn't move. I shook my head and crawled into his lap, inhaled his skin, kissed him.

We didn't make love that night but rather the next morning. Reeking. Our entombed hangover processes released into the air, whatever happens inside a body to convert poison into harmless agony. We weren't embarrassed or anxious or sad, just tired and needing grease and salt and soap and hot water, but first thin, breathless kisses, then thicker, surer, bodies twisted up together like tree branches growing around each other, so close and so deep and I was nothing but Ralph's then and he was nothing but mine.

"Do you like that?" he'd asked in the middle of it, and not in the clenched, rhetorical way of an unsavory for whom anything but an enthusiastic yes would have been unheard of or, worse, just unheard. I'd felt like a ghost, suddenly addressed by a mortal after a thousand years unseen, stuttered a bewildered yes because, though I can't remember what he was doing, I'd liked that he'd asked me. Loved that he'd asked me. Had never enjoyed sex more than in that moment when he'd asked me.

We were never apart again, save for work. My apartment became just an expensive storage locker for a few months until we decided I'd move into his place, officially, that old apartment, a satellite branch of heaven, how every day there I could love him more, all the ways he'd learned to handle life, like the meticulous way he packed an overnight bag: tightly rolled T-shirts, pants trifolded, flattened; a sack for dirty underwear and another for extra shoes. His morning routine: two alarms and then shit and shower, fruit and cereal for breakfast, plucking keys, wallet, bus pass, from a sacred spot, never lost, never scrambling to leave the house. Merciless about socks, a single threadbare heel and the pair was done, tossed in the garbage without a second thought. Life isn't so bad when you do it the way that Ralph taught me, learning from him, slowly untangling all the bad habits from my mother. Being inseparable from Ralph felt like something I'd been missing from the chemistry of my marrow, a bond that I could never have with her, that might have made everything different. A real live Couchy Motherthing, finally making me whole and real and connected to the rest of the world.

10

RALPH BLASTS THROUGH THE SCREEN DOOR in a nice plaid shirt and dark jeans and thick white gauze wrapped around his hand. I look at it, I can't help it. He sees me looking. I don't want to have to ask again and it's like he can read my mind.

"It was an accident."

"An accident." I don't mean to sound as skeptical as I do.

"Yes, an accident. I really don't want to talk about it right now. I'm sorry."

"It's okay." I put my hand on his neck, pull him close for a kiss, and his skin scatters from my touch.

We're quiet on the walk. Shoulders up, drawing cold air into our warm lungs where it's tagged, white now, released again into the world like an endangered species. It's the kind of night where even though it's dark, you can still see some clouds, sketched and smudged by the fat of a palm across the sky. Ralph is looking up at them too, we're both looking at them together, these night clouds, and I know that even if Ralph is halfway in the dark, we're still lucky to love each other as much as we do. My mom was never this lucky. His mom was never this lucky. They both chose the kind of man who could stop loving a person all of a sudden. Laura burned only once, then never again. My mother over and over and over.

If someone looked at the data, I wonder if they'd see that divorce is hereditary. And Ralph and I, we're anomalies: two red, beating dots far from data's long dead curve, high above and looking down and feeling bad that so many people are doomed to repeat their parents' mistakes. But not us. We call to the lifeless points plotted along the curve, *Join us! Come up here where it's blank and we can build the whole world ourselves!* But they can't hear us, the rush of the curve is too powerful, thunder in their ears and all they can see. Farther and farther away the curve is massive. Farther and farther away Ralph and I start to look like just one single, perfect dot.

Then we're at Aunt Tony's, waiting to be seated, standing next to a wooden waiter with smooth, exaggerated features, hip height and holding a tray of miscellaneous business cards, hopeful patrons after the monthly meatball draw. The last time we were here was with Laura. She'd sifted through the pile the way you might throw the pages of a magazine back and forth in a waiting room, a busy little performance, quiet assimilation to the room and its purposes. But then she scoffed, communicating to Ralph that he was to ask what was wrong, so, despite what his BPD printouts warned, he indulged what would most certainly be another "maladaptive negative thought" and he asked her.

"Just look at this." She'd shaken her head. "A lawyer, an obstetrician—can you imagine finding your lawyer or your doctor competing for free meatballs?"

Laura knew I'd thrown my own business card in there more than once. Not even mine because I didn't have one, but a generic card for the Northern Star that I'd scribbled my name and phone number on. I'd begged Ralph to throw his card in too, to double our odds, but he claimed to not have any: *Who still has business cards?*

"What does it matter if your lawyer wants a free meatball? What difference would that make?" Ralph defending me without either of us acknowledging it.

"It demonstrates poor judgment," Laura spat. "Hopefulness from *anyone* is proof of poor judgment, but especially from a professional."

"All right, Mom." Ralph squeezed my hand, indirectly conceding her cruelty.

A man who looks nothing like the wooden waiter walks toward us, two menus pressed under his arm. He leads us to a little table with a checkerboard tablecloth. We've had this waiter before. Once I heard him describe Ralph and me as a "deuce" to the hostess. "I guess because there's two of us," Ralph had said, pushing his bottom lip up the way people do when they learn something new. "Deuce," I repeated, and we laughed somewhat giddily, ordered expensive Long Island iced teas without even discussing it first. A nice night just the two of us. A deuce.

Across from me now Ralph's mouth is a line pressed down at the corners. He's paler than usual too. He puts his hands on the table and I see blood worming its way through the gauze. An ominous splotch, not quite red, just damp in his palm. Oily. He smiles at me. The waiter pours us some water, steals a glance at Ralph's wrapped hand, then asks if we'd like anything to drink.

"Do you have coolers?" Ralph asks.

"A few. We've got these cherry-flavored hard colas that people seem to like." I notice the waiter has an earring, a thick silver cuff through the cartilage.

Ralph looks at me and I consider declining a cooler, on account of Cal's potential rooting, but he'll think it's strange if I don't, he'll ask questions, and I don't want to be a killjoy tonight with the two of us out and maybe about to have a good time for the first time in too long. Maybe all Ralph needs right now is a good time. One good time and everything will be better. So I'll be a good time. I'll have a cooler. I'm sorry, Cal, your first sacrifice for your family. I think of something my mother once told me, that you can do anything you want until the pregnancy test. I choose to believe that's true even though I know for a fact that she was loaded with terrible information. I nod and Ralph says, "We'll take two please, and then two more after that when you see we're done. Oh, and some of those cheesy rice balls too, with the tomato sauce."

"Coming right up," says the waiter.

"You really took charge there."

"I've always wanted to order like that."

"What an ambitious bucket list." I crack open the menu and lay it out in front of me.

Ralph smiles, but it's strange, the top half of his face, eyes, brows, forehead, hasn't moved at all. Like he'd been injected with whatever they use to numb you at the dentist and it hadn't quite made its way down to his mouth yet. He leans back in his chair, lets both hands crawl up over his face, inhales so deeply that I can smell blood and gauze too. "Abby, I've got to tell you something." His voice is muffled by his palms.

I lean over the table, pry his wrists down, and look into his bloated, worn-out eyes. If they weren't eyes, you'd have considered them spent, tossed them out, and gotten new ones by now.

"What is it, Ralphie?"

"You're going to think I'm nuts." He's staring at my hands, where I'm touching him.

I hunch low, try to force my face into his sight line. "I would never think you're nuts." I've got him now, he's looking me in the eyes. "Even if it sounds nuts, I will always believe you. Remember after we watched *Face/Off*? The promise we made?"

"Yeah, sure, but obviously I never thought it would actually come up."

"Well, it's a good thing we talked about it then."

He pulls his hands back, rubs his eyes with the heels of his palms, then peers over at the bar, anxious for our coolers.

"Look at me." I take his hands again. "Just spit it out. It can't be that bad."

He chews his lip, punishing it with so much nervous energy it's hard to watch. What could be so bad that he can't just tell me? Unless he doesn't love me anymore, he's going to leave, we're not an anomaly after all but just like all the other children of divorced parents. I hear them shrieking along the curve, laughing at us for thinking we were better than them. I'll smash the cooler bottle, I'll kill us both before I let us get dragged down to the horrible curve with everyone else.

"Abby, Mom is back."

The words batter against something in my head so that even though I hear him I don't really understand. "What?"

"My mother is back. She's in the basement." A cold-blooded thing spirals up my spine, tailbone to skull. The way he said it, he really believes it. I glance back at the waiter. I need that cherry hard cola, right now, badly. He's behind the bar, cracking them open, placing them on a tray alongside two ice-packed glasses. I turn back to Ralph. He's staring at me. His eyes don't seem tired or worn anymore. They seem cold and rotten, dead flesh artificially animated, sparking a visceral reaction in the living: kill it, make it dead again.

"Okay" is all I can say.

"You don't believe me."

"No, it's not that exactly." I rub my temples, try to tenderize the information I've just received so my brain can digest it.

"Abby, you said you'd believe me. You promised." He's frustrated, antsy in his seat, scoffing as he declares, "I'm *not* crazy."

"I *know* you're not crazy, Ralph." I rub my temples harder, desperate to produce the right words. "Okay, just, help me understand. Your mother is back. From . . . the dead?"

"Yes. No. *Back* isn't the right word. She's—ah, fuck, what's the point, I can see, I can see you think I'm crazy."

"Stop, I don't think you're crazy. I really don't, but I do think, ugh, God, I do think you're maybe, a bit depressed again, and—"

"I'm not depressed either, Abby, you think I don't know the difference? Yeah, I'm sad about Mom, yes, I could be taking it better. I should have gone into work today, I shouldn't have done this." He lifts his gauzed hand.

"I thought you said that was an accident."

Ralph puts both of his hands flat on the table, stares between them, knuckles jumping. He breathes deep through his nose, gathering strength. "I fell down the basement stairs today. I'm fine, I'm completely fine, but it was a bad fall. I was knocked out for a second—here, feel." He guides my hand to the back of his head, where a golf-ball-size lump radiates beneath my fingers.

"That's really bad." I pull my hand back. "You might have a concussion."

"It's fine." He elbows himself forward, as close to me as he can, whispering, "But when I woke up"—closer, quieter—"my mother was *there*. Just sitting there on the couch, *staring at me*."

And I'm worried that she's told him about the ring. Even though that's completely insane, I'm worried now that he knows. This is exactly why you shouldn't do bad things. A bad thing will make you completely insane. "What did she say?" I ask, half expecting him to confront me.

I jump when the waiter drops off our hard cherry colas. He smiles and apologizes for startling me and asks if we're ready to order.

"Not quite," I say, still shaken, and he spins around to tend to another table, leaving us with the feeling that we've wasted the time and energy of a very busy man.

Ralph pours my hard cherry cola into a glass full of ice, which is quite gentlemanly. He slides it toward me. It sizzles like regular cola, sparkly and cosmic. I take down a long, many-glugged drink, imagine Ralph's spirit floating in the glittering cosmos of a just-cracked cherry cola cooler. He's weightless there, a wise and satisfied energy. No connection to what's sitting across from me here at Aunt Tony's: all bloated eyes and wind moaning through hollows. The thing sitting across from me is a fingernail clipping; a fan of hair, cut and landed spread on the floor; overgrowth snipped from its animating force—Laura's illness—and left with the mystifying puzzle of who he is now.

Together they'd been a pattern, black-and-white, and now all the black is gone and what's left over is an infinite white void.

"What did she say, Ralph?"

"Well, nothing at first. I screamed and ran up the stairs and jammed a chair under the door handle. I thought I'd just hit my head, that I was seeing things. But she looked so real, I just, I had to go down and make sure. And there she was, sitting there, staring at me. She asked me how my head was. She was wearing her blue dress. I was scared shitless."

"Did she have her ring?" My voice rattles like a warped drawer. Another glug of cooler to steady it. I grab my bottom lip between my teeth and feel my eyes inflate with the cautious guilt of an incontinent dog who's trying to enjoy the first few minutes of its master's return before the horror of what it's done in the living room is discovered.

"No," he says easily, not hiding anything. No, she doesn't have her ring, and Ralph still has no idea where it is. He sips his cooler, taking in a few shards of ice, which he moves around his mouth, against his teeth, as he speaks. "At least I don't think so. She kept sort of tuning in and out like a radio station; sometimes it was just this crunching sound, really loud, like if static were somehow eating corn nuts, then other times I could hear her and sense her and even see her a bit. She said she kept losing the frequency, like it was hard work to stay put. I put on the murder shows for her, the ones she liked. That seemed to help."

"Did you ask her why the fuck she's here?" My hand, still clutching my cooler, is getting uncomfortably cold. Dead. I shiver. Protect it in the warmth of my lap.

"Of course I did, but she didn't really know anything. She said she'd just never really left. Woke up on the basement floor, realized that we couldn't see her. She watched you clean that night. She said it was sweet of you to let me sleep."

"Okay, *bull*shit."

"What?"

"She didn't say that. If she's really down there, she didn't say that."

Ralph stares at me. "She did."

I know he's lying. That's the thing, I know he's lying. I can tell. He's not lying about seeing his mother, about the ring, but he is lying about this. These were the kinds of fights we had when we first moved into the house, Laura pummeling me with what I was certain were insults, about my cooking or my job or my family, out of nowhere, for no reason at all; Ralph insisting that I'd misunderstood something, that her intentions were pure.

"Swear she said that. Swear on your half of the rice balls."

Just as the words leave my mouth, the rice balls appear between us, landing with two hard knocks, brown and sizzling and half-submerged in an unsettled red sauce. When things like that happen, when I say rice balls and they appear like magic, it makes me think for a split second that there really is something intelligent about the universe, a sense of humor or something. And maybe Ralph really did see his mother today. She's still here. A cosmic mistake. A joke. That's sort of funny maybe, when you think about it. One day, when I'm a few lifetimes away from all this, I might think it's funny too.

"Fine." Ralph drags a rice ball through some sauce. "She wondered why you didn't think to borrow Irena's steamer for the basement carpet before ripping it up." He bites the rice ball in half, and the steam from what's left in his hand is thick and swirling as a spell. "Are you happy?"

"She *wondered*."

"Abby, come on."

"No, I love it. I love that she *wondered*. I *wonder* why she can't tell you straight out that she thinks I'm an idiot instead of pretending to *wonder* about all the idiotic things I do."

"You see? I told you." Ralph finished off the rest of the rice ball. "She's still here."

Except she's not. For all the regular reasons having to do with the limits of the physical world, but also because Ralph clearly doesn't know about the ring, and if she were back, if she were *really* back, it would have been the first thing out of her mouth: *Abby stole my ring, pulled it from my dying finger, she's terrible, Ralph, a Kay Jewelers lowlife through and through.*

Which means maybe it's actually Ralph who *wondered* why I didn't ask Irena to borrow her steamer. Ralph who's upset that I destroyed the basement carpet. But it's not our basement, Ralph, it's not *our carpet.* "Listen, I'm sorry I didn't think of the steamer, I just, I was trying to get rid of all that, of all the—"

"Oh, I know. Listen, I would have done the same thing. You're not going to just knock on Irena's door and lug the steamer out of her attic or wherever, Cud after your shoelace the whole time like it's some flailing ladynapper." He bisects another steaming rice ball.

"Right." I watch him pop the rest of the rice ball into his mouth. "Okay, how are these things not melting your mouth out right now?"

"I don't know. I don't feel anything. Like this." He lifts his hand. "I don't feel this either."

"You have to tell me what happened there."

"It was dumb." He coats another rice ball in sauce. "I thought she asked me to."

"Your mother?"

"I misunderstood. That static. I thought she needed my blood, but then, I don't know, I misunderstood her."

"*Your* blood?" Hairs on the back of my neck come to life, awakening like some unholy flora. I'm frightened, for the first time in years, of a thing that I know isn't real. "Ralph, what on earth would she need *your blood* for?"

"I said I misunderstood, all right? Just"—he hides his bandaged hand in his lap—"just forget about it. Please."

"Ralph . . . ," I start, but can't seem to finish. I'm nervous to press him, the way that he is right now. So instead I grab a rice ball too, coat it in the red sauce. "These must not be that hot." I shove the whole thing in my mouth. It's like I'm chewing on a burning coal: my eyes water and I can't fully close my mouth but I keep chewing, boiling rice spilling out like lava, steam spewing from my mouth in frantic, huffing *ha cha cha cha*s. When I'm able to, I chug half my hard cola. Ralph is doing that weird smile again, like the back of his skull is pulled off and Laura is manipulating his folds with her hands.

"Abby, you've gotta believe me."

"I know, Ralph."

"I'm not crazy."

"I *know,* Ralph."

The waiter comes back, raises his nose at our table because we're a deuce dropped in the middle of his section. "How is the arancini?"

"Hot," I say.

"Are you ready to order?"

"I'll just have the spaghetti and meatballs," I say.

"Very good." He turns to Ralph.

"I'll have a steak. As rare as can be. Fries on the side. Some of that creamed spinach too."

"Coming right up." The waiter, visibly lifted by Ralph's expensive order, plucks our menus from our hands at the exact same time.

It takes us a moment to recover from such a normal inter-action. Ralph scratches his elbow. I clear my throat and take another drink. I wish we could be quiet now for a while. Sit simply, comfortably, out in the world together like nothing is wrong, but Ralph has a lot more to say.

"Do you think that when you don't want to be alive any-more, I mean really don't want to be alive anymore, badly, that it's possible to just die?"

I shake my head. "No." I know it doesn't work like that. On Couchy Motherthing in my old house, staring outside, listen-ing to her fight with Rick or Randy or whoever was out there freezing to death, I wanted to die but nothing happened. I wanted to not be alive anymore but I had to be. Alive still, in this terrible moment too, even though frankly I have that feel-ing again where I wouldn't mind not being alive.

"But why not? You've got to have a will to live, don't you? Something's got to happen when you don't have one anymore, right?"

I drop my head into my stiffened fingers, stare into the table. "I need another drink."

And again the universe delivers it to me. It wants me to know that it's warm and thick around me, controlling every moment. Magical things happen. Ralph's mother is down in the basement, and maybe not for the ring either, but for *his blood,* exploiting the gene inside him that's just like hers. The one that aches to destroy its host; the one that, when nurtured, the way only a Motherthing can nurture, will develop into something unstoppable.

"Thanks," Ralph says to the waiter, then leans closer to me. "What about your patients at work? Isn't that what happens to them? At a certain point they must just really stop wanting to be alive. What else would make a heart stop beating after ninety, ninety-five, one hundred years, when nothing changes, nothing happens to make it stop? It's because the person is just done. Really fucking done. Maybe Mom didn't really mean what she did. Maybe she killed her body, but her will to live, it's still thriving."

I breathe deep in through my nose and the tears begin to settle back inside and in that same moment the waiter brings our food. Ralph's arteries barely finish their wolf whistle before he digs in. Like he's never eaten before, pinching up fries by the bundle, scooping spinach, hacking triangles from his steak. His hands don't stop, a pair of Ferris wheels depositing their contents into his mouth and down the front of his shirt. More stains of the tormented, accumulating like raindrops. He hasn't eaten like this ever, really, and certainly not since he found out about Laura.

I roll my meatballs around on their plate, thinking that maybe I'll try to make my own meatballs soon. Make meatballs and save your family. I feel myself sliding, drawn to the appeal of simply believing him, or at least acting like I do, living my life as though his mother were still alive and haunting the basement. Right now it seems like the easiest, most harmless way to live, a *lifestyle choice,* like owning a hot tub. Much better than calling a doctor, having them lug Ralph to short-term mental health, where he'll hate me more and more as they experiment with drug after drug, which might work for a while then stop, or never work at all, or amplify his suicidal ideations and send him howling through the swinging double doors of a psych ward, and all the while I'm just living in the house alone or mostly alone, because maybe Laura is really there, watching from dark corners as I clean, criticisms unuttered, settling instead in the crags of her skull, percolating, potent, just like in real life—the way I work a sponge, the way I fold sheets, the way my fork pirouettes in spaghetti like I think I'm something—Ralph actually sane the whole time, decomposing now in a padded cell all because of me.

A third cooler and a shared tiramisu. Ralph leaves a very good tip and the waiter says, "*Thank* you, sir," emphasizing it like that. *Not a deuce after all, are we, mister.*

We're walking home and I tell Ralph that I need to see his mother, that to believe any of this, I'm going to have to see her too.

"Even Joan Allen needed proof in *Face/Off*," I insist.

"Okay, we can try."

All I've got to do is stand in the basement in the dark and wait for her to come out.

That's all.

11

WE CHANGE INTO OUR PAJAMAS as soon as we get home because that's what we always do, no matter who's haunting the basement, a precious custom from our old life that we've managed to preserve here in hell.

Ralph opens us a couple more coolers, and together we head down. I see that he's covered the windows, stuffed some old couch cushions into each squat little rectangle of glass, so that when he turns off the light down here, it's like trying to see through ink.

He takes a swig of his cooler. "Okay." He sets it down on top of the coffee table. "So I'm going to go up the stairs, turn off the light, and shut the door, and you just wait, okay? Maybe try saying her name, you know, call out to her. I don't really know how it works. You've got to think about her too. Think about her face, maybe, or a memory you have. I must have been thinking about her when I was unconscious."

"Must have been." I take a swig from my cooler too and

set it next to Ralph's, where I also spot the large, sharp kitchen knife that Laura used that night to score her arms. Cleaned and gleaming and down here with Ralph all day. *I thought she needed my blood.*

"You might not see her, but I do appreciate you trying." He gives me a fast hug, which I savor with my eyes closed like a good smell, then he disappears up the stairs.

The second he's gone, I carefully shove the knife into the waist of my pajama pants, cover the top of it with my shirt. The metal is unpleasant against the soft warmth of my lower back. Before I have time to scan the room, the lights are off and the basement door is closed and I'm all alone in the blackest dark I've ever been in.

I wish that a few seconds ago I'd had the good sense to grab my cooler and sit down on the couch, because who knows how long I'll be standing here. I have to give it a decent amount of time because I don't want Ralph to think that I don't want to see his mother. I mean, I don't really. No one wants to see a ghost, do they? Or their mother-in-law, for that matter. The woman who first colonized your husband's brain, defenses now fortified with all the darkest powers of the afterlife. Fun.

I could have loved you so much, Laura, you stupid fucking asshole, but you just couldn't do it, you were just too mean, sucking everything pleasant from a room. The private alarm of losing track of a spider on your ceiling, that was what it felt like to be in a room with you. But I'm not going to think about her because I don't want to see her. I'm not going to see her. I'm not going to see her. I'm not going to see her sketched gray hair or her eyes, deep-set thumbprints; how she always looked wrong in daylight. Like a possum. Hissing. Curved back, hands limp as dishrags, shuffling around in her blue dress the way she used to on those thin legs, feeble ankles, barely lifting her feet, so the sound made you crazy, then made you feel bad for being mad at an old woman who couldn't lift her feet. Wouldn't lift her feet. She could have if she wanted to, but she liked to make noise, liked to insinuate herself into people's ears. How did a hissing possum like you raise Ralph, the perfect good? Ralph the Perfect Good, as truly good as a person can be. You didn't really do it though, did you? It happened accidentally, didn't it, a reaction to your dangerous gloom like those rare prairie flowers that only grow in cemeteries, beauty formed and nourished by the dead.

Something's growing in my chest, small at first but hard as ice, then bigger and bigger till it's difficult to breathe around. Dread, this is dread, dread that my body could feel before I even noticed, but I notice it now. And a little sound, almost not there at all: tap . . . tap . . . tap . . . tap . . . tap, from somewhere behind me, deep in the pitch dark, a tap, or is it a crackle?—a slow dialing into my frequency, just like Ralph said. Happening. Real. A sound that wasn't here before is here now, tap tap tap tap tap tap tap, faster, less careful, because she knows I can hear.

The dread and the tapping, I reach around my back and grip the handle of the knife, hands trembling. I don't want to, I can't believe it, but I have to say her name out loud: "Laura?"—my voice slippery, unstable, avoiding the ball of dread in my chest. If my voice meets the ball of dread, I'll scream. I wonder if Ralph's heard me say her name, if he's got his ear pressed against the basement door.

I hear the rustle of hard carpet beneath crispy heels, one foot after the other. I can feel it too, not alone, walking toward me now, I catch her scent, how it was at the end, sleep-sweaty, untended caverns, her whole body dusted in a pollen of build-ups. I smell you. I can smell you, Laura, I swear to God. I close my eyes even though I can't see anything at all, shut my mouth, press a tight fist against it so my breathing scrapes loud and fast against my fingers. Other fist still clutching the knife, I pull it out, hold it in front of me. The coolers rattle. I jab at the darkness. Coffee table nudged by her shuffling foot. Another sound. Another jab. Was that the couch? Did she just bump into the couch? Could she really be this close now? I squeeze my eyes shut tighter, press harder around my mouth, and drop into a squat, low, close to the floor, like maybe it's better if I'm small and compact because I can't let her touch me, can't let her infect me, the darkness is trying to get inside me and I can't take it anymore. I honestly can't take it anymore, I honestly can't. I can't I can't I can't—

"*RAAAAAAAAAAAAAAAAAAALPH!*" I scream.

He flicks on the lights right away and I open my eyes. The room is empty. No Laura breathing into my face.

His feet are thunder down the stairs behind me. I spin around and tuck the knife back into the waist of my pajama pants. When he grabs me, the relief is immediate, bracing, like catching yourself just before a bad fall. I feel his heart beating against my cheek, and the sound of it, the way he's holding me, he's *here,* he's *really* here. Not like yesterday or this morning or even a few hours ago when he pressed himself up against the wall to avoid touching me. I believed him about his mother. I really believed him, enough to scream. I screamed and now he's here. I can scream at his monsters and bring him back to life.

He holds me out by the shoulders and looks into my eyes.

I'm trying to mirror his focus, but my eyes scribble over his, powerless against the quake of deep, dark drunkenness. "Did you see her?" he whispers.

"Yes." I clutch him tight because he's letting me. "No. I didn't see her. But, ugh, fuck, Ralph! I'm fucking drunk. I'm extremely fucking drunk." The muscles in my face are tired, my tongue a great, hot burden.

"I know you saw her." He holds me close again, loves me again because I might believe him. "I can tell you did." He's drunk too, each word gummed to the other.

I'm crying, my face hot and leaking. "What does this mean?" I whisper.

"I don't know what it means." Ralph holds me so tight my cheek squishes into his chest, pressing my eye and nostril closed, lips squeezed open like a coin purse, a diamond of my exposed teeth and gums. If Laura could see me right now, she'd laugh.

"Can we go upstairs?" I never want to come down here again. I want to hide the knife somewhere. I want to tell him about the ring. I want to pee.

"Of course." Ralph holds my hand, grips the rail as he pulls me up the stairs, and if believing in his dead mother is what I have to do to lure Ralph back to life, touching me, holding me, if that's what it takes, then I believe you, Ralph, I believe everything you say, she was down there all right. I heard her and smelled her and felt her breath in my face.

I shove the knife between the mattress and the box spring beneath my head, then slip in next to Ralph, who is already asleep before the covers make it to his chin, rolled toward me, facing me, for the first time since Laura died.

12

Scene: Ralph, Abby, and Laura are sitting at the round kitchen table. The room is modest, functional. The appliances old but well taken care of. Someone in this family knew how to charm every bit of life from a thing, and it shows. They've just finished dinner. Ralph's and Abby's plates are streaked with food, but Laura's plate is clean. She rolls the lit end of a cigarette along its edge. Behind her the neighbor is visible through the window, passing back and forth, bending out of sight to offer table scraps to her small dog.

LAURA: *[Incredulous, more heated than the situation calls for.]* Abby, for God's sake, of course you've noticed his head, don't lie.

ABBY: *[Hoping her deliberate calm will bring Laura down too.]* What do you mean though *ridges*? Where are these ridges? *[Naturally Abby had clocked the way Ralph's skull seemed to crest along the sides, how the crests joined at his*

crown like a wishbone. But it was so slight, so absolutely noth-
ing, that she didn't see why in the world they should ever have
to talk about it.]

RALPH: *[Uncomfortable, shifting in his chair.]* Mom, you're
fucking obsessed with my head.

LAURA: It was shocking. When you were born, honestly,
you looked like a lizard or something. I almost dumped
you in the sewer. *[Laura lets breeze from an open window*
catch smoke from her mouth and pull it out like a silk scarf.]

ABBY: *[Collecting their plates.]* I think lizards look regal.
[Ralph scoffs.] What? I really do! And besides, I've never
even noticed your head before. *[Reaches for Laura's plate,*
but then stops and leaves it for ashing.] I really haven't,
Ralph, I'm not just saying that.

RALPH: *[Exasperated.]* Abby, it's *fine,* I don't *care* that I've
got a weird-shaped head. *[To Laura.]* Honestly, I don't.

LAURA: *[Stubbing her cigarette.]* I made it a point to never
stroke your head when I was breastfeeding you *[Ralph rolls*
his eyes, gets up from the table to help Abby at the sink], just
in case it somehow wired you to like the feeling of having
your head stroked. *[Laura lights another one, handling it*
like a wand, something innately tied to her essence, her power.
She draws upon it deeply, not sure if they're even paying atten-
tion to her now.] Then you'd have to deal with it later in
life. You let your guard down, some woman strokes your
ridges and she recoils, rejects you for it.

RALPH: *[Paying attention of course, but he wishes he hadn't been.]* Mom, that's crazy.

LAURA: It's not crazy, it's called being a mother. Just you wait. Abby will know one day, won't you, Abby? Actually, wait, maybe not. *[Laughing, an affect of innocence, of mere curiosity.]* How old are you again?

13

A FEW HOURS LATER my eyelids peel open and take half my corneas with them. I try to rub some moisture back in with my knuckles, but then I realize everything needs this level of attention: my mouth needs water, my bowels need voiding, my spirit is leaking from my pores. I curl into my own hangover stench and loathe every second I've spent alive.

Ralph is on his side snoring gently, hands tucked up together under his cheek. I love him so much I want to take a bite out of the wedge of muscle that runs along his side. I think a lot about eating him, about eating everything I love—burying my teeth into Cal's undercooked baby feet, of course, but also Mrs. Bondy's big, fat heart, tearing up flesh, sinew snapping, flipping my head back and letting it all slide down my throat, warm and happy, then horrified because I've killed the thing I love. Eating, love's natural, bloody conclusion that can never, ever be indulged, because then the thing you love is destroyed. And maybe not destroying the thing you love, resisting that impulse, is the highest expression of love. So instead I just drool over Ralph's wedge of muscle, sniff it top to bottom till it settles my cooler-roiled stomach.

Hopefully after yesterday he feels a bit better. I believe him, as far as he knows. Like Joan Allen in the movie *Face/Off,* who must believe that her husband's sworn enemy, the man who murdered their son, is actually her husband, the victim of a violent, forced face-swap surgery.

I have to go to work. *You have to go to work, Abby, you have to get up, because if he's not going to work, you've got to.* One of the only things my mother taught me, a nonnegotiable rule of life: "You're not allowed to call in sick for a hangover. You're just not. Only real pieces of shit call in sick for hangovers. Those pay-'em-Friday, fall-on-their-ass boozers who can't be trusted with their money before the week is through. That's not you, honey."

That's not me.

Just before I swing my legs over the bed, I imagine Ralph's mother underneath it, flat on her stomach and looking up through greasy hair, grinning, waiting for me to leave so she can climb into bed and eat her son, because that's how much she loves him. And she doesn't have to resist it, not now, because she's dead and the rules don't apply to her anymore.

Not there, she's not there. I was very drunk last night, and very desperate not to have an insane husband. *Did you say something? What was that?* Someone had been speaking to him for a while. Someone who wasn't me.

Auditory hallucinations. Major depression with psychotic features. He'd never gone into much detail about it. He couldn't, he said, that time of his life too foggy, pinned to his psyche only by the facts of the illness: dates and medications

and diagnoses. It had happened to someone else, a character in
a book.

I brace myself, throw my head down between my legs, and
stare into the dusty, empty floor beneath. She's not there. Of
course. But I do remember the knife, hidden now between the
mattress and box spring on my side. I pry between them with
my fingers, reach in carefully, connect with the handle.

The bathroom stings, cold floor, too bright. I sit on the toilet, unleash a fury of liquid evil. *I'm sorry, Cal, I'm sorry that I
drank the way that I did, and that you had to share space in one
way or another with that hot hell sludge.* I don't have time to
shower, which is so disappointing I almost cry. I rinse my face,
rub my eyes, brush my teeth, throw on my scrubs, and head to
work. The subway ride is a blur: tamping vomit, gripping the
pole with a sweaty palm, scanning desperately for a seat that
never materializes.

At the station I buy a greasy egg sandwich, protect its warm
potency with the front of my winter coat on the short walk to
the Northern Star.

When I get to work, Linda, freshly braided, is already at
the front desk. She smiles at me, sitting small and straight and
organized, biceps snug to her sides, forearms busy as a mantis,
unwrapping the same buttered bagel, seedless and tidy, that she
eats every single morning. There's something so pleasing about
her routines that it almost makes you envy her uncluttered life:
single, childless, the way everyone should live. A cup that never
spills. Maybe I'm jealous of Linda. Maybe I don't want anyone
in my life after all, no Ralph or Cal or Motherthings. But that's
not true. I wish it were, but it's not.

The halls are so quiet here, patients sealed in their rooms,
carpets of thick white bread. I pass a corkboard that our activi-

ties coordinator, Jerri, set up, thumbtacked pictures of our residents when they were young and beautiful. The game was to guess who's who: *Can you believe that that's Doris? Yes,* that *Doris, quivering Doris with the floor-length whiskers and the oozing bedsores. Can you believe she ever looked this beautiful?* Everyone seemed to think the corkboard was *adorable,* a word that should be considered a slur in an old age parlor. One of our residents, Marie, walked by when Jerri was setting it up. *Which one are you, Marie?*

Marie leaned over, studied the board for a minute, bent her finger back against a photo of a woman standing in a train station, hair whipped into dark, wild strips. *Oh, Marie, that's not you!* shrieked Jerri. *That's Doris. . . . Yes,* that *Doris! I guess it's been a while, huh, Marie? This is you.* Jerri pointed to a picture of another dark-haired woman, this one at a parade, standing straight, fingers hooked together at her hip. *Oh, Marie, you're adorable.* Marie shrugged, shuffled back to her room. I nearly burst into tears.

Marie died a few months later, and I know it sounds crazy, but I'm sure it was because of the corkboard. Because what else is there to do but drop dead at that point? When you don't even recognize yourself anymore, when the person you spent your whole life becoming is a stranger in a photograph and everyone thinks it's funny that you didn't realize you're No One now. Unceremoniously absorbed by the great homogenous colony, the leaking, aching, voiceless elderly, looking and sounding and treated the same no matter what they'd accomplished before they started shitting themselves again.

Thankfully the kitchen is empty. I'm able to quickly scarf my greasy egg sandwich and chug my orange juice like the desperate animal my hangover has reduced me to. I close my eyes.

Remember how beautiful I was the night I met Ralph, when I was drinking my strawberry coolers at the bar all alone. Sometimes when I went to the bar alone, I didn't look so beautiful. Those were the nights I'd attract unsavories. Men who weren't sweet. Who bought me too many drinks so when we got back to my place I stumbled around like a remote-controlled toy, bumping into things, knocking them to the ground, a jar of change toppled over and smashed and scattered across the floor. Scorched flashes of dry, dead-eyed humping. Humping. Making hump. Becoming hump. Over and over and over till I'm all rub burned and swollen through the seat. Unsavories leave in the morning, either before you get up or while you're pretending to be asleep. Unsavories understand—they don't say goodbye and you don't want them to. You'll never see an unsavory again, not because you'll literally never see him again, but because even if you did, you wouldn't recognize him. For all intents and purposes, unsavories die after you're done with them. Wither up from their hangovers, turn to dust, and scatter.

Daniel. My first real boyfriend. He was an unsavory.

One time we went out to a bar with his friends, guzzled a million pitchers of draft beer, then walked home at the end of the night, blowing around haphazard as trash, laughing about God knows what, then fighting for no good reason. We got through our front door, dropped our coats and bags and pulled off our shoes and shed as much of our clothing as we could manage before landing flat on the bed like a pair of logs.

But then Daniel wasn't ready to go to bed yet. He wanted to have sex. He pawed at me, dragged his stubble along my neck. I knew what he wanted but I didn't want to, "No, Dan-

iel," I murmured, "I'm exhausted, I'm drunk, please come on, *no*," batted at his incessant hands, he grumbled, "Fine fine fine fine," he was annoyed, I could tell, but sleep was after me, relentless, no resisting it.

I passed out the way you do after guzzling a million pitchers, mouth open, breath rattling like wind through a cave. Restless drunken sleep, the kind you wake up from a bit later, maybe a few minutes, maybe an hour, needing to puke or chug water or cry. When I did, I was lying on my back and my bra was off, underwear pulled down, hanging from one of my ankles. Daniel was lying on his side against me, his leg hooked around mine, holding my legs apart. He was masturbating, the undeniable squish and pace of it, fondling me with his other hand like I was one of those sensory boards for babies with the beads and the fabric and the plastic chains, humping at me and feeling me and whapping away, and I didn't know what to do so I just didn't do anything. I pretended to be sleeping until the inevitable shock hot across my thigh, but I kept it contained, muffled like a jar, everything inside me muted like a jar. Jarred Abby. He didn't notice anything, wiped me off with a T-shirt, my T-shirt it would turn out, and fell asleep himself.

The next day I rinsed my T-shirt in the bathroom, balled it up, and hid it in my purse. I wore one of his home. *Where's yours?* he asked. I shrugged, didn't say anything about what he'd done, let alone break up with him. Boys are boys and they do what they want. Women want things too sometimes, but mostly they're just warm sensory boards for men to tweak and rub and learn about themselves and the world through.

By the time I met Ralph, I was desperately tired of attracting unsavories. I wanted to do the kind of classy drinking that attracts sweet, good men who'd never masturbate all over you while you pretended to sleep. Or if they did, it's because they knew you were pretending. *Wanted* to be pretending.

I wore a pair of tall brown boots and a dress with flowers on it that I'd borrowed from my mom before we stopped talking. She was the person who gave me my first cooler. I'd asked if it was juice and she laughed and shook her head. *It's better,* she'd said, and she was right.

It's sort of a boring fantasy to act out, just looking nice in a bar, but things happen to women seen sitting and looking beautiful somewhere. A beacon attracting the kind of excitement that men make; that women aren't allowed to make for themselves. So you look great, and some man comes up to you and changes your life. Which is what Ralph did. A sweet. Sweeter than amniotic fluid. Sweeter than breast milk.

With my eyes closed I almost see it again, my body starving, suckling for it: the picture projected, latching to my eyelids, shaking a bit, then settling down, grays and whites and black burns around the corners. The picture is silent but I remember what it sounded like: Ralph's drunk friend had just asked if he could buy me a drink when Ralph burst through, apologizing, dragging his friend away. "Wait!" I said, because I was already a bit drunk myself and I liked Ralph's clean white T-shirt and his plain jacket and his honest-to-goodness khakis and the way his whole face grew lines when he smiled because it meant that one day he'd wrinkle up that way, and it would look like he was smiling all the time. He'd said, "This isn't how people meet anymore, just at a bar like this." That made me feel like what was happening was so special, like we'd stepped through a secret tear in time, except for the coolers, which of course are very modern.

"Morning, Abby."

I open my eyes to find Rouslana bending into the open fridge, carefully relocating a tower of clamshell containers to make room for her own sealable glass dish.

"Morning," I reply too cheerfully.

I fold my sandwich wrapper, throw it in the garbage, and head down the hall to Mrs. Bondy's room, where I find my baby sound asleep. I look at her face. How her skin pools on the bed so her head seems like a melted candle, lips parted, mouth empty, small hard skull a hidden treasure buried in wax.

"Sweet dreams, my baby," I say so quietly just in case anyone else is around. I lay my hand on her floured head, stroke her hair back the way that mothers do, fill my eyes with this helpless thing that loves me best.

Then I leave for the rest of my morning rounds, lunch duty, laundry. The hours are too bright and busy, but they move at a good clip, and I successfully override every anxious hungover thought about the very real possibility that Ralph is sinking into another psychotic depression.

14

Scene: Ralph's apartment, the morning after they first met. It's tidy, but not sterile. The cream walls of his bedroom are bright from the morning sun. Ralph and Abby are baked naked into his gray comforter like sausages in dough, legs wrapped up, a foot poking out the bottom. He's behind her, tracing pictures on her back: bicycles and cherries and even the quadratic equation that she'd identified, most impressively in Ralph's opinion, as "something mathy."

RALPH: Okay, if you get this next one right, I'll make us breakfast.

ABBY: You weren't going to make breakfast?

RALPH: Just, shh, pay attention now. *[Ralph clears his throat and starts to draw.]*

ABBY: Wait! *Wait!*

RALPH: *[Startled, he pulls his hand back.]* What is it?

ABBY: You can't just go right over the quadratic equation with a new drawing, especially not now that breakfast is on the line. Are you trying to throw my sensors off? Are you a *cheat*, Ralph Lamb?

RALPH: No, of course not! Okay, what do I do? How do I reset your sensors?

ABBY: You've gotta erase. *Eraaaaaaaassssssssse.* *[Stretching the word with mock condescension.]*

RALPH: Oh, okay, yes, you're right. *[Ralph dusts over the quadratic equation with quick, gentle pats, then uses his palm to wipe the little pats away.]* Is that good?

ABBY: *[Closes her eyes, takes time to consider her back.]* Yes, that's a fresh canvas. Go ahead.

[Abby focuses on his fingertip, which is moving slowly along her spine, over her basket of ribs, grazing her fleshier parts purposefully. She accuses him of trying to distract her and he denies it dramatically, knowing he's been caught. When he's finally done, he lifts his hand with a flourish, buries it back beneath the covers. Her eyebrows furrow, she laughs.]

RALPH: All right, guess.

ABBY: I have no fucking clue.

RALPH: Guess!

ABBY: A spaceship?

RALPH: No.

ABBY: A-a-aaaaaaaaa tree? *[Laughing.]*

RALPH: Oh my God, you're getting colder. Okay, go back. You were right about it being a vessel of some sort, not a spaceship, but that's close.

ABBY: A submarine?

RALPH: So close! Wow, you are honestly so good at this.

ABBY: A yacht?

RALPH: Okay, I'm realizing now that what I chose is ridiculous. Yacht, that's close enough. It was a freighter.

ABBY: A *freighter?* What kind of—that's a very specific vessel.

RALPH: Well, I don't know, you almost guessed quadratic equation, I figured I had to go harder.

ABBY: "Something mathy" isn't almost the quadratic equation. You're giving me far too much credit. Here, turn around, I'll show you it's not that hard.

[Ralph elbows himself over. Abby pulls down the blanket, readies her canvas using Ralph's pat-and-brush method, and starts to draw. Ralph opens his mouth to say something and she shushes him until she's finished.]

RALPH: Uh, I have no clue.

ABBY: Just guess.

RALPH: Is it bacon?

ABBY: *Bacon!* No!

RALPH: A skyscraper?

ABBY: Good Lord. It's a *freighter*.

RALPH: Come on. That wasn't—have you ever seen a freighter before?

ABBY: I just saw one actually. One of our clients at the Northern Star wanted to go to the beach and watch them pass by last week. Awfully slow.

RALPH: Was it quite boring?

ABBY: It was. But in a nice way. The folks there, they know how to make events out of nothing, out of just, people doing their jobs. Freighters. Or when the motel next door was installing a pool last year, everyone crowded around the window to watch. It was good. The whole summer felt like it was all about that pool.

RALPH: I guess it was all about that pool. Do you take them to the beach often?

ABBY: Not really.

RALPH: I hate the beach.

ABBY: How come?

RALPH: I just, I never know what to do with my wallet.

ABBY: *[Laughing.]* That's why you hate the beach? The whole beach? Because of your little wallet?

RALPH: Like, do you bury it in the sand? Do you leave it in the car? You can't leave your wallet in the car, someone will break your window.

ABBY: *[In a mocking voice, like a seagull's.]* My wallet! My wallet!

RALPH: It's terrible to have your wallet stolen! Or I imagine it is. It's never happened to me.

ABBY: Of course it hasn't, look how cautious you are. You won't even go to the beach because you've got to protect this danged wallet.

RALPH: Okay, what's wrong with being cautious, by the way? I'm asking your opinion, as a woman, what is so unattractive about caution? And what kind of a world have we created that caution should be mocked and, you know, deemed physically unattractive. That's stupid. Just, from a survival-of-the-fittest perspective, turning caution into a quality you don't want to mate with, that has to be some kind of bug we've introduced into the evolutionary process.

ABBY: Or maybe it's on purpose. We're not supposed to last forever you know.

RALPH: Like planned obsolescence.

ABBY: Exactly. We're supposed to want to die. A little bit.

[And then Abby gulps, remembering their conversation from last night. How Ralph gets sometimes, depressed. She can't remember enough from last night to know if she's put her foot in her mouth. Did Ralph ever want to die? She's too suddenly silent, plucking her bottom lip with her fingers.

He rolls her over, resumes tracing shapes on her back, adding detail to his freighter. Windows. A few stacks of cargo, she could tell now.]

ABBY: Can I ask you something? You don't have to answer it if you don't want to, I don't want to bring something up that's going to make you feel embarrassed or, I don't know, that's going to hurt you.

RALPH: *[The pace of his tracing unchanged. He's calm, knowing already that she would never do or say or ask anything to hurt him.]* Of course.

ABBY: Can you tell me again what it feels like to be depressed?

RALPH: *[Tracing, thinking.]* I mean, I don't really remember what I said last night, but *[the pop and hiss of a space heater in his bedroom, reminding them of its power]* it's like being dead, only without peace. Your sense of yourself, the thing in you that loves your family and your friends and, you know, experiences joy or even pain, that thing is gone and you're just left with your walking corpse and it's just as dreadful as any corpse is, but it's you. You're the corpse.

ABBY: Are you depressed now?

RALPH: No. Not for a long time. I take medication now, and I used to go to therapy. I should go back, really. And I meditate sometimes, that's helpful.

[Abby nods, almost speaks but decides at the last second not to share the fact that she has no idea what he means by this sense of yourself. This thing inside you that makes you who you are. Abby didn't have one of those. If she had any sense of herself at all, it was as a seed, carried by some shuddering and indifferent wind, waiting to be dropped into the place that would finally make her real. To lose this sense of yourself must surely be awful, but maybe, she thinks, it's worse to die without ever knowing yourself at all.]

But that Ralph has one, and one so solid that it could be lost and found again; that it'd slipped from his interiors like some small but significant organ, and he'd been able to build a path back to it, this matters to Abby. This is important, very specifically to her, in a way that is as moving as it is mystifying.]

ABBY: I'm sorry that happened to you. *[And because she's hungover or maybe even still drunk from last night, she begins to cry a little.]*

RALPH: Abby, it's okay. *[He gathers her in his arms, their skin the exact same temperature so Abby feels like she's dissolving, passing into him.]* I'm okay. In fact, I'm great. I feel so good. I feel so lucky. I can't believe I met you last night.

ABBY: *[Sniffing, smiling.]* I can't believe I met you.

[Ralph kisses the back of her neck, her hair, behind her ears. She knows then what it all means, meeting Ralph, their opening up to each other the way they had. It means that there's a thing inside her too. A thing that makes her her. Because otherwise Ralph would never have noticed her. His feelers would have passed over her in that bar, finding nothing to sink themselves into. But instead they found her right away, wove themselves beneath her skin, through her muscles, grabbed her by the thing and pulled her in deep. She also knows now that eventually, with time and effort and care, in the same way he'd done it for himself, Ralph will show her who she is too.]

15

RALPH IS BACK in Laura's bed again when I get home, where I learn he's spent almost the entire day, a chalk outline sprawled at a crime scene.

He asks me point-blank if I believe him, and even though I'm very tempted to say yes, dying to say yes, I have to say no. Because I can't lie to him about this. I can't *really* pretend his mother is alive just so he'll keep touching me, for God's sake.

He rolls away from me, stares at her troll dolls: round eyes, smudged noses, stiff hair. It's a dangerous kind of stare he's doing. I think of a time my mother was baking chicken breasts for Randy or Doug or Todd, two of them, raw, glistening side by side on a parchment-lined pan like the *before* lungs in a smoking-cessation ad. I wanted to bite them, a singular snap to the raw flesh, cold on the gums. The possibility of a sickness so exquisitely consuming; the possibility that she might choose me over him, lie in my bed, use a gathered bit of cool cloth to clear my face of sweat and strips of hair.

I stared at the chicken breasts the way that Ralph is staring at these dolls, and they started to breathe, expand and contract so the light sidled over their slick surfaces and I nearly lost my mind.

I want to intercept his staring, knowing it leads to madness, but I can't because he's too focused, trying to bottle, save, preserve his spirit, that thing that makes him who he is, it's trickling from him again slowly but steadily, the way it has before. He hasn't changed the bandage on his hand. It's frayed, turning black around the edges.

I begin to pluck fuzz from his pajamas, work a crunchy stain from his flannel with my nail. I plow his hair with my fingernails, lick my hand and flatten a cowlick affecting the shortest hairs on the back of his neck.

I want to ask if he saw her today, if she's becoming clearer, finding the right frequency. I want to ask if she still moves her mouth as though warding off devils, chewing cigarettes and cough drops and her own fingers in a pinch, or if she's been freed of that impulse, now that she's the one who's a devil.

That's not your mother, Ralph. That's a hallucination. You're depressed and we're going to take you to the hospital.

He squirms from my grooming fingers, hangs from the edge of the bed like a tree sloth. I bite back tears. Think of The Book. A chapter on how to protect your kitchen from vermin. I recite the names of the most common house ants in my head: *pavement ants, carpenter ants, odorous house ants, thief ants, acrobat ants, pharaoh ants, sugar ants*—almost all of these ants have the same palate as we do, craving sweets and meats and starches and liquids, not so different, are we, except ants are rude I guess, they don't realize that we have to pay for our sweets and meats and starches and liquids. The Book explains how to seal your cupboards. How to trick the ants into lugging poison back to their queen.

And then Ralph asks if he can be alone. I can't believe it. I'm stunned, blinking. He doesn't want me there, for the first time since we met he doesn't want me near him. I've never felt so worthless in all my life. I say okay and go to our room, get into bed with my clothes still on, and stretch my mouth open as wide as it can go, squeeze my eyes shut and pretend that I'm screaming: take a deep breath and squeeze my throat around the sound. It feels good the way that screaming would but I'm not making all that racket. I silent scream and silent scream over and over again until a few tears squeeze out and roll down the sides of my face, and after a while I exhaust myself enough to fall asleep.

16

Scene: A bar, typical for the city—long and narrow and dimly lit by gobbed little candles set in the bottom of stout tumblers, mismatched, vintage, like most of the glassware. Like the bar itself, ancient carvings preserved in fresh lacquer and updated with hooks underneath to hang coats and bags. The stools are backless but comfortable. The few tables are packed with patrons—two become four become six as the night hurtles onward, the room reconfigures to suit the crowd, tables dragged together, chairs squeezed in, servers shimmying sideways between every imaginable obstacle. The music is nice though, working in combination with somewhat steep drink prices to keep the place calm.

RALPH: *[Thumbing at his friend, who wanders wobbly back to their table.]* Sorry about him.

ABBY: That's okay, he didn't bother me.

[Ralph smiles, turns to leave.]

ABBY: *[Feigning a damsel's distress, knowing it's better to mask what you want in a joke rather than be seen* wanting *in public.]* Oh, um, don't go!

RALPH: *[Skeptical, hopeful.]* Yeah? Should I— *[Gestures at the chair.]*

ABBY: Yeah, sit down.

RALPH: *[Mounting the stool.]* Okay, thanks. I guess you're not meeting someone then? I assumed you must be meeting someone.

ABBY: *[Scooting closer to him.]* No, I'm not. This is it, this is what I'm doing. *[She lifts her drink.]*

RALPH: *[Uses one finger to drag a coaster into his orbit, then sets his beer on it.]* Do you do this a lot? Come to a bar alone?

ABBY: *[Looking down into her drink.]* No, not really.

RALPH: I've—

ABBY: *[Looking back up at him.]* Actually, yes, I do. I come to bars alone all the time. Do you?

RALPH: I haven't really, no.

ABBY: *[Leaning back, wishing she hadn't blurted such an unflattering truth.]* Makes sense. You don't seem like a weirdo.

RALPH: *[Leaning closer to her.]* It's not that, I'm plenty weird! It just feels like a lot of work for nothing to go somewhere alone. Don't you find that? To get dressed, spend the money, be far from your own bathroom, just to be alone?

ABBY: I never really thought about it that way. *[Sipping from her cooler.]* I mean, I'd rather if someone was here with me, if that's what you mean, I just, I don't have anyone to come with.

[Once again Abby's blurted an uncomfortable thing. You're supposed to make people think you've got a lot of friends, you're supposed to make people think you're happy—content in your work and connected to others, with a family who have become real friends, and friends who've become real family. You're not supposed to embody the energy of some ill-tempered dolphin, banished from the pod, blocking swimmers from shore just for the company. She pinches the skin on top of her hand and twists till it won't budge anymore.]

RALPH: Why not?

[He lays a hand over hers and like magic she stops pinching. It's the nicest thing anyone's done for her—the most observant, interested, sweetest—a sweet! This Ralph is a real live sweet and she's got him

now next to her, blocked from the shore. The boots and the dress, all of it must have worked because here he is, still interested despite her pinching and conspicuous loneliness.]

ABBY: *[Lifting her hand, still patched with pink from her pinching, to remind him of the weird thing she was just doing.]* Because I'm a weirdo I guess.

RALPH: Well, you don't look like a weirdo.

ABBY: *[Self-consciously smearing ripples from her dress over her thighs.]* I don't always look this nice when I come out.

RALPH: How come you look so nice tonight?

ABBY: *[Laughing.]* I guess, I don't know, I just had that feeling. Like I was tired of coming out and looking bad to everyone.

RALPH: *[Not laughing.]* You look great.

ABBY: *[Stops laughing too, taking her attractiveness as seriously as he does.]* Oh, well, thank you.

RALPH: I wonder if, when that happens, when you get that feeling that you want to look nice, it's because you're feeling especially good about yourself, or if it's because you're feeling especially bad about yourself.

ABBY: I'd say . . . I'd say I'm feeling especially good tonight.

RALPH: *[Smiling.]* Yeah?

ABBY: *[Smiling.]* Yeah, I mean, I am now. I probably wasn't before you sat down, but right now I'm feeling especially good.

RALPH: *[Blushing.]* That's a nice compliment I think.

ABBY: I'd say so.

RALPH: I wonder if you had your feeling because you knew that out here somewhere I'd been dragged out of the house by my friends for a birthday party.

[He finishes off his beer. Places it next to the coaster to indicate that he's ready for another, something Abby identifies immediately as a clear, clever little efficiency, presumably one of many.]

ABBY: *[Looking at the table.]* That's a lot of friends you've got.

RALPH: Yeah, well, they're coworkers, really. *[Noticing Abby's empty drink, he waves down the bartender. Abby leans closer to Ralph, smiling.]* Excuse me, can we get a couple more? Two of whatever she's having. *[The bartender nods, trots off.]*

ABBY: *[Mimicking the bartender's British accent, the word he uses instead of* cooler.*]* You like alcopops?

RALPH: I've never had one.

ABBY: Well, you're in for a goddamn treat.

[The bartender drops off two coolers with ice. Ralph's has an excessive number of maraschino cherries in it.]

ABBY: Thanks. Oh, look. You see how many maraschino cherries he's put in yours compared to mine? He's trying to make you feel like a little bitch.

RALPH: Why?

ABBY: For ordering this drink. This alcopop.

RALPH: No. That can't be. I'm pretty sure I asked for six thousand maraschino cherries, didn't I?

ABBY: I don't remember you asking for six thousand maraschino cherries.

RALPH: Well, I'm happy to have them, I fucking love these things. *[Popping a cherry into his mouth.]*

ABBY: *[Retrieving a single sword of cherries from her drink.]* Me too. Except I've heard they're not actually food. *[She pulls one off with her teeth.]*

RALPH: Really?

ABBY: I mean, you can eat them, but they're just supposed to be garnish. *[Pulling another off, then another, then laying the bested sword next to her drink.]*

RALPH: Are they bad for you?

ABBY: I think if they're not classified as food they can't be *good* for you.

RALPH: Honestly, I don't really care. Do you?

ABBY: No. I do not.

RALPH: Here. *[He pulls one of the extra cherry swords from his drink, drops it into Abby's glass.]*

ABBY: Ha, Ralph, you don't have to—

[He leans in and kisses her.]

RALPH: Was that okay?

ABBY: Yes.

RALPH: Can I do it again?

ABBY: Yes.

[He kisses her again, longer, his mouth sweet from the cherries. A sweet, not an unsavory, an actual sweet. She reaches up behind him, splays her fingers up along his neck and through his hair, pressing him closer to her; his arm finds its way around her lower back, and if they don't stop now, someone will have to ask them to. The English bartender will tell them to go snog somewhere else. Abby pulls away first. Ralph's table of coworkers try to make

it seem like they haven't noticed, quickly start up conversations again.]

ABBY: Do you wanna get out of here after this one?

RALPH: Really? Yes, definitely. My place isn't far.

[They're facing each other now, his knees spread wide to accommodate hers, pressed together politely—your knees should be friends, a Motherthing once said—arches of her boots fastened to the bottom rung of the barstool.]

ABBY: You know, I like that you invited me to your place. Because I always thought that a murderer probably wouldn't invite you over.

RALPH: No? Why not?

ABBY: Because it would be much easier to kill someone and just leave them at their house where they belong anyway, rather than try to get rid of a body from your own house.

RALPH: Okay, now I'm starting to think that you're a murderer. Maybe we should go to your place.

ABBY: No way, José. You're way more likely to murder me, so I get to choose. That is what "ladies' choice" means.

RALPH: I don't think that's what that means. Listen. *[Waving down the bartender, gesturing for the bill.]* I'm going to buy all your drinks from tonight and you can't stop me.

ABBY: I won't try to stop you. You can buy me other stuff too, actually. I need a new humidifier, a new shower curtain, paper towels, laundry detergent.

RALPH: Done. There's a superstore near here, isn't there? We can pop in before we go home and . . . you know.

ABBY: *[Grabbing his collar, pulling him closer.]* No, I don't know, buddy, what are you saying?

RALPH: *[Leaning in.]* You know, before we go home and I murder you.

17

AT WORK I'M ASSIGNED TO RECREATION until 5:00 p.m., but I switch with Rouslana and try to spend as much of the day as possible hiding in Mrs. Bondy's closet, doing a nice thing for her, a quiet task that always makes me feel better: neatly folding her blouses and trousers and nighties and socks and organizing them in her drawer. Like most of the women who live here, her clothes come from stores named after reliable-sounding women: Karen Miller, Eileen Fisher, Suzanne Davis. Realtors and insurance brokers and bookkeepers, the best you've ever known.

And though the clothes are often as sturdy as their names, no professional woman could wear them to an office and be taken seriously. The assaults of color and pattern and texture you find in clothes for baby girls, but not boys, who get to enjoy the same dignified denims and plaids from the cradle to the grave. The work of women's clothes never more important than at the beginning and the end of their lives when it's tasked with broadcasting, as loudly as possible: please don't try to have sex with me.

When I emerge from the closet, Mrs. Bondy is awake, smiling at me. She reaches out a hand for me to take in thanks.

"Of course." I squeeze her hand, but I can't let go. I keep squeezing it. She pulls me down to sit at the side of her bed, and I realize I'm about to cry. I pluck a tissue from the box next to her bed. "I'm sorry."

She shakes her head with more vigor than I knew she was capable of. She clears her throat and with effort manages to say, "Tell me."

"Ralph," I whisper.

"Has he hurt you?" The way she asks it, matter-of-factly, without alarm. Life has never been easy for women.

I shake my head. "He's sick. Depressed."

She nods sympathetically. "Men get that way, don't they." She pulls me in close for a hug, strokes the back of my head. "He's had a rough time. It'll pass, honey. You'll be all right." The way she smells is nice, clean, with that tweak of ammonia at the end from her hair dye. Her bones are small, brittle, beneath a wilt of warm flesh. I could hold her forever. Until she dies. Latch on tight and don't let go till the very end, so she wouldn't have to experience it alone. She doesn't twitch, boundless commitment to this hug, I know she'll hold on until I let go because she's my baby and she loves me best of all.

But I don't want anyone to see us. Not that we're not allowed to hug our babies here, but I realize I don't want anyone asking questions about it either, talking about me behind my back. Why is she sad and why is she hugging Mrs. Bondy, and where's her own mother, her friends, her husband, to hug her?

I start to squirm, the prickle of a thousand eyes roving over

the scene, Mrs. Bondy's daughter, Janet, suddenly and inex-
plicably standing in the doorway: *Just what do you think you're
doing with* my *mother?*

I reluctantly disengage from Mrs. Bondy's gentle arms,
return to standing. "I'm sorry." I straighten the sheets where
I'd just been sitting. "I shouldn't be bothering you with this."

She shakes her head, confused, because I always bother her
with things like this. She reaches out for me to come back, but
I ignore it, pretend I don't see.

"We'll be fine. I've got to be off now, okay?" Head turned,
avoiding her reaching arms and her pleading eyes, all she can
do without much voice, to stop me from walking out the door.
"See you tomorrow!" I shout too cheerfully, just before I leave.

I rub and sniff all evidence of sadness from my face as I
make my way to the staff kitchen, distract myself from the guilt
of leaving her that way, reaching for me, by collecting dishes
from rooms along the way. Perfectly normal. Perfectly fine. I
just didn't see. She was reaching but I just didn't see.

Linda calls me to the front desk. She's leaned over the check-
in binder. "Do you know who this is?" She points to an illegible
signature crammed into a cell on Mrs. Bondy's otherwise bare
page.

I spin the binder to face me, peer at an abundance of restless cursive. Another Bondy maybe? Or maybe not. The person
dropped in on one of my bereavement days, and I feel a shameful ripple of irritation at Laura for causing this unsettling mys-
tery. *Who's been in to see my baby?* I shake my head. "No clue."

"It says right here, clear as day, please *print* your name.
Print. I don't know why that's so hard for people." Linda flings
a few more pages as though to prove her point.

I shrug. Rouslana approaches the desk, eager to make small

talk. Her mother has been visiting from Kyiv so Rouslana doesn't want to go home either, but soon we all run out of things to say to one another. Rouslana is tall and pretty and glamorous. I couldn't even fathom the kind of food she buys or what the labels of her real clothes look like. We all pull on our coats. Linda walks to her car, while Rouslana and I head to the subway. She goes east toward downtown and I go west toward certain gloom, vexed the whole way by that excess of ink marring my baby's sign-in page.

18

ANOTHER DAY, another pause in our front doorway, one hand on the place where Cal is rooting, and the other on the frame, so many layers of cool, old paint that it gives like mushroom. Porous insides, where the fantasy lives, leaks out, swirling, fills the space with a gentle, intoxicating steam: a room with new couches, lots of big, soft pillows, and a massive, overbaked ottoman where everyone has room to perch their feet. Every foot in a tight, new sock, so thick you can't tell when you're touching someone else anyway, but each foot knows it's warmer there together, moving, like a family of rats in one dark little den. A family. The type of family that could be born from me and Ralph and our perfect, supernatural love.

I turn on the light. I see our living room couch, never new to us, pulled seams and embarrassingly well-worn, like all we do all day and all night is sit on that couch. No baked fat ottoman, no feet or noise or family. It's cold in here and a tap is dripping and everything is dreadful as a coma, and I wonder if I should just go into the kitchen and get the meat mallet, find Ralph, wind up and crack him across the head with it, again and again till the job is done. It'll be hard of course, I'm saying it like it's nothing but it'll be hard. Then I'd find a box cutter, or I saw in a magazine once that you can sharpen a knife against the bottom of a porcelain mug. I could do that. Find something sharp and run a bath and carve frowns into my arms like Laura did. Empty into a tub though, so it's more considerate for whoever finds us, not the flashy, carpet-destroying mess that Laura left behind. Then this is all over: Ralph relieved of his miserable hallucinations and me not tortured by him anymore. And it's even more comforting than my fantasy about the sweet family and the little rat feet; murder so much more manageable right now than creating a whole entire family.

Ralph is in the basement of course because when he's not in her bedroom with her troll dolls, he's in the basement with her. A den dweller just like she was, like Jack Russells are, and badgers. They like when their home is hugging them.

And each night I ask him how he's feeling. *Fine.* I ask him if he's seen Laura. *Yes.* If he wants any dinner. *No.* If he's spoken to anyone from work. *No.* If he wants me to turn the light on. *No.*

Tonight though, things are a bit different. Tonight a dim green light is shooting from between the keys of an old electric piano, hoisted waist-high on lean crossed legs. I don't know where it came from, but here it is, and it's glowing bright. Ralph's face is so darling in this green light. His scoop of nose and squinty eyes. But he's a captive down here, the darkness coiled around him like chains, prying open his mouth, filling his insides, *Mine now,* says the darkness, voice strummed across low, angry strings, sucking nutrition from a little hole it's made in Ralph's body somewhere.

"Where'd you find this?"

I've startled him. He fidgets in his seat, realizing now, in the presence of another pair of eyes, that he might look a bit strange, sitting there glowing in the dark. "Found it in the alley." He's still in his pajamas of course, plaid pants with the ragged bloodstain, white T-shirt, smeared and spattered. Tormented. "My mother played the piano when she was small, did you know that? She was very good, might have even been great if my grandmother had been more supportive. And now here this is."

It's hard to determine how he's feeling in this green light, his expression so obscured by it, like ooze running down his face. Though it's not a good sign that he's reciting one of Laura's grand mythologies: her innate artistic abilities, which her mother refused to nurture; the sacrifices Laura had made for Ralph, especially when it came to men, so that sometimes the way Ralph and his mother interacted was more like flirting: he'd pop out from behind a door and spook her, tickle her till she screamed and slapped him gently on the arm. Then they'd fizzle from the interaction as though it had never happened, like a pair of actors working in a haunted house doing the same scene over and over again.

"The alley." I'm thinking about him so dangerously close to the bare, brain-shaped bush, that disloyal patch of turned soil shrieking my crime. "What made you go back there?"

"The gate was open, I went out to close it and saw this. Seemed like too much of a coincidence not to bring it inside."

Strange that the gate should be open, the metal latch so

corroded it rained rust every time it lifted. It crossed my mind that if Laura were still lingering, unlatching the gate would be a good way to draw Ralph back there, where just below the bare, brain-shaped bush a patch of unsettled soil might be just noticeable enough.

"Before you ask, yes, I saw her today." He taps lightly at a few keys.

"Okay."

"I'm not making it up."

"I know that."

"And I'm going to learn to play this." He taps the same keys again.

"I think that's a good idea. Do you wanna bring it upstairs?"

When I sit down next to him, the cushion belches an invisible fug of dust and skin cells. If I were a dog, I'd snap at it, startled, and my teeth would crash into one another.

"Down here is fine." Ralph fidgets a bit of distance between us and scratches his elbow.

I lean over, press down on the lowest key. "Down here with Laura."

He smiles at me, the strange new smile.

"What about a Beethoven wig?" I press the key again. "Do you need a Beethoven wig?"

"I don't wanna be a poseur."

"My Ralphie, so cool."

"Listen." He waves me away from the keys and plays "Hot Cross Buns," demanding silence with a slow, luxurious pace. When he's finished, he says, "Maybe I am ready for that Beethoven wig."

I misinterpret this brief lapse in gloom and reach for his hand.

He pulls it away. "I'm sorry." He stares at the keyboard.

"How's this going to work if I can't touch you?"

He turns soberly, looks into my eyes. "It's for your own good, Abby."

"How's that?"

He presses his hands between his knees, shakes his head. "I don't want to say," he whispers.

I move to touch him again, an impulse I regret almost immediately when he shouts, in a desperate, terrified voice I've never heard before, "Abby, *please! Stop!*"

I throw my hands up, then immediately dig them beneath my thighs. "Ralph, you've gotta tell me *why*."

"Because I'm *dead*. I'm dead and it's going to kill you too, living with me, being with me, every day we're living together in this house is killing you too."

"You're not *dead*," I whisper, shivering. *Dead.* Not just seeing her now, but dead himself. And then what am I? If I'm seeing Ralph and Ralph is dead, then am I dead too? *Am I dead too, Ralph?* But of course I'm not dead, because Cal is here, I can feel her, press a hand against her and close my eyes, and because I'm desperate, because I don't know what else to do, I say, "I'm late."

"For what?"

"*Late,* Ralph. The *big* late."

"No, you're not."

I wait for the current of glee to soar through his spine and light up his face and make everything better, but it doesn't come. Instead he slumps down farther, runs his hands up his face, fingers in his hair, which he clutches and yanks in frustration. My Ralph. Who loves babies openly, shamelessly, like no other man on earth. Who couldn't wait to be a father. He's positively devastated by this information.

"I thought you'd be happy." I curve my spine, tuck in, bury my hands farther beneath my thighs. Not happy about a baby, about our pure love baby, Cal, who might save the world one day, who would transform us into our final forms: Mom and Dad, two people who'd had more love than they could handle, sick with it in fact, because too much of anything eventually becomes poison. But then Cal is born, ready to collect all that toxic spillover, and we're saved.

Ralph and I sitting at his table in the old apartment, playing cards and drinking coolers, Ralph explaining how we'd prepare for Cal, how we'd keep our intentions and instincts uncorrupted. "We'll need nothing from her," he'd said, "not ever, only giving her everything, always." And I'd felt so overwhelmingly in love with him as he spoke, the pragmatism he applied to everything in his life, applied to this too. His reverence for this most precious responsibility, my knowing that it came from a place of pain, knowing that he'd never let Cal experience anything like what he had. "You have to know your fleas," he'd said, a tip from the Borderline Parent, referring to the little bugs of dysfunction that mothers like ours leave crawling all over and inside you. "If you know you've got them and you know what they are, you won't give them to anyone else." We'd kill our fleas, together, raise our pure love baby in perfect, pest-free bliss.

"Abby, I can't."

In an instant my vision blurs and sharpens. "Of course you can." My voice is shaking, like I'm operating it from outside my body. "This is the plan, this was always the plan."

"There's a plague in me, Abby, in Mom. I can't pass this along to someone else, our child, who had no choice. It's not right. I won't do it."

"Well, your mom had it, and she had you. Do you wish you were never born?"

He presses into his eyes with the heels of his palms. "I can't give you what you want."

"Yes, you can. You already have." A hand on my stomach.

"How late are you?"

"Just a day."

"Have you taken a test?"

"Not yet."

"Okay, so it could still be nothing." He sees me wince. "I'm sorry, Abby, I just—you're still young and you're beautiful and funny and—you're going to be a great mother one day, the best, all right? I just—I—don't know."

He exhales, deflating as gloriously as a parade float. Something rotten on his breath, in the air now, makes my stomach turn. This true whiff of a Ralph-less life, as unfathomable as the universe. To even get close to it makes me sick. Insane. I'm not me without Ralph, I'm not human. Dragged back into the dark, lonely cell I'd spent decades trapped in, screaming, clawing, torn fingernails wedged in the walls. Worse for me because I've been there, worse for me because I *know*. Like a baby knows, so crushingly alone in that dark womb so it screams itself hoarse if it's ever alone in the dark again.

I'll never leave you alone in the dark, Cal, not ever. I won't care what anyone thinks, I won't care if I never sleep a wink again. Never alone, never ever alone, never ever alone.

I'm staring at the keyboard. The keys are long and white as fangs and I imagine that for every glowing piano keyboard in the world there's some beast left toothless and vulnerable, wandering the wilds of Wyoming or the Arctic or wherever long-toothed beasts live.

I press a piano key. I don't know which one but it's low and I don't let go till he lifts his face from his hands and looks at me. His face glowing green, strange shadows so he looks like my Ralph but not quite. Just enough light to make us both green and strange but not enough to reveal the dark wood panel walls all around us or the concrete patch beneath our feet so it looks like neither of us even has any feet. We're just faces and chests, hovering consciousnesses, staring into this light. It's what we do. It's what we are. A pair of green energy faces and chests existing in a basement in a house full of blood. That would be nice if that was all we were.

"I'm going to make some food." I stand and check my phone. Six forty-five now and dinner is going to be late. Not that it matters, it's just us. For now. When Cal comes, it will matter more because it's important that kids eat at the same time every day.

I crouch up the stairs, duck into the bathroom, and silent scream into a wad of toilet paper I've banged from the roll.

I should be screaming into tissues, not toilet paper. Tissues. For faces. And not the dusty off-brand tatters that Ralph has filled Laura's bed with, either. We need brand-name tissues. Kleenex. We need to be a house that never runs out of Kleenex.

We need a new couch. We need to be the kind of house that euthanizes couches tenderly, before they begin to decompose.

We need a new house. We need to be the kind of house that isn't this house.

But that's not possible right now, so I just have to try harder to make this house ours and not hers.

"It's ours," I mutter out loud, "do you hear me, Laura?"

As though in response, Ralph plays a note on the keyboard. Or maybe it was Laura, hiding from me while I was down there, out again now and whispering to Ralph that he's doing the right thing, that this is his house and I have no right to make him feel bad in it.

19

I WASN'T GOING TO HAVE MORE COOLERS till I knew for sure about Cal, but here I am again, cracking one open, sucking it down.

You're only managing the preliminaries right now, Cal, early stages, sipping nutrients from your yolk sac and doing paperwork. Not the real labor yet of growing organs and developing brain cells. I'll stop drinking coolers when I *really* miss my period, how's that? When it's a whole week late. I press a hand low on my stomach, get a sense from her that she thinks that's okay, reasonable, then take a long swig from the cooler.

I can't give you what you want.

Gelatin comes in thin, rectangular leaves, which I lay in a Tupperware container filled with cold water. They soak ten minutes, then I pour it all into a pot and heat it over the stove. I imagine I learned this from my mother, but I didn't. I imagine it's an old recipe passed from her mother to her to me, but really it came from The Book, of course.

I beat the salad dressing, mix it with the salmon, stir in the prepared gelatin, then pour all of the ingredients into my foot-long fish mold so they can mingle in the fridge for a while, become firm and delicious together. When Cal comes, I'll show her how to use gelatin. I'll give her my copy of *Secrets of a Famous Chef* and impart to her how important it is to only cook from This Book, my spells for a long and happy life like ours.

I open another cooler, dig the gummy bears out of the cupboard, and open The Book to the "Mother and Children" section, *carefully compiled by leading authorities.* Reading it helps me to not cry.

The baby's growth and development require plenty of lime (I pull a green gummy bear from the bag), *iron* (I pull a red gummy bear from the bag), *and phosphorus* (a white gummy bear from the bag. I line them up in front of me and continue reading). *If the mother doesn't eat enough lime, iron, and phosphorus* (I glance up at my army of nutrients), *the supply will be taken from her own body, resulting in rapid decay of the teeth. Many infants are born with a tendency to rickets because of the faulty diet of the mother.* (I quickly gobble up the gummy bears, rinse them from my mouth with a few big, healthy chugs of cooler, and set out three more.)

A healthy, full-blooded woman (That's me!) *should not be allowed to satisfy all her whims in her desire for harmful foods.* Except there's a grease splotch over the *r* in *harmful* so it looks like *hamful,* which makes me laugh, especially because I would say that I *do* crave particularly *hamful* foods, whatever that means. I finish off the cooler and find another one, a hard lemonade. Hard, hard lemonade for hard, hard people. Wooden dolls. Stone cherubs. That waiter figurine at Aunt Tony's holding out a tray of business cards, all of them together at a party enjoying hard lemonade for hard people. You work hard, you are hard, enjoy a nice hard drink.

In the case of a pale, anemic, delicate woman (like Laura!), *a more liberal allowance of proper food should be made in an effort to build up her own body and give her strength to continue her expectancy successfully.*

So Laura gets hamful foods and I do not, even though I love hamful foods and she does not. She would eat them, though, just to spite me, right in front of me, complaining about every bite.

I remember a time she described ketchup as "too heavy," and I had to glue my tongue to the roof of my mouth.

Laura liked to talk about how her body was "eighty pounds soaking wet," how difficult it was for her to keep food down in general, but especially when she was pregnant with Ralph. She just wasn't built for the body's harsher processes. Ralph was born cesarean. An emergency. Prolonged labor, weak contractions, and then ultimately Ralph made the call by filling the womb with his inaugural dump, having to be extracted within minutes or die. He'd been fine ultimately, if a bit more disgusting upon extraction, but the experience traumatized Laura so much that she couldn't bear to go through it again.

She left Ralph's father when Ralph was nine, put in a great deal of effort to make it difficult for Ralph to see him. Ralph's own memories of his father have mostly been wiped out by Laura's stories about him, delivered like gospel, row after row of big-bellied trolls echoing her like a chorus: *And what did the father do? He stole from her! He lay with other women! He abused her emotionally, spiritually, mentally! No regard for the boy!*

Ralph was never angry with her. Instead Ralph worked very

hard to prove that her leaving his father had had absolutely no effect on him; every move he made in life was designed to alleviate her guilt: *Look at me, I'm totally fine, even though you took me away from my dad, I've grown into a perfectly well-adjusted man. I have a great job, I'm married. I moved us in with you to help you through your darkest days because you raised me so well and I don't resent you at all. What other son do you know would do that? You must have been the best mother in the whole wide world to have a kid like me who would do that.*

Stability was survival to Ralph, and that's what I loved about him too, both Laura and me leaning on him without mercy, the both of us taking and taking and taking from him till there was nothing left.

I drink more of my cooler, press my forehead into the soft sides of both fists. *I'm sorry, I'm sorry. You don't deserve this, Ralph. I can do better. I can save you. With* Secrets of a Famous Chef *I can save you.*

Laura didn't believe in *Secrets of a Famous Chef. My mother had a copy and she died when she was fifty-one, so what does that tell you?*

In fact, Laura didn't believe in anything at all. Religion, miracles, karma, what have you, it was all for the weak and stupid. And when Ralph confronted her about her good-luck charms (after I mentioned something about fate and had to endure a battering of barely veiled insults too egregious to ignore), she simply said they were different, because they were hers, and if you knew her, which Ralph did, then that should be enough of an explanation.

This was exactly the way she was a hypocrite: the whole world as mercilessly random as a cancer, except to her, on whom it'd fixed a cruel and obsessive eye, screwing her over at every turn. Stubbing her toe, spilling her coffee, catching her blue dress on the head of a nail, all part of a pattern of assaults for which she'd been targeted for no reason. Negativity was Laura's mysticism, and maybe that powerful negativity has kept her here on earth. The universe *would* deny her peace, wouldn't it. Just like it denied her the ability to ever spread peanut butter without getting it on her knuckles.

She and Ralph ate a lot of peanut butter. And a lot of take-out. Because Laura didn't care about serving good foods to save your family. Maybe if you'd fed him good foods from The Book, he wouldn't have had his breakdown, an event of remarkably disparate details depending on who you asked. According to Ralph, the doctors in the hospital made much of Laura's parenting style. The prevailing theory at the time, or at least where he was being treated, was that certain blends of maternal rejection and overprotection could trigger psychological breakdowns in children. The doctors brought her into his sessions, tried to coach her on boundaries and codependency, explained how Ralph, as her child, had had no choice but to engage with her in unhealthy habits. It all made sense to him, and it helped him. He was able to build himself back up based on these facts and theories and explanations, for the most part, and keep loving her all the same.

But according to Laura, the doctors were a bunch of sexist quacks with mommy complexes, looking to punish their own mothers vicariously through their patients. She admits Ralph dug himself out of his depression, but it was no thanks to them. He read their books and interpreted their lessons and cured *himself. I hate to hear him give them credit,* that's *what bothers me.*

But she didn't know anything about Ralph. Not his real self.

Not ever. She never knew how badly he wanted to be a father, for example.

Or, back when he was small, she didn't know about his house of stones: an arrangement of large, flat rocks embedded in a field a few blocks from their home, a place where little Ralph could be alone. He pretended it was his own apartment, each stone a room, and made a fantasy of basic life skills—cooking up tasty meals in the kitchen stone and taking naps before work in the living room stone. He eventually brought that same sacred care to his real apartment, the one he invited me to, which became my fantasy too. A real home, where everything had its place; where the sheets were always clean and the fridge full and every inch of it perfectly safe for public viewing.

Laura always had something to say about his apartment. The size, the neighborhood. The dangerous space heater for which he should be compensated by his landlord: *you signed a rental agreement that included* heat, *Ralph, you never agreed to pay his bills* for *him.*

> LAURA: I told him he wouldn't be there long, and he wasn't, was he. A couple years, then he was back with me.

> ABBY: *Because* of you, Laura. You didn't *predict* anything. You're not a *mystic.*

> LAURA: Of course I am. I'm dead but I'm here. Doesn't get more mystical than that. You think you're a mystic too, filled with gems of knowledge like Ralphie said, because you've suffered some, like that makes you different from everyone else on earth.

ABBY: I have suffered.

LAURA: And you think you should be rewarded for it? With gems? With an *opal*? That's why mothers don't love you, Abby, you think you're so fucking special.

ABBY: I am special.

LAURA: You're not. Your gems are discount gems. Two-for-one. Remember what she said? Remember it.

ABBY: No.

LAURA: You can have us both.

ABBY: No.

LAURA: You can have us both.

ABBY: Shut up. You're not mystical. The Book is mystical. You're just dead.

LAURA: Are you going to save him? Are you going to use your gems for good and stop him from doing what I did?

ABBY: I'm trying, Laura.

LAURA: You need to save him, Abby. He'll die if you don't do something.

ABBY: Cal can do something. Cal will save him.

LAURA: You're not pregnant, Abby.

ABBY: Yes, I am.

LAURA: You're not.

"I am too!" I shout, then immediately laugh to myself, not because it's funny but because after you talk to yourself it feels better, less crazy, to fill the air with more sound. Laughter. Because you know it's crazy, you were just trying to be funny. I pluck my drunk-numb lower lip a few times before finishing off my last cooler, a *hard* cola, in one big swig. One, two, three, four, five empty cooler bottles. I don't want any jellied salmon tonight. The flavors will have to mingle till morning.

I stand up, the kitchen chair grinds against the linoleum. I'm even drunker than I thought, have to lean against the table, then the wall, for support, flick off lights, leaving dark rooms in my wake all the way upstairs, where I take off my clothes, get right into bed. Massive and empty.

Ralph is downstairs still, banging away on the piano.

I hope he's going easy on his hand.

I can't give you what you want.

I stretch open my mouth, try to silent scream myself to sleep, but it's not working.

The coolers are burning me up inside, leaving my senses raw and tuned-in to every strange creak and shadow inside the house. I need water. I need to pee. I wish I were a sleepwalker, animated only by my physical needs, so I could wade unconscious through Ralph's imaginary night horrors: Laura's long fingers reaching at me from dark corners, raking gently through my hair, threatening to wrap around my ankle at the top of the stairs, but I don't care because I'm not there, I'm somewhere deep in my sleeping brain. Sleepwalking, you're sleepwalking, Abby, and nothing can hurt you.

Somewhere deep inside my sleeping brain, I throw my legs over the side of the bed, still wobbly from the coolers, lean against the bedroom doorframe, run my hand along the wall for support, all the way to the bathroom, where I feel for one of the shell-shaped night-lights that callus the walls, find it, flick it on.

Weak, warm light trickles into the darkness, just enough for me to see the toilet. Coolers quadruple inside you, meaning that for every cooler you drink, you end up with four times the amount of pee, meaning I have twentysomething coolers' worth of liquid inside me. It's one of their only drawbacks, really. That and the hot, sugary hangovers that riddle your insides like a decayed tooth. I remember my mother called them sugar bugs, sugar bugs burrowing through your teeth like an ant farm and that's why you've gotta brush every night.

I'll have earned at least a bit of a hangover tomorrow, that's for sure. Even my pee stinks like a cavity. I get up and wipe and drag a glistening gob of blood with it.

Cal.

I close my eyes. A trick. The house is playing tricks on both of us, me with this blood and Ralph with his mother. I open my eyes again. She's still there. My Cal. Smeared. Obliterated.

I bring the gob of blood up to my face, listen closely. *Sorry,* she squeaks, *this wasn't our month.* I take a deep breath. I'm the mother so I have to be strong. I nod solemnly and I flush her. The coolers, acting evil tonight, want me to cry, but I won't. It's fine. We're barely trying, really, what do I expect, I don't even know when I ovulate, so shut up coolers, you glamorous fucking whores, skinny around the middle and plastered in good-time colors, clanking together, laughing at me. You'll see, when I really try, when I really get going, I'll get so fucking pregnant.

"I told you you weren't pregnant."

"Shut up," I say, leaned over, steadying myself with the side of the tub, digging a pad out from beneath the sink. I set the pad squarely on my underwear, then stand at the sink and fill a little cup with water, watch my throat move in the mirror as I swallow it down.

Fill up another, swish it around in my mouth, then stop, realizing that someone has spoken. Someone real.

"I told you you weren't pregnant," she says again, exactly the same way, a crackled recording, words floating in white noise. My eyes widen around what I now see reflected behind me in the mirror, a shape behind the shower curtain, swaying slightly the way a living thing does, fighting gravity and involuntary bodily processes. The shape, human, lifts one hand, rests its fingers against the curtain, four dark points, pressing forward. I can't swallow, I let the water tremble out over my lip and into the sink and I clear my throat and close my eyes, pretend I haven't seen it because I'm sleepwalking, deep inside my sleeping brain, and this isn't real. The crunch of shower curtain, I keep my eyes closed, no, no, not happening, grope for the knob, fling open the door and race down the hall and slam our bedroom door behind me.

Back into bed, fistfuls of blanket hoisted up to my chin, I pretend not to hear the shower curtain rattle gently along the bar, the bathroom door open and close and footsteps, bare, dragging, making their way down the hall and, from my count, stopping just outside our closed bedroom door. Then silence. Standing. The swaying un-still of a beating, living body, and my flesh crawls, relentless, all night long, can't settle, can't sleep, snatching only fitful, drunken bouts of half consciousness.

I dream our bedroom door is creaking open and I tear myself awake violently, sweaty, twisted up in the sheets. I see the door is closed, settle back down, and do the whole thing over and over, until finally, just as cars start honking, struggling out of their snowy parking spots, I really crash.

20

MAYBE I'VE DEVELOPED A SUPERPOWER, which is that I can
see ghosts, but only when I'm shit-faced. I am the Incredible
Drinking Woman. If I'm going to defeat the Evil Ghost, I have
to keep getting hammered. In the first issue, titled *Failure to
Thrive,* the need to be constantly drunk kills my unborn child.
She drowns in my womb, a bog of digested coolers, no mouth
yet to scream, but enough flipper to author a spectacular final
thrash, made more dramatic by a vacuous, sizzling aftermath.
Now this is personal, says my dialogue bubble, defeating the
ghost no longer just some obligation thrust upon me by cir-
cumstance, but a smoldering need to exact revenge for killing
my Cal.

I silent scream for a second, then grab Ralph's pillow and
drag it over my head. These pillows used to be Laura's too.
Heavy from decades of her skin cells. I wonder for just a frac-
tion of a second if maybe the *pillows* were the problem the

whole time, for both of them, Ralph and Laura, sleeping on cursed pillows their whole lives. *The pillows* are what whisper hexes into their ears at night, and if I get rid of them, Ralph will be cured.

I don't let myself think of that for too long though, it's a flash more than a thought, and then it's gone. Because it's not true. Pillows don't make people kill themselves. Neither do the angry ghosts of unsettled mothers.

What's happening is that Ralph is getting in my head now, his delusions becoming mine, easily, because I'm nothing. Still just a seed floating in the wind. Landing on Ralph, rooting in Ralph, becoming Ralph instead of becoming *me*. And that doesn't work here. If I'm going to save him, I can't keep being nothing. I have to be something. Somehow.

I make my way into the bathroom, wrap my hand around the shower curtain, tear it open. Empty. Ordinary.

I sit on the toilet, pull the pad, Cal-soaked, from my underwear. I'll miss you, Cal. But it's okay, it's okay, because I'm going to mark this down in my calendar, really start tracking things. Only you can make Cal real, Abby. You're the magic one. You've endured the suffering that makes mystics; that fills them with gems of transcendent wisdom. Not mall gems. Good gems. Remember what Ralph said, what suffering is: throbbing little irritants, sand in an oyster, rubbing and rubbing and rubbing into beautiful, glittering lozenges of magic and you're full of them.

I look like shit. I'm not sleeping well. I'm not eating good things from The Book. Ralph's darkness thumbs at my skin, marked like clay. Maybe when I get new pillows, I'll get some of those anti-aging ones I saw on the Shopping Channel. I didn't realize it, but if you're a side sleeper, which I am, you can get more wrinkles all over that side of your face. Even in your sleep you could be doing better!

I wash my face and rub in cream from a massive, industrial-size tub of moisturizer that also used to belong to Laura. It came from a coworker's daughter who worked at the Pond's factory. Laura called it cold cream. She also called conditioner *cream rinse. Cream* must have been a big buzzword in marketing to women back in Laura's day. It's a nice word, *cream.* A nice idea, *cream.* Cool. Soothing. Clouding imperfections and filling gaps, making everything look smoother, even coffee. Then some unsavory came along and turned it into a verb and ruined it for everyone.

I pull on my scrubs and secure my hair in a ponytail, then grab the massive tub of *cold cream* and head toward the stairs. *Cream.* It's the size of a baby, I think. The weight of a baby, resting on my hip. I resist the urge to bounce it. *Cream. Cream. Not a baby, but cream, a baby's worth of cream.* "I'm throwing away your *cold cream,* Laura," I say to the upstairs hallway, imagine her on some invisible plane behind me, arms crossed, shaking her head, complaining to Ralph later about how I don't know the value of a dollar: *She's so wasteful, Abigail, you're just so wasteful. Were you always this wasteful? Or just since marrying Ralph? A person could learn to be wasteful on that salary, I'm just saying.*

I hear the TV on in the living room and I know that Ralph isn't going into work again today, because this is our life now: Ralph is an unemployed madman, and I'm his worthless familiar, playing the dangerous game of dipping in and out of his delusion like it's a warm, soothing tub of ORGANICA.

He's sprawled on the couch, a handful of tossed spaghetti,

watching Laura's favorite murder show. Eyes and mouth open a little bit, wet slits in his face. He's like a baby, half-asleep but still hungry. Everything and everyone is a baby and that's just how my brain is now. I move toward the couch, tap his feet so he tucks them in, a reflex like when you poke a snail in the eye. I sit down. He keeps his feet tucked up close to him. I don't want to leave.

"Ralph."

When he sits up, dry Rice Krispies drizzle from his pajamas. I'm making the conscious decision not to pick them up. They'll get stepped on, become dust, invite every variety of ant from The Book: come one, come all, these humans have given up.

"Did you take a test?" Worry mars his forehead.

I wait for the gems to give me guidance, but they don't, just watch me sit there like a goon, staring at Ralph as his posture involuntarily resumes its potato-bug curl. Ralph was more comfortable being small. He once said his height, a hair above six feet, two inches, felt like a curse from his father. I hated to hear that. I was proud of his height, like a fisherman grinning behind some massive conquest. *Abby Lamb, oh, boy, would you look at the size of her husband!*

I'm trying not to cry, but it's impossible right now, like trying to hold a ladleful of soup in my cupped hands. "I got my period."

He exhales. "I'm sorry, Abby. I know how bad you want this, I—"

"*We* want this. How bad *we* want this."

He frowns. Blinks. Ralph's eyes but not Ralph's eyes. How eyes that love you look so different from eyes that don't. They're like a pair of once-precious jewels that have now lost all value, the same but worthless, like every other rock in the world. I want to bite him. See if he tastes the same, but I think it might push him over the edge if I tried.

I try to imagine that my tear ducts are totally empty, wrung out and dry enough to panfry. From *Secrets of a Famous Chef*: Start by carving a fresh tear duct out of the face, making your first cut about an inch down from the inside corner of the eye. Bury the knife until you can't anymore. You don't want to force it through the skull. Drag the knife up so it follows parallel to the nose, all the way to the eyelid, making sure to keep the depth as uniform as possible. Peel back this flap of skin and you should see the lacrimal duct and sac. Etch away any connective tissue and the duct should slide out easily. Pat dry with paper towel completely before panfrying (see Giblet Bites recipe for exact frying directions).

I leave him on the couch and go to the kitchen, stand in the middle of the room and pull myself together; deep breaths work. In and out and in and out and I see that *Secrets of a Famous Chef* is still open on the table where I left it, the chapter about what mothers should eat while nursing: *A breastfed baby has little fear of summer complaint, surgical tuberculosis, convulsions, or bowlegs. A nursing mother should try to cultivate a cheerful frame of mind.* A cheerful frame of mind. Just the phrase makes me laugh. How could I have ever expected Cal to root in my gloomy uterus? I need to put a smile on this uterus, make Ralph well again so it can be loamy and joyful as a cornfield.

I pick up The Book to put it away and discover the kitchen knife beneath it, the one I'd shoved beneath the mattress. I don't remember leaving it out on the table like this. I don't remember pulling it out at all. I picture a Laura made of static, squeezing her hand between my mattress and box spring while I sleep, retrieving the knife and setting it on the table for Ralph to find. It's not safe here, not with their shared gene drawn to it like warmth. I bury it in my purse, then grab our biggest Tupperware container, the one I used to soak the gelatin, and I fill it with the rest of our sharpest knives, including steak knives, anything Ralph could use from here to slice himself up, then fill the container with water and cram it into the freezer. All the knives frozen soon: deactivated. I'll keep the cursed knife with me always.

21

I'D EXTRACTED THE JELLIED SALMON *almost* successfully from the foot-long fish mold (everything made it but the tail) and dumped it on an aluminum tray, the kind that bucks at absolute random and makes a person terrified they might launch jellied salmon all over the floor. I strapped it into the back seat of Laura's car and drove to work instead of taking the subway.

At the front entrance I press the activation switch with my elbow and the door opens for me. When the tray bucks, it's loud as a gong, but no one notices or comes to help me, not that they really could, only one person at a time should ever hold a bucking aluminum tray, but they could at least come near me and walk near me and give me the peace of mind that they're there and ready to help if the salmon bucks right out of my hands, spatters its guts all over the floor.

It takes some time to fit the tray into the fridge. Only women work here so the fridge is tidy, bricked with labeled salads and yogurts and cubed, colorful fruit; Diet Cokes and slim cans of soda water and chocolate bars of various sizes, resealed with elastic, that we all nibble from, mice slowly picking from a baited trap. I know that amniotic fluid is sweet and breast milk is sweet and every baby is born loving sweet things. When I'm pregnant next time, actually pregnant, mine will be the sweetest womb. I'll eat mango and chocolate and ice cream and spoonfuls of Cool Whip right from the tub. Cal will spend nine months floating in syrup. I'll give her heaven for a while.

A few people come in and out of the kitchen, needing things from the fridge, standing behind me, so I get out of their way and they smile and say sorry and I nod and wave my hand and mostly they don't ask what's on the tray. One person, Carlie, who brings in the slim cans of soda water, asks what's on the tray and I answer, "You'll just have to wait and see!" which sort of kills the conversation because all she could do then was just smile and nod and move along with her morning.

It's time for the breakfast service, where I get to pretend to be a waitress—straighten my back and stick my chest out and raise my chin.

When I was young, all the most beautiful people I'd ever seen were waitresses, and after we were done eating, Mom's boyfriends stuffed small fortunes into their sticky black folders. A *restaurant*: where you step inside and are instantly transformed into a *guest*. Money in your pocket the mana that makes this magic possible.

You can choose to be a *good guest* or a *bad guest,* a benevolent master or an abusive monster to the flock of friendly, gorgeous humanoids who magically deliver your nearly every wish. Assuming of course that Northern Star residents wish for cheerless eggs and watery decaf and mandarin orange slices suspended in goo, like tiny lungs or livers or kidneys awaiting transplant, indifferent as manicurists about who they end up with.

All the other care professionals find serving food demeaning and they adopt noticeably terrible attitudes to protect themselves from the feeling: dropping plates of food in front of people too loudly, rolling their eyes when a resident asks for more water or an extra napkin, especially rude when a visitor joins to dine.

Usually I'm able to simply observe this bad behavior, maybe shake my head a little, mostly let it go. But today it's gnawing at me, seeing our *guests* hesitate to ask for things they need, the energy from Carlie so palpably *hostile*. And I know why I'm feeling so raw. It's because I have to look inside myself, produce enough *ME-ness* to keep anchored in reality while Ralph drifts deeper into the dark. There is no threshold I can cross to perform this magic, no mana I can spend to make *something* from *nothing*.

Nothing.

I am nothing.

I am nothing so Ralph will die.

Mrs. Bondy's not at breakfast, which isn't uncommon for her. I often make her a tray and bring it to her room after service, leave it on her side table so she can eat as soon as she wakes up. Quite a few residents are still in bed today, so Carlie, *annoyingly* desperate to get out of the dining room, offers to load a cart with meal trays and deliver them.

I finish service alone, then do my rounds, then before I know it it's nearly noon. I go into the break room to set up my jellied salmon, shake crackers into a couple of abandoned Tupperware containers from the cupboard. The break room is unnecessarily bright and the lights seem to tremble, buzz, a sound that makes the whole room feel rigged up somehow. Like if you opened the fridge, you'd get electrocuted. An extremely aggressive dieting technique.

In this light the jellied salmon looks quite unappetizing. It's staring at me. Sliced-olive eye catching light the way a real eye does. I move a little to the left and it does too, portraits in an old mansion, haunted by generations of unsmiling salmon, successful enough to have filled a mansion with commissioned portraits.

Carol walks into the break room, stopped in her tracks by my jellied salmon. "Now what's this?" she says, intrigued.

"Jellied salmon." I stand up straight next to it like it's my science fair project. A human sign. I've been placed here instead of a toothpick with a little bit of paper on it that says *jellied salmon*. I was too distracted by the salmon's eye to cover up the broken tail with a lettuce leaf, but that's okay. Maybe if I just leave it exposed, people will think that other people have already eaten some and not be so scared of it. *God, Abby, that's some quick positive thinking. Good for you,* sarcastically. Like it's Laura saying it. I stick my pinkie fingers in my ears and shake my hands vigorously. "You're not real," I whisper.

"What's that?" asks Carol.

"Oh, nothing. Everything is fine."

"My God." Carol takes in the jellied salmon with her hands on her hips. "You *made* this?" She leans over it cautiously, ready to recoil if it flaps awake and snaps at her. The salmon is staring at her now, watching her move slowly into its line of vision, hair hanging around her face like a broken net, all of her skin drooping straight down. It makes you realize just how much gravity has to do with the way your face has settled, how different you'd look if you walked on your hands your whole life instead of your feet: eyebrows halfway up your forehead, drooping into your hairline, top lip hanging open and showing your teeth.

"Yes, you should try some! It's high in protein, low in carbs." I hold out a bowl of crackers. "Oh, except for the crackers of course. Those are all carbs." I clear my throat, dig one of the crackers into the jellied salmon, and eat it, just to show her that it's not poison. It really is good.

"No thanks." She turns around toward the fridge. I'm so *annoyed* again that it shorts the fluorescent light above us. It shudders, dark, then light, and the room is changed: the second Carol's hand wraps around the fridge handle a jolt tears through her, shakes her so hard she lands seemingly boneless on the floor, twitching, bowels and bladder evacuated, her hand is black, twisted as a branch, and her teeth are black and her eyes have exploded, popped, bloody pus leaking down her face, sockets sizzling. Toothless and blind, exactly my specialty here at the old age parlor, then she'd see just how important my job is, just how nice I am to lug in any kind of snack at all. People love snacks at work, people *live* for snacks at work, Carol, *you fucking fuck*.

The light shudders again. "They should fix that." She gestures up at the fixture with a small spoon, a baby spoon.

Safer to be *nothing*. Safer to drift into oblivion with Ralph.

Carol leans back on the fridge door, peels the lid from a tiny yogurt cup, presses her tongue fat along it, then tosses the lid into the garbage can. The whole scene could be a commercial. She is the ultimate yogurt type—clean and kind and intimate with the fragile chemistry of her gut flora. I am a jellied salmon type. I am a jellied salmon type, and Laura is dead. Ashes now. Burned without her ring.

Without her ring.

And there's nothing I can do about it. Not now. And even if there *were*, it wouldn't make a difference because she's *not fucking here.*

Carol takes infuriatingly small bites. As though eating is some charming hobby she's picked up, and not crucial to her survival.

I know from yogurt commercials that an epidemic is happening right now: constipated women, *dangerously* constipated, dying for probiotics. A perk of being a jellied salmon type is that I shit regular as a clock every morning. I don't need yogurt for anything. In a way it makes me proud; the sort of pride I'd feel if I were particularly fertile: fertilized and fertilizing, birthing and shitting with ease is as naturally woman as a woman can be. I'm in an ad, squatting in a field, emptying myself into a pixelated blur, "as naturally woman as a woman can be," I say, then nip a bite of jellied salmon from a baby spoon.

I want Carol to feel bad for turning down my salmon. I want her to know that she's not better than me.

"Carol?"

"Hmm?" She pulls the spoon upside down over her bottom lip.

"Do you eat that yogurt because you need help shitting?"

She juts her head forward, eyes wide. "Cripes, Abby!"

Her expression, the tone of her voice, the instant realization that what I've asked is inappropriate and strange; that I've succeeded in nothing but making myself look like a weirdo, or worse, like *I* might be the one who needs help shitting. Safer to be *nothing, god*dammit. Safer to drift into oblivion with Ralph.

"Oh, Carol, I'm so sorry, I was just asking because . . . I shit so regularly and I never eat yogurt, and—" I'm trying to fix something that simply can't be fixed, stomping on the nose of the *Titanic,* trying to keep the ass end from sinking. I want to stop, but, also, I'm just so fucking *annoyed.* How dare she not even *try* the salmon. I know she likes canned salmon, I've seen her eat it before, Carol, I see you eat salmon all the time, spreading it from those little blue tins stamped with sustainability certifications, onto crackers lighter than air. It's sweet the way you do it, sort of special how you drag a wad of it onto every bite as opposed to spreading it across the whole cracker and eating it that way. I'm sorry, Carol. I'm not actually mad at you at all.

"Okay, okay, okay, Abby, it's fine, you don't have to be *that* sorry."

I nod. Stand there quietly, try to be the right kind of sorry, scared to say anything else because my brain and my mouth are absolutely fucked now it seems.

"I just like yogurt, but, you're right, all of the commercials these days basically talk about it like it's a laxative. That's funny."

I laugh a bit. "Yeah, I just, a woman should be able to shit." I don't know what's happening to me. I don't know what I'm saying.

Carol shrugs, smiles politely, and leaves without having a bite of my jellied salmon.

I need Mrs. Bondy. I need to touch her soft hands. I start making my way toward her room, nod at the other women on duty: Rouslana, tall and slim, stretching up high, one heel pulled off the ground, changing the channel on the muted TV in the main room. Shanitra, frowning over a pile of pills to be sorted. Ellen, rolling Mr. Phibbs, and Carlie, with the snack cart, rolling from room to room.

Mrs. Bondy's eyes are open, big and clear and wide, when I walk through the door. "Morning, Mrs. Bondy."

She waves hello and I get to work tidying her kitchenette, wash her teacup and set it to dry on a dish towel, rinse a grainy settle of cereal milk from the bottom of her bowl. I picture Ralph staring into the TV right now, maybe eating a bowl of cereal, string of milk down his chin, Laura sidling up next to him, catching the milk, slurping it off her own fingers.

You're imagining things, Abby. You have a wild imagination. Major depression with psychotic features. Psychotic. Abby, HELLO! I wish you'd just call me. I could talk you out of this, I could always talk you out of things, remember the thing you thought you heard, "You can have us both," *I talked you out of it, you see?* Lessons in how to become *nothing*; how to hear things, then not hear them, feel them, then not feel them, strap yourself to someone else, then let go and endure the ride.

Mrs. Bondy is trying to say something. I lean in close to her so that my ear is almost pressed up against her lips, and I make out that she's thirsty.

"Well, why didn't ya say so!" I shout, and she smiles at my joke. The doctor said that most patients with her set of symptoms usually stop trying to talk by now, but I think that maybe she keeps trying because I still understand her. Like how parents can always understand their kids. When someone understands you, it motivates you to keep going. Sometimes it doesn't feel like an accident, that Mrs. Bondy and I get along so well, like she's another mystic like me, some precious gem of wisdom, tumbled in her suffering, trapped in her body, and only I can extract it.

I fill her water glass and get her a new straw and she lifts both hands for it and drinks, a set of long, deep pulls, gives me back the glass. I place it on her night table and she squeezes my hand in thanks. I turn her hand over in mine, she makes our sign for "manicure." I knew she might want this today so I've brought nearly black nail polish in from home.

Back when Mrs. Bondy could speak a little more, she told me that she used to wear black nail polish and dye her hair black and wear black eyeliner and try to make her lips the same color as her skin, "like a witch," she'd said.

I pull a chair up next to her bed, lay a towel over my lap, and set her hand on it, spread her fingers apart, lift the first one, and drag an emery board along the top, over and over in the same direction because that's the right way to do it. If you go back and forth, your nail is more susceptible to breakage.

She looks at my face while I do it because when you get older, you do whatever you want. Young people don't stare at each other like this—there's too much bouncing around inside us still: insecurity and rage and fight and *What are you looking at, what's your problem?* But old people, they don't give a shit. They want to see people's faces, examine them in a way they were never allowed to before. Most of us will get to eventually, look at people's faces like never before, especially those of us who eat good recipes from The Book and live forever, we'll get to stare deep into a thousand faces one day and that's something to look forward to.

She clears her throat, so I look up at her. She mouths, "How's Ralph?"

I move on to her next nail. "He's better!" I say too loudly. "Much better. It was just, I guess it was just a phase, like you said. Sorry about that the other day, honestly I shouldn't have said anything." I shake my head. She raises her eyebrows, holds me in the kind of stare mothers use to will truth from their children, Mrs. Bondy my mother, my real mother, switched at birth and she's known it all along, holding it in until now, right now, when she finally reveals her secret, the whole reason she chose the Northern Star, to be with me, her final days made blissful because she got to be near me. But then she lowers her eyebrows, stops staring at me, lets my lie go, the way a mother never would, reminding me, cruelly, that I'm not her child.

But, no, Abby, she's not doing that. Not on purpose. She doesn't know that she's your baby, and that you're hers. You've never told her before.

I squeeze the tip of her next finger.

Tell her, Abby. Tell her she's your baby. An elderly baby and a tormented husband and an undead mother-in-law, you really can have it all!

I work her nail with the emery board again, grind a mist of keratin I can taste. My mother never taught me to file my nails the right way, I read it in a magazine, which is perfectly fine, but I wonder if Mrs. Bondy taught her daughter the right way to file her nails. Then magic again, how thinking of Laura had maybe made her appear, I'm thinking about Mrs. Bondy's daughter and she appears, for the first time in a year. I smell her first, the cracked-open spine of a fashion magazine, the kind we keep scattered across the terrible table in the lobby that draws people's shins to its sharp corners.

"Hi, Mom," she says, and I spin around, accidentally fling the emery board so it lands just in front of her black boots, wool leggings, tight pencil skirt, crisp white blouse, pulled and tucked to look like a cloud. Hair perfectly set and glossy as a doll's before it disappears into a scribble of screaming, greedy children. She's made the whole room smell different, dangerous, malignant. And feel different too, dingy and unacceptable now. Photographs in some sort of exposé on the inhumane condition of old age homes. Except this is a wonderful place, well taken care of, staff like me who treat the residents like their own sweet little babies.

I turn back to Mrs. Bondy, whose whole face breaks into a smile, biology preventing her from recognizing that her daughter is a fucking asshole. Her fucking asshole daughter rushes to the other side of the bed in a hummingbird burst. "I *told* you I'd be back," she says, pencil skirt tight as a fist so that her legs move like she's trying to escape it. She gathers Mrs. Bondy up in her arms, and they hold each other for a while. I see the unfinished half of Mrs. Bondy's nails turn white, squeezing this woman with more strength than I knew she had in her. I don't know what to do so I just sit there, forgotten in a haze of fragrance. I don't want to leave them alone together. I can't bring myself to do it. Mrs. Bondy is my baby and this scented woman is a stranger. She's not technically, but she is.

"I didn't expect you back so soon" is all Mrs. Bondy can manage before erupting into a violent coughing fit.

Janet Bondy finally notices me. "Shouldn't you be helping her?" she barks, waving an arm into her mother's exploding face.

"This is why we have a no-fragrance rule." I shoo Janet away, grab the glass of water from the nightstand, and settle Mrs. Bondy down.

"Oh," she says, pulling the corner of her blouse to her nose and breathing in like she doesn't even notice it anymore.

"Are you all right, Mother?" Janet's made her way to the other side of the bed, leaning in again.

Mrs. Bondy mouths the words *thank you* at me.

"Yes, yes, thank you." Janet turns to me. "I'm Janet Bondy, by the way, I don't think we've met."

"I'm Abigail. I work with your mother. We have met before, actually." I stick my hand out over Mrs. Bondy. Janet picks it up and drops it like a used tissue. Her eyes are big and wander in their sockets like a tiny-skulled dog. Her lips, artificially plump and pink and glossy as raw poultry, barely move when she speaks. I'm bubbling inside, fizzing up like a just-poured cooler, so jealous it's boiling my guts. Touching Janet's powdery hand has excavated even more of my jellied-salmon insides—the parts of me that want to grab her arms, pull them behind her, kick her straight out the door, bloodied stump arms still in my hands, beat her to death with them in the hallway, run out the front door with them, still flailing, terrify the parking lot pigeons so they whoosh up and take me with them.

"We have? Sorry about that."

"That's all right. It's been a very long time."

"Right." Janet receives my passive-aggressiveness, forces a smile, and wonders why I'm not gone yet.

Mrs. Bondy is plucking her half-filed nails with her thumb. I grab the nail polish. "We can finish this later, Mrs. Bondy."

She nods, squeezes my wrist.

"Oh, I can do that." Janet holds her hand out for the nail polish.

I squeeze it into my palm, actively stop my whole body from whipping it in her face, hold it, hold it, Abby, don't throw it, Abby; a rogue nerve that can't take it anymore begins to twitch just beneath my eye. I'm barely able to fight it, slowly extend my arm forward, drop the nail polish into Janet's outstretched hand.

"Thanks."

"You're welcome," I press through clenched teeth. It's the perfect time to leave. A more natural break has never existed in the whole entire world. When you don't leave during a natural break, pressure starts to build in a room, people get anxious. It's just not how things are done. But I don't leave. I keep standing there next to the bed, not moving, and would have all day if Carol, sweet, kind Carol, hadn't come to save me, leaning into the doorway, asking if I've got a minute to help her move chairs for Jerri's art lesson this afternoon.

I take a deep breath. "Sure." I smile insincerely at Janet.

22

CAROL HUFFS STRAY HAIRS from her face as she lifts an impressive stack of chairs and shuffles them to the wall. She stands up, refastens her ponytail, and says, "Wonder what she's after."

"Who, Janet?" I wrangle an impressive stack of chairs too. We're a good team of hardworking women, and no matter what kind of work you're doing, it's always nice to be doing it with people like that, a certain satisfaction that comes from everyone respecting each other's time and bodies, no one valuing their own more than yours. This mutual respect is a sort of way of being close to people, for a jellied-salmon type like me. I try to hold this positivity in my mind, but it leaks out quickly.

"She's been by a couple times now," says Carol. "I'd never met her before."

"Aha." Dawning on me now, the swirling signature on Mrs. Bondy's visitor page in the book. "I was wondering who'd signed in to see her."

"It's probably something to do with money. It always is. Next thing you know we'll be moving her out."

"Moving Mrs. Bondy?"

"That's how it usually goes. The family starts showing up out of nowhere, complaining, 'Why isn't this clean? Who's taking care of that? Paying too much for this to be dirty and that to be ignored.' Next thing you know our client's out the door, on the way to Kingsmere."

The violence flares again, tight around my spine. "She wouldn't." I set my stack of chairs down, lean on the arms. "It would be murder to move Mrs. Bondy."

Carol shrugs, opens her mouth to speak, but stops, blinking. She rests her knuckles against her forehead, the elegant way a yogurt type's body expresses distress.

"Are you okay?" I ask.

"Yeah, yes, I'm just, I got dizzy there for a second."

"Let's get you something to eat."

Carol nods appreciatively. We make our way to the kitchen.

"Todd's been out of town," she says. "Sometimes I get scared in the apartment at night and don't sleep well. He keeps talking about moving out to the suburbs, but I don't know, I think I'd be even more scared out there."

I start to pull the salmon out of the fridge.

"Oh, no thanks, Abby, I think I'll just have a Diet Coke."

"It's for me," I lie, meat between my vertebrae shrinking to jerky, this fucking bitch refusing my fucking salmon *again,* giving me back my coolers just so she didn't have to look at them in her fridge. These annoyed feelings, this rage, vibrating so quickly inside me it's become pleasure, like taking a shit while having an incredible orgasm, while somehow also scratching Janet so hard my nails pack backward with her flesh.

I've got both hands on either side of the bucking salmon tray while Carol blathers on about restless nights in her California king.

I'm going to smash the tray across Carol's head. Shitting and coming and smashing Carol across the face, every point of contact an explosion of relief. This is it, this is what Ralph needs, the cure is shitting and coming and killing at the same time.

Carol is staring at me.

"What?" I snap.

"I'm just . . . gonna . . ." She points at the fridge behind me. I'm in her way.

"Oh! I'm sorry!" I step aside so she can grab a buxom bottle of Diet Coke.

"Anyway, maybe Todd's right. Maybe we should move."

"We're almost nearly in the suburbs. It's not scary."

"That's right, I forgot, you're in Ralph's mom's house. God, what a lucky break."

"Yeah, it was lucky." I skid a cracker through the jellied salmon, shovel it fold-loaded into my mouth so I have an excuse not to say anything else, just chew and breathe carefully through the crumbs.

"Oh, shit." Carol palms her forehead, realizing what she's said. "I'm such a complete idiot, Abby, Jesus, I'm so sorry, that was a terrible thing to say. This real estate market, it turns people into cretins, it really does."

"No, no." I wave my hand at her, notice some crumbs on my shirt and bat them off. "I knew what you meant. And you're right, it's crazy out there, we lucked out in a way, even though it was for an awful reason."

"Are you mad at me?" She pouts.

"Of course not, no, it's really okay." I smile, traces of shitting and coming and smashing her brains palpable, but retreating.

"All right, Abby, give me one of those crackers."

I hold the box out for her and she loads a cracker with an amount of salmon that is more than just politeness. She's really having a bite.

And it's nice the way she says Abby.

I do like Carol. I do like her. She's had me over to her house, right in her own house, and maybe giving me back my coolers was a friendly thing to do. If she's not going to drink them, then why should they go to waste? It's not her fault she doesn't like cooler fuzz all over her brain and tongue, candy coating all of her words so they're sticky, indistinct. I love you, Carol. I'm sorry I wanted to kill you for a minute there, but I'm over it now.

23

RALPH HAS NOW REJECTED all forms of therapeutic grooming, including a blow job, which was such a humiliating disaster that the intrusive memory takes the form of me, dressed up like a horse, lipping desperately for a raw carrot.

I gather flesh between my thumb and finger, have to keep pinching harder and harder to make the thought go away.

I have nowhere to go.

No friends.

No mother.

I'm nothing.

I'm *nothing*.

I run into my mother's room, find the rolling hillside of two bodies. There's a bear in there, sleeping next to her. A man, though. Dragging long, stale lungfuls of air through his unfamiliar throat. I wish he wasn't there but I'm so scared. I need my mother. I saw something in my room, a crouching thing with eyes like watermelon seeds and ropes of greasy hair hanging in front of its grimace. It peered at me from the closet, glistening teeth, deep, rasping pulls of breath that inflated its chest so much I could see every branch of its black veins.

I erupt from my blanket, run to the side of her bed, poke her cheek. She's drunk. I'm young but I can tell, her insides full of glue, eyes peel open slowly one after the other. How she stinks.

Mommy, there's something in my room and every time I close my eyes it gets closer.

She mumbles something like *Come on then* and makes space for me, scoots in closer to the man. I lift the blanket a bit, careful not to jostle anything too much, and snuggle into her. I really wish this man wasn't here, but I have no choice, it's either sleep with this man or sleep with the closet thing. I breathe in deep, prickly sweat-and-fart-and-booze-filled breaths of their hot sleeping, until I finally fall asleep too.

In the middle of the night I wake up, crack open an eye to see the man on the other side of my sleeping mother sitting up on the bed. Constellations of acne mar his curved back. I can't see his head. Hung low somewhere in front, heavy and kneaded by yellow fingers. He stands up, flings his arms up high to stretch, twists left, then right, then turns around. Through my slivered eye I see his face. I see his hollow, pocked chest. I see that pudge of wrinkled flesh peeking from a tangle of hair. It makes my stomach turn. Just sitting there. Fat and sleepy as an overfed mouse. He'd been naked this whole time I've been in here. She was probably naked too, me pressed up against her bare, just-fucked body. I never checked to see if she was naked too, just closed my eyes, tucked my body up small. Waited for him to come back to bed, his snoring to steady, then went back into my room with the goblin.

I HAVE *SECRETS OF A FAMOUS CHEF* in bed with me tonight, lie on my side with my head hoisted up on my palm like a picture frame, flip through its calming pages. An illustration, called a colored plate in The Book, of a chicken and a pig nosing through long grass. Another colored plate, a rabbit burrow packed tight with scooped softness. The glisten of a single red eye.

One of the chief reasons that the meat supply doesn't meet human demands is that man has concentrated his appetite on fewer and fewer animals for meat. By following these instructions, you can safely eat the heads, brains, kidneys, tongues, ribs, shanks, hocks, feet, and tails of not just pig, fowl, goat, and cow, but also discover the pungent, sumptuous delights of bear, deer, rabbit, woodchuck, and opossum. Meat is good for you, a high-quality protein providing energy, health, and vigor. This chapter is intended to help families conduct the butchering and safe preparation of any animal at all with pleasure and pride.

I close The Book, close my eyes. Anxious, scowling. It would seem, as evidenced by the fact that all recent attempts at excavation have produced only horrible, violent impulses, that if there ever was some*thing* inside me, a thing that made me *me,* it's certainly spoiled now, riddled with galleries of hollowed-out tunnels, distinct to carpenter ant infestations according to The Book, a particularly disturbing colored plate featuring the cross section of a secretly overrun wood beam. I will sink to the depths of Ralph's despair with him, and both of us will succumb to the stains of the tormented.

I flip over, still scowling. I need sleep. Everything will be less bleak in the morning if I can only iron out this scowling, find the softness my face needs to rest. I beg the room for help, beg the pillow, beg the bed, but their indifference has the opposite effect, my face twists more, finds its familiar rotation: mouth open, tongue out resting just behind my bottom teeth; eyes shut tight, tears generating, overflowing, finding their paths down my face and wetting my pillow.

I bury my face in the soft wet, and from somewhere low, the place where food emulsifies to poison, a scream starts to brew. It moves heavy and hot up through my body and out of my mouth and into the pillow, Ralph's mother's old pillow, filled with screams, hungry for more, and that's it, I've fucking had it, I've fucking had it with these screampuffs, storing all our pain and then hissing it back into our ears all night: *He's mine now, I'm bringing him with me, it's only a matter of time before you come home and find him just like me, blood everywhere.*

I sit up, drag the pillow off the bed, and carry it downstairs.

Every time I turn a corner I expect to see Laura, sitting there, splayed across the living room couch in a hiked-up housecoat with the fattiest part of her arm over her eyes, smoking a cigarette at the kitchen table, watching a murder show on the little TV she'd rigged up in there.

LAURA: What are you doing with my pillow, Abigail?

[Her voice isn't right. It's a thousand voices, strummed in unison, some of them growling, some of them too high.]

ABBY: I'm getting rid of it.

At the front door I dig my feet into my boots and pull my coat over a long T-shirt with a flirtatious-looking horse on it, an outfit that makes me look like a woman who regularly falls asleep with lit cigarettes.

And speaking of which, I paw Laura's smokes and a book of matches from the kitchen junk drawer where she kept them. Outside in the backyard I throw the screaming pillow on the grass and stare at it.

LAURA: Wow, looks like you were exactly right. Problem solved. Evil pillow deactivated. Ralph is cured.

ABBY: Shut up, Laura.

I light one of her cigarettes and stare at the pillow. Drop to sit on the grass, still staring. The grass is half-frozen, wet, soaks through my underwear. I feel the vibrations of everything alive underneath me. All the bugs, tortured by their cravings to eat and build and reproduce. I've never seen a bug sleep before, the poor things. Exhausted, terrorized by their instincts to stay alive. I lean forward, plant my elbows on the bulges of flesh above my knees, wonder how any living thing can endure such a wild and terrible life.

I smoke another cigarette, stare at the pillow till it has a face, two folds that look like sad, broken eyes, a wide, wailing mouth.

"You shut up too," I say to it.

I lob my cigarette at it so it lands securely, caught in the pillow's wide, wailing mouth. I watch the concentrated ash grow and grow until the tiniest flame begins to lick around it, filling the space between each flake with orange heat. The flame grows. Not taller, but wider, spreading through the pillow's mouth, a bright orange perimeter opening up quickly, revealing the pillow's interiors, which at first seem infinite, as though you could reach your hand into this fiery hole and not see any trace of it on the other side. I'm terrified, my whole face hard with alarm, until I realize that the white stuffing is just dissolving from the heat faster than my brain can make sense of it. The sight of a charred black tip, like the break of a wave, brings reality into focus and settles me completely.

I see everything the way that it is now. Darkness reveals the truth. The stuffing is on fire, burning high and wild as a campfire. I light another cigarette, watch it burn, and I'm not scared, the grass is too wet and cold to light. But even if it did, who fucking cares? I hate this house. Filled with an evil, crawling grime that wants to get inside you, wants to infect you with misery.

Something moves behind the flame, along the perimeter of the yard.

I shoot up to standing, whip the cigarette into the fire. "Hello?" I whisper, stretch myself up onto my toes as though that might help me see better in the dark.

I can't see anything though, my eyes so filled with bright hot flames that the darkness beyond it is absolute. I hear it again. A stick breaks. The shuffle of feet, barely lifting from the grass. The ridges and valleys of the brain-shaped bush rustle, disturbed.

She's here.

In the spot I buried her ring.

With quivering fingers I draw another cigarette from the pack, struggle to meet the match. Lit, finally, then drag, drag, drag to keep from crying. Another pull, then another, then another, then it's done. I flick it into the flame, which is still burning but not as brightly, licking at its natural end.

"Laura?" I whisper, and the moment I do I start to cry. "Laura, please, I'm sorry," I sob. Then the fire dies abruptly, my eyes still so filled with its ferocious light I can't see anything at all, let alone a creeping Laura. Creeping Laura. I step toward the bush where she's hiding, where her ring is buried, past the burned black pillow.

Then Irena's back door opens and I nearly scream. I remember Laura mentioning Cud couldn't hold his pee anymore. Irena has to get up in the middle of the night to let him out. Cud, all dogs really, must think they're magic. They can do a thing like bark at the back door, and it immediately opens for them.

Kids too, at least for a while. They cry and someone runs to them. They stretch their arms at a thing they want and the thing appears in their hands. They believe they're magic until grudgingly, painfully, they learn they're not. And all their powers, pointing and crying and screaming and hitting, stop working. They're punished for their magic instead. For thinking they were special. It's no wonder people kill each other.

Then I see it, a big black hole where the ring was. Empty. The ring is gone. Really gone. Not a shadow behind a shower curtain or a feeling in the basement when I'm drunk and sad and susceptible to Ralph's residue, but a real, live, empty hole where once there'd been a ring stolen from a dying woman.

Cud is stalking the fence that separates our yards, sniffing. He senses Laura is here too. I move closer to the hole, eyes still adjusting, knees meet ground, cold, hard, uneven soil digging into my skin. This is where I'd buried it, this is where it was.

Cud growls, smelling her, catching glimpses of her between the slats in the fence, he yips once, a warning that she's lurching up behind me, then unleashes a torrent of harsh barks, not his usual little sounds. I spin around, sure that Laura will be standing there, arms out, ring dangling from her finger, but she's not there. There's nothing there. I'm all alone.

I stand back up quickly, the blood rushing from my head and never finding it again. Everything feels off now. I'm looking at the yard backward through binoculars. This isn't the same world, not the world I know. Because Laura really is still here, the dead walk among us, it's true, and now that I know, everything is different.

I kick dirt over the hole, some feral instinct to obscure my scent. Irena opens the back door. "What the hell is the matter with you?" she hisses, and Cud scurries toward her, rattled and ashamed, the jingle of his collar sealed up by the house.

<h1 style="text-align:center">25</h1>

THE NEXT MORNING I'm drawn to her bedroom door like a magnet, press my forehead against it, force a message to Ralph through its thickness: *I'm sorry. I believe you. I'm sorry.*

In the bathroom, getting ready for work, I open the garbage can to toss away the final drippings of my period, and a lashless, almond-shaped eye stares back at me. I pick it up, accidentally smear a dollop of Cal across the iris. *Find out why. Find out why.* The medium's business card, the woman with the bottomless browns. *Find out why.* One of my gems shimmers, voice multiplied, crazed, reflected a thousand times, *A message,* it whispers, *from Cal.* A message that only a mystic could receive, not a real voice exactly, but a special kind of guidance, and it's my job, as the mystic, to interpret it.

On the subway car, fingers hooked around a bar along the ceiling, swinging like a sock on a laundry line. Everyone's body touching, swayed by the same sloppy inertia, syncopated melody of gasps at every abrupt stop. Mine is an uncommon stop, so I have to work my way up out of the crowd like ground-water. *Thank you, excuse me, thank you, thank you, excuse me. Excuse me. Mystic here, mind the gems.*

At work there's only the tiniest tip of the salmon's nose left in the fridge, which means that everyone tried a bit of him and maybe some even came back for more. People like my jellied salmon, they trust me enough to put something I made into their mouths, swallow it down, introduce material from my personal kitchen at home into their bodies. No one saw me prepare it but they believe I did a good, clean job. That's very special. These yogurt types must really not think I'm disgusting. But I am still different from them, disconnected, because Laura is real and I know it now. But it's okay. It's going to be okay. Because there's logic to a ghost, rules and methods for getting rid of one, unlike depression, for which there is nothing but stubborn despair.

I check in with Linda at the front desk. I'm on rounds and first up is Mrs. Bondy, which feels like a good sign. Except when I walk through her door, I see Janet again, hovering over her body like the grim reaper.

"Hi," I say.

Janet spins around. Mrs. Bondy's face looks heavy, wet in the creases. "Is this not a private residence? Would you walk into someone's house without knocking?"

"Sorry, it's just, it's the routine."

Janet scowls, maybe whispering to her mother, *This is the reason why, this is it right here, Mother, this is uncivilized, you deserve more respect than this.*

"Would you excuse me?" I step between them without waiting for a response, nudge Janet purposely as I bring Mrs. Bondy's water glass to her lips. I have strength now. I'm going to banish a ghost from our house. Janet is scandalized by my nudging, her pug eyes open so wide they might dry up and fall out like ripe apples.

"Could I have a word?" she snaps, and motions toward the foot of the bed where she steps close to me, too close, I can smell her skin, sun-cooked despite the season and too sweet. "I've been trying to be nice to you people," she whispers. "But honestly I don't really care what you think. I don't have to explain myself to you. You all get paid every month, taking whatever you need for extras, and I don't say anything."

"That's because we don't need your permission, Janet. Anything additional to your mother's monthly rent is for her comfort, like this heating blanket"—I press a finger into her bed—"which is absolutely essential to managing her back pain. The pain of being abandoned by her only daughter, though, that's pain we can't manage unfortunately."

Janet's expression doesn't change, which makes me more furious. Did I not just say an absolutely scandalous thing? What is *wrong* with this woman?

"Leave us alone," she says calmly.

I step even closer to her, staring into her eyes. "No."

"Abigail, *leave us alone.*" She steps closer still. I could kiss her if I wanted to. I could drag my tongue up her face, drive it into her mouth, disarm her completely, then bite her nose off.

I look at Mrs. Bondy, her eyes distorted with concern, mouth open, arms up and reaching. She's upset, and I don't want that. I step down, back away from Janet, whose smug, stupid face tells me she thinks she's won. A knot in my chest. It hurts to breathe. I can't look at Janet. If I look at Janet, I'll kill Janet and that's the truth. I'm saving her life right now, by spinning around and marching out the door, ready to let this knot in my chest dissolve and become tears in the bathroom, but when I turn the corner, I run right into Carol.

"Sorry!"

"It's okay," I mumble, and move around her, but she grabs my arm.

"Do you have a sec?"

"Sure," I say, even though I don't have a sec, because every *sec* that passes without this knot becoming tears it becomes poison instead.

She huddles me in close to her. Her mouth is hooked in the corner, an almost undetectable smile.

"What is it?"

She looks down at her feet, pulls more smile into her face when she looks back up at me again. "Remember I was telling you how I was feeling tired yesterday?"

"Yeah."

"Well"—she looks around and I really wish she'd just spit it out already—"I'm pregnant." From her dopey, beaming grin comes a long, unimaginable squeak. Insanely long, still squeaking, still making eye contact with me. I imagine I'll have to slap her if she doesn't stop but thankfully she does on her own.

I don't know what to say. I feel the same roiling boil inside that I felt with Janet. Definitely jealous. Definitely, definitely. The most hideous, twisted feeling, to hate someone's happiness, and I don't want to feel it for Carol. *Carol, you ate my jellied salmon and gave me back my coolers. You're a good yogurt person who deserves everything you want in life.*

I can't think of anything to say so I reach out and grab her up and hug her tight and she hugs me back and I can feel how excited she is, it's leaking out of her and into me, souring when it touches my boiling jealous skin. I don't know what to say. I start to squeal like she did but my heart's not in it and it sounds demented. Luckily she interrupts it and just starts talking again.

"I can't believe it, honestly. Todd's been away so much, we really weren't, you know, *trying* like that." She laughs to herself. She's so happy, from the inside out she's just so happy that laughs are escaping from her like butterflies. I want to be happy to even be near this much happiness. I want to just be able to appreciate that instead of feeling like I could kick her in the stomach and all my problems would go away. She's still talking, no idea what I'm thinking about. "I mean I probably shouldn't even be saying anything yet, it's still so early, six weeks, I just, I really can't believe it, I had to tell someone or I was going to explode."

"Well, don't explode yet!"

She laughs because I've made a joke about how she's going to be exploding eventually now that she's pregnant, ha ha, two of her punctuating holes merging into one, a soft-boned solid working its way out and it cries! It's alive! Her life has meaning now! Her family of rats warm together, a fount of unconditional love—all a human really needs, said Ralph—will flow forever. What a nice goddamn thing for her. It's good. I'm happy for you, Carol. I am happy for you I am happy for you I am happy for you I am happy for you, Carol, I am I am I am I am. I don't want anything bad to happen to you or your baby, I really, in my heart of hearts, actually, seriously do not, but right now we've got a darkness in the house. Maybe. And there's no telling what I could do. So get away from me, Carol, get away from me before I hurt you.

She's talking about renovations: yellow-plaid-and-cream curtains and modern-cottage vibes. Rouslana wanders down the hall, Carol pulls me in closer. She doesn't want anyone else to know yet, it's still so early in the pregnancy. I realize that I'm a person Carol wouldn't mind revealing her miscarriage to, if that should happen, and I really hope it doesn't, I really do. I need to get away from Carol.

"Listen, Carol, I'm really happy for you, but actually I'm kind of feeling sick, I was going to the bathroom, to, you know—too much yogurt! Ha!" I gulp, swallow a bullet of air, which sits uncomfortably in my chest. "That was a joke." I can still see the residue of Carol's smile in her now deeply concerned face. "So I'm going to go home, actually. I'm sorry, I don't mean to change the subject or anything, I wanna talk more about this tomorrow, I promise, I'm just, I'm really feeling nauseous."

"Oh no." It's genuine. She's so genuine, goddammit, Carol, you're going to be an incredible mother. You really are. "Who knows, maybe you're pregnant too!"

Tears fill my eyes. I drop my head into my hands.

"Oh, sweetie, are you okay?"

"I—I'm fine." I pull my head up again, sniffing. "I just, I need to go home."

"Go." She puts her arm around my shoulders, leads me to the front closet to get my coat. "I can cover for you. Do you want me to talk to Big Beauty?"

"Could you? I just really have to go."

Carol smiles and hugs me again. "Of course."

In the parking lot I see Janet's car. I know it's hers because Mrs. Bondy has told me about Janet's precious poodle, who is now staring at me from the passenger-side window. White once, now yellow, cigarette stained, garbage water trickling from its eyes. When I get close, she barks fog all over the windows, faster, faster, legs pressed stiff against the door, leathery nose leaving frantic streaks on the glass. This little thing loves Janet. Loves Janet most of all. This thing, just like Mrs. Bondy, is bound by blood and instinct to love a greedy whore like Janet.

I cup darkness around my eyes, peer inside. It barks into my face but I can still see it, a folder for another old age home. Kingsmere. Carol was right. The cheapest home in the city, as well as the site of two widely publicized sexual assault allegations, bedbugs, regular STI outbreaks. It's the first catchall, the place that old folks go while waiting out someone's death at a good place like the Northern Star. Janet wants to send Mrs. Bondy there because it's cheap and no one cares if you visit or not. My baby in a place like that; the thought makes my stomach shrivel and drop like a stone. I want to puke but instead I pace next to her car and wrap my hand around the kitchen knife handle in my purse, safe with me, safe from Ralph.

26

I'M THINKING ABOUT LAURA'S CIGARETTES. Her lungs. Ralph's lungs secondhand, inhaling all those toxins, combustion ravaging the only set of breathers she's got so she might have ended up like Mr. Phibbs at work, hacking all the time into a handkerchief he keeps next to his bed, sober and stiff as a little soldier collecting its superior's phlegm, never complaining and never slouching, lucky to be at Mr. Phibbs's side. Carol told me that his lungs grew boils that popped, growing and popping and growing and popping all the time, like the thick, dented cheeks of some soggy teen.

A pregnant woman passes me on the sidewalk.

Some women are pregnant, but most aren't.

Carol is a pregnant woman and I'm not.

Some women are pregnant, but most aren't.

Carol is a pregnant woman and I'm not.

Some women are pregnant.

But most aren't.

Carol is a pregnant woman.

And I'm not.

Somehow it's dark by the time I get home and my feet are snow-stiff and aching. Irena has left a large centerpiece on the porch, a freshly repurposed burst of pink roses, blue hydrangeas, a jolly mist of baby's breath, unacceptably cheerful for the occasion, but thoughtful all the same. A note reads, *Sorry for your loss. We're here for you. Love Irena and Cud.*

It starts to snow. Succulent flakes disappear on the porch steps. Notes from Ralph's keyboard, not yet a melody, thud against the basement window.

Find out why.

The world *must* crack open from time to time, unsettled spirits drawn to the commotion and sucked back to earth, otherwise why would there be this business card? We'd call a plumber to service our pipes, an electrician for the wiring—why wouldn't I go to a medium to help with our ghost?

I leave the centerpiece, get in the car, and drive to the address on the card.

In front of the Laundromat door, I breathe heat into my hands, take in the street, quiet as a pond. I think of those first late nights in Ralph's apartment, enjoying the rhythms of his deepest, most restorative sleep, but too happy to drift off myself, in disbelief still to find myself layered in clean, crisp sheets, my head on a good, unstained pillow. Just a few feet away, a cupboard with Q-tips and toilet paper, real *supplies*; and a fridge full of sensible food, coffee all ready to go for the morning. Ralph would make eggs too, not specially because I was there, but because a person has eggs for breakfast. And soon, I remember thinking, clutching fistfuls of duvet to steady my overwhelming joy, *I would be a person too.*

There's a white buzzer next to the door beneath a small drawing of the same lashless eye from the business card. I square myself up—shoulders back, face forward—reach out, and press on it, long and hard. Bolstered with a big, cool lungful of winter air, waiting for the creak of shifted weight on the floor inside, a shadow over the peephole, but nothing happens. I exhale steam, reach out to press again, but before my finger lands on the buzzer, the door whooshes open, nearly sucks me in with it. And there she is, the woman in the red dress with her bottomless browns, inkwells that might drip down her cheeks at any minute. Except she isn't wearing a red dress now, she's wearing an oversize white sweatshirt stamped in textured snowflakes, black tights, woolly socks, and her long white-blond hair is swept and knotted securely on top of her head. She's younger than I was expecting. Much younger. As though a potion had restored her youth, but her taste in loud, seasonal prints remained.

"Huh." She tilts her head. "The suicide."

"That's me." That she remembers is somehow proof of her legitimacy, like she doesn't hand her card out to just anyone.

"We'd almost given up on you." She steps aside. "Come on in." Guides me past her and closes the door behind me, her fearlessness unsettling. I'm a stranger and she serves ambrosia salad at church picnics, Ralph was right about that. The accent though, as surprising as her youth. Polish maybe. Ukrainian.

"How did you know we'd need you?"

"She had a feeling. Your jacket." She waves at a hook drilled into a slobber of yellow paint. I take it off, hang it up, and smile at her, seeking approval from this unsettlingly wholesome medium for having hung my coat up well.

"She?"

"Up there." She herds me up a set of steep, sopping steps, smiling when I look back at her, polite as a beauty queen. Every moaning step lifts me into a pricklier density of spent matches and tuneless, rattling music until I'm standing in the thick of it, the threshold of a shadowy attic room, lit only by street light from a small window, open despite the cold, a plastic baby doll, naked and eyeless, wedged between the frame and the sill. The long, thin curtains on either side of the window are so animated by winter wind that it's easy to miss the woman sitting between them, hands folded over a round table, staring at me with her opal eye.

The skin on the back of my neck scrambles to hide beneath my sweatshirt. The young woman touches the small of my back and I jump, startled. "Sit."

"You," I say to the old woman, "I saw you." She doesn't respond, just blinks, and every wrinkle in her face blinks too. I knock my knee against something as I scoot in under the heavy, black tablecloth. "Sorry," I say, I guess to the table.

"We spend a lot of nights there," the young woman says, moving behind the old woman. "It's easier to connect with the dead when you're present for their passing."

"Sure, I guess I just didn't realize you were together."

She shrugs. "Did you happen to bring the card I gave your husband?"

"I did." I reach into my pocket, hand it over. "What do you need it for?"

She takes a moment to examine it. "I'm not really sure." She smiles and hands it to Opal-eye, whose opal shimmers when it passes over the Cal smear. She taps the smear with a branch-like finger, hums approvingly, then plants her nostrils against it like a pair of suction cups on a piece of glass, inhales deeply. *Wait! I want to say. No! Oh, God, that's my dried-up old period blood!* But I can't say it, it's too embarrassing. And I'm relieved when she lifts her nostrils from the card that the smear is still there, that she hasn't somehow loosened it from the card-stock fibers, painting the inside of her sinuses. She looks up at me and tilts her head. She knows it's my blood, as an animal would, bury its nose between my legs, bay to its master, *This is it, this is the kill site!*

Opal-eye knows everything, I can tell: that Cal was almost here but now she's gone, that she was going to be amazing, a pure love baby who might one day have saved the world. This understanding of the old woman's power, my absolute certainty that this is exactly where I need to be, is draining the air from my lungs, too fast, like a pair of unknotted balloons thrashing across the sky.

"Are you all right?" asks the young woman.

"I'm fine"—though my body is refusing oxygen now, gasps barely skidding past my throat.

"Good. Her fee is one hundred dollars."

I hand the young woman a wad of cold, stale bills. The transaction somehow triggering my ability to breathe again.

"Thank you." She slips the money somewhere inside her snowflake sweatshirt. The old woman hands the card over as well, and the young woman disappears with it behind us, the squeal-grind of a drawer pulled open, filing away my money and my little piece of Cal. I turn around, an instinctive reaction to the sound of the drawer and see that the room isn't small at all; if you squint, you can see length in the darkness, vast, empty, impossible space that didn't quite connect with the shape of the building from the outside. The young woman stands a few feet from the table in front of a hulking wooden bureau loaded with drawers and cupboards, catches me peering into the deep, endless dark. I smile guiltily, turn back around, and find Opal-eye with both hands flat on the table: long, transparent fingernails, filed to sharp points, stacks of silver bracelets and rings and a pattern of liver spots that might once have belonged to a leopard that she killed and ate with her bare hands.

She reaches for me, cautiously, like she can't see me, like she's in another world, with only the vaguest sense of what's going on in this one. She finds my hand, hers ice-cold, resistant to my warmth. She's pulling me closer, out of my seat, my elbows marching half across the table, mere inches from her cool, odorless breath and opal eye. I can see my reflection in it, scared, blinking, trapped, hysterical, pounding against the opaque orb.

A single drop of blood escapes over her bottom lip, shrinks to nothing down her chin, then abruptly she spits onto the black tablecloth, a spatter across my forearm, which I'm shocked to find I can't yank back out of her grip. She smears the spatter with her other hand, leaves little trails like shooting stars, lets her opal roam the pattern, then starts to mutter, and the young woman, staring at her, translates:

"The suicide, your mother-in-law, she's always been vulnerable to self-harm, always dark. Your husband, he's always been scared of it."

"Yes," I whisper.

"She's tried it before. The same way, with a knife. Your husband, he has too."

An invasion of blurriness, blinking, shaking my head. "No, that's not true."

"It is true," says the young woman, translating.

Opal-eye draws my forearm to her nostrils like she did with my little Cal smear, closes her eyes, takes a deep breath, mutters, "Yes, yes, yes." The young woman translates, "You're not alone. Something is with us now, something that's attached to you."

My face burns. Not alone, we're not alone. "To me?"

"To both of you, but it's here with us now."

"Is it her?" I whimper—any louder and I'll cry.

"We'll have to meet it and see."

The young woman reaches behind the old woman, pulls the baby doll from the sill, and lets the window slam shut. The sound startles me, I immediately look at the young woman, betrayed by the lack of warning.

"Sorry. We don't want to invite anyone else in." She glides over to the bureau, buries the doll in a drawer, makes a pouch with the front of her sweatshirt, and fills it with pudgy candles, a black lighter, a dinner roll she frees with great effort from a clingy plastic bag. She walks, hunched over her pouch, back to the table, where she empties its contents across the tablecloth.

I wonder how much of this old woman's stale, spattered blood is hidden in the black of the tablecloth. Smart to use black. Adds to the drama, but also, black never stains, it just sort of gets heartier, stiffer. The darker Ralph's mother got, the filthier her clothes got, so sometimes when I was doing laundry, it was as though I were pulling those wooden carnival cutouts from the hamper, the ones where you stick your face in the hole and take a picture, cracking them in half, in quarters, in eighths over my knee just so I could fit them into the washing machine. Ralph's would be that way now, carnival-cutout clothes, false wooden exterior, nothing left behind it. *I'm dead,* he'd said. And maybe he is. Maybe these two will summon Ralph into the room. *A twist!* He's been dead the whole time! Dead and attached to me, the most unsavory unsavory of all.

The young woman places the dinner roll in front of Opaleye, sets the candles in a circle on the table, and says, "I'll be joining too. Better with three, I hope you don't mind." She tightens the knot in her hair before she sits down next to me.

"Not at all. I'm sorry, I just realized that I don't know your names."

"Oh, right, okay. I'm Annie." The young woman places a hand on her chest. "And you can call her . . . Joan." The old woman, leaned over the table, smiles for the first time, crescent of speckled barnacles glistening in the candlelight.

I smile back. "I'm Abby."

They nod like they knew that already. We all endure a moment of silence together before Annie lays her hands knuckle side down on the table and then motions to form a circle.

Joan clears her throat, closes her good eye, lets the opal ramble over us and behind us and all over the room. She begins to chant, long, slow sounds that draw her mouth open. Annie follows. Once I get the hang of it, I join in too, over and over, over and over and over until my throat craves the vibrations: stretched soft vowels shaking everything hard out of my face so it hangs like slime from my skull. The circle begins to sway: a mysterious twitch of energy, passing through us, gaining momentum as insidiously as a germ.

Laura behind the shower curtain, gleeful because Cal was gone.

I'm telling you, Ralphie, she took my ring, right off my finger, no good, never good, and she knew the whole time because a mother knows. But I'm a mother too, even if I'm not yet, I'm a mother too.

The room is getting brighter, brighter, like the table's on fire. *SHHHHH!*

We stop, dazed from the chant. I open my eyes; opal-eyed Joan grabs the dinner roll, holds it out, her opal eye searching and finally landing in the endless darkness just behind me. More muttering. Annie clears her throat, translates nervously, "Come, come, my sweet one, come to the light, have a taste of our offering, it's for you, don't be scared." Joan's voice gets higher, faster, Annie continues to translate: "We won't hurt you, my sweet, come to us, come to us, enter me if you wish, I'm open for you, my darling, while the circle is formed, while there is food on this table, you are welcome here."

The candlelight dancing in her opal eye, trapped inside it, pounding against it, begging to be freed, like I'd been. She's not blinking either, just staring at something behind me, and a strange jolt in my body keeps trying to get me to turn around, like the spark inside you that catches just before you jump off a diving board, go, go, *go*: turn around, see what's back there, see who she's talking to. But I can't, I'm too scared, I just stare into Joan's opal eye. *You're not alone candlelight, I'm with you, trapped with you inside the eye,* and then it's really not alone, there's another reflection trapped inside with it, getting bigger, lurching forward: the jabbering ghoul from my closet, strips of long blood-hard hair growing from the center of its head, barely concealing the angles and scabs and hollows of its grinning face. Laura's blue dress, tattered, greasy around the neck, bloody down the arms.

"Come, sweet one," and Joan's kissing at it, wrinkles multiplying around her lips. "Come, come, come," she purrs. This is how Joan spoke to her own children, grandchildren, great-grandchildren, to Annie when she was small, luring them toward her with a dinner roll, then devouring them, slurping up their essences so they would become her slaves, a brood of child familiars roaming the ink dark of this room's unknown ends, waiting to be dispatched to the ICU waiting room to bring back fresh prey.

One of the candles sputters, extinguishes, and Joan's face changes, she opens her opal eye wider and begins to scream, only she screams words, different from our chant, and Annie isn't translating anymore, she's screaming something back at her, repeating the same word over and over again when Joan goes limp in her chair, arms and legs hanging over the sides, eyes closed.

"What is it?" I whisper to Annie, who shakes her head like she has no idea, sits back in her chair, and watches with me as Joan stirs. Her hands shoot up first, startling us both, wrists limp like she's being pulled by them, forward, over the table. Her face is different, winched into a grin on one side. She grabs the dinner roll, gobbles it down, then, with her mouth full of half-masticated bread, she begins to chant again, moving the mound of bread to either side of her mouth, pelting the table with hunks of starchy paste.

A gob touches me and I yelp. Annie looks at me, urges me to chant with her, so we do, faster this time, and I keep my eyes shut so I don't have to see the hot roll of wet bread spilling from Joan's mouth.

Joan stops chanting abruptly and I open my eyes. She erupts with laughter: head back, webs of thickened drool connecting her teeth. She brings her head down slowly to stare at me.

"Feed me," she says, her voice deep, her mouth strange, working hard to make its way around the unfamiliar language. She smiles wide, chewed bread caulked across her barnacle teeth, filling every nook and cavity with soft, striking white.

She tilts her head, sorrow strung tight through her face, and lifts a hand gently, reaches across the table to drag her palm along my cheek. A heavy glob of bready drool stretches from her lip as she wraps her hand around the side of my head, palm against my ear. "*Feeeeeeeed meeeeeeeeeeee,*" deeper, echoing against the contours of whatever dimension she's trapped in.

I lean back out of her grip and her expression changes, she's pouting, hurt. "I'm hungry and cold, Abby. Abby, help me, Abby, my feet, they're splitting, my heels, it's so *dank* here, Abby. It's so *wet. Help me, Abby.*"

I open my mouth to reply, but Annie snatches my arm, shakes her head firmly. Joan's expression changes again, furious now, I see the gums gleaming above her barnacles. "I said *help me*, you *thief!* You *sneaky little thief!* If you want him, you have to take us both, you understand?" She rears her head back and laughs hysterically, screams, "*You can have us both, you can have us both!*" Laughing hard. Roaring. "Now feed me, you stupid fucking bitch! Feed me, you fucking whore. I'm going to eat, I'm going to eat whether you feed me or not you bitch bitch bitch bitch bitch." She lays her hands flat, bares her pasty teeth, lunges forward halfway across the table, launching Annie and me out of our chairs. She screams so loud it shakes the walls; bullets of bread paste fire at me. I cover my ears. The screaming stops and her body goes limp again, lands with a thud, unconscious on the table, her arm still out toward me.

Annie rights her chair, hustles over to Joan, who stirs before Annie can touch her, she's mumbling something.

Annie responds quietly, scared, then Joan rests her head on the table and closes her eyes and Annie turns to me. Her voice is different. Her face too. Suddenly I'm looking at a much-older woman. I think. Or had she always looked this way? The confusion makes me nauseous, disoriented, like she pretended to be young to collect me and now something had gone so seriously wrong that she doesn't have the strength for her disguise anymore.

"Okay." Annie squeezes the bridge of her nose. "Your mother-in-law, she's with you, with your husband technically, and she's very angry. She'd rather see her son dead with her than alive with you. You must understand, she's not herself anymore, more like a demon now."

"My God." I feel disassembled, mind spun to dust, no idea what to do with the winding miles of my body. I right my chair and sit down.

"You have to feed him something *special*. Something that proves your devotion to him. Not love, you understand? *Devotion.* A mother's love is *devoted. Consuming.* And you have to do it soon. When a spirit gets like this, becomes more fiend than ghost, it starts to feed on darkness, cultivates it in whoever they're attached to. Like a farmer, like crops. The longer she's with your husband, the darker he's going to get and he will hurt himself. He's done it before."

I lean forward, both hands on the table. "You have to tell me what to feed him."

Her face is grave and grown-up as a stone saint. "I can't."

"You *have* to. I can't lose him, you don't understand, I can't *lose him*." My eyes fill with tears. "Annie, *please*." Begging her, I'm begging her now, hands clasped together. "Please."

"I don't *know* what you should feed him. He's *your* husband, she's *your* demon. You have to figure that out yourself."

"I—no. I need more. You have to tell me *something*."

"I'm sorry, no." Annie claps her hands together with finality. "I've told you everything I can. It's time to go." She stands up.

I stand up too, paw at her, beg her more. "Please, I can't lose him, you don't understand."

"I'm sorry, I can't tell you any more than I already have. I don't know any more. We don't encounter this often."

"But you have encountered it before—"

"Yes." She guides me to the door. Joan is still out cold.

"And what happened?"

She shakes her head solemnly, opens the door. "Just try to feed him something, take care of him, do your best."

"This is ridiculous." Like I'm at a restaurant that's just served me a plate of pubic hair. "Just ridiculous." At the bottom of the stairs I put on my coat, turn to admonish her some more, but the door is already closed. She turns the dead bolt with remarkably communicative force.

Back in the car I feel cold and confused and alone, a coal of dread burning in my stomach. Cal, Cal, Cal, what do I do now? What do I feed him?

I glance at the bright green lines of the digital clock: 9:37 p.m. The car takes till 9:41 to get warm enough to drive. Ralph's mother's old car. Her loose change, her old gas receipts, her expired air freshener hanging from the mirror, which I'm scared to look into in case she's back there, more than half demon, leering at me from the back seat.

I have to feed it. Feed Ralph, something that will poison his queen. Anemic Laura who could proudly never keep food down.

"I am devoted. I *am* devoted, you bitch bitch bitch bitch bitch," mitten mounds embellished with the icy jewels of my hissing, hissing, "Bitch bitch bitch," all the way home.

27

I KEEP FINDING CHUNKS of hardened bread paste in my hair, feeling them lodged in the folds of my neck like ticks, but when I go to scrape them out with my finger, there's nothing there. No one will know I'm dealing with phantom bread burrs all day long. Just like I might not know who has a canker sore today or who is constipated, but they're out there in the world, and they're dealing with it.

I wave at Linda, who might be teeming with hot white canker sores, whose digestive tract might well be backed up to her teeth, but who is sitting at the front desk acting like a normal, comfortable, happy person. She waves back at me as I pass, head to the kitchen, where Carol's leaned against the counter, thumbing through pages of maternity clothes on her phone. She's going to be such a beautiful pregnant woman. It makes me want to cry. And stab her.

"Hey, Carol."

"Oh, hey, Abby." She turns off her phone and puts it in her pocket. "Listen, Big Beauty's looking for you."

"Oh, God." I drop my bag on the table. It's too loud. The knife clangs.

Carol glances. "Cripes, what's in there?"

"A very large kitchen knife."

"Ha."

She thinks I'm joking because she always thinks I'm joking. When I talk to her about bowel movements or bring coolers to her house, I'm serious about those things and she thinks it's all a big fucking joke.

Big Beauty is the boss of everyone, the nurses, the caregivers, the dietitians. Even the doctors are a little bit scared of her because she's thick joints and broad planes and as certain in her movements as a wild animal. Big Beauty has no favorites, Big Beauty has no friends. Big Beauty could be an omnipotent computer system rigged up through the whole place, and it's good that way, the best kind of boss. But if she wants to see you, that's usually bad, because it means you're a bug, a defect, the kind of thing that Ralph and his team work very hard to keep out of their software.

Her door is always open so she knows how often people go out for smokes and who's taking too long sitting in the grass in the back, eating lunch. She sees everyone here with little stats over their head: ratings and duties and a timer. My stats say that I'm five minutes early, that today I've got to give three baths and work lunch and have an hour break scheduled at two.

I take a deep breath and sweep my skin one last time for hardened bread chunks before I step into her office, drag my knuckle politely on the door.

"Hi, Ellen," I say, never *Big Beauty* to her face of course.

"Abigail, hello. Have a seat." She stands up, presents a wide chair upholstered in polished orange vinyl. The desk is white linoleum, profoundly uncluttered, nothing but her trademark turquoise mug and a beige file folder. Something about the room suggests that Big Beauty might have an affinity for the American Southwest, or at the very least the American Southwest that exists in this careful arrangement of orange and turquoise and tan, but no one would ever know, because Big Beauty would sooner cut off her thumbs than reveal anything that might humanize her.

I smile, shut the door behind me, sit obediently in the chair. Sitting has altered the careful arrangement of my underwear so it feels full of hard bread paste now too, ticks burrowing their way inside. I grind myself into the chair discreetly, clear my throat.

Big Beauty sits again, lays fingers gently on the tan file folder as though it were a Ouija board's planchette, about to fly around the desk guided by spirits. The folder is perfect: clean and smooth like everything else in the room. Folders, chairs, papers, pens, none would dare mar in Big Beauty's presence. To be near her was to seek her approval, her quiet tolerance a reward.

"I'll get to the point. This is a formal complaint from Janet Bondy." Her fingers are interlocked, pulled in close to her chest.

I shoot forward in my chair, eyes bulging. "What?"

"She claims that you made cruel and disparaging remarks about her, and that you behaved unprofessionally in front of her mother. She doesn't believe your standard of care is up to par, and for this reason, among others, she wants to remove Mrs. Bondy from the Northern Star."

"She *said* all that?" I lean forward, stare down the perfect file folder as though it's somehow entangled in this affront.

"She did. She was quite upset."

"Ellen, I, listen, I know how this sounds, but she *started* it."

"The loved ones of our clients aren't always on their best behavior. It can be very emotionally draining to see someone you care about here, and you know that. This"—she bops the perfect folder with both fists—"is unacceptable."

Loved ones, I nearly spit, but instead bite my lips together, lean back in the chair.

"She claims that you accused her of abandoning her mother, that you willfully agitated Mrs. Bondy, and that you wouldn't leave when politely asked to. Is that about right?"

"Those things happened, yes, but she's leaving out very important context." I'm raising my voice, clock specks of my saliva on the perfect file folder, which surely Big Beauty has clocked too. "She wants to move her mother to *Kingsmere*."

"That's her choice."

"But, *Ellen,* how can we—sometimes I just can't—are we just supposed to stand by and let someone like that, a *stranger,* who doesn't care and doesn't know anything, we're just supposed to let them touch our bab—the clients? Just handle them after all that we've done? All of our careful work keeping this, this body alive and healthy and even sometimes happy, even happy sometimes, we're just supposed to let Janet undo all of that good work and send her to a place like Kingsmere?"

"That's her daughter, Abby. Janet is Mrs. Bondy's child."

"I shouldn't have lost my temper, you're right, but she was going to move Mrs. Bondy to Kingsmere anyway, that's the only reason she came here at all. I saw the orientation documents in her car."

"Her car. Why were you in her car?"

"What?" I heard her of course, Big Beauty never mumbles.

"Why were you in her car?"

"What?" I repeat, no question now that I'm stalling.

"*Why* were you in her *car*?" Her patience dangerously thin.

"No! I wasn't *in* her car. I just looked inside it when it was parked in the lot."

"But why?"

"I don't know. She'd left her dog in there and I recognized it and I just wanted to look. It's not a big deal."

"Abby"—she brings her fingers to her temples, rubs gently— "I'm going to remove you from Mrs. Bondy's care strategy."

My breath grinds to a halt, slips backward, catching in my throat. "No," I whisper. "Please, no, you can't do this to me."

"I know you and Mrs. Bondy are close, but her daughter calls the shots now, and I'm just not sure, from the details of this complaint, that she'd be satisfied with anything else. I'm not happy about it either. You make Mrs. Bondy very happy. And I plan to tell Janet that too. But my hands are tied here. If we want Mrs. Bondy to be able to stay, if *that's* the ultimate objective, then you can't work with her anymore."

My eyes fill with tears, I hate that it's happening, but I can't stop it, and before I can excuse myself, Big Beauty has hauled her great presence around to my side of the desk. She kneels at my side, places a hand on my back. She feels genuinely sorry for me, maybe even . . . could it be? A *kinship* with me? As though before she'd been Big Beauty, she too had once succumbed to the metastasizing impotence of a gross injustice.

She produces a box of tissues from somewhere, somehow. I conjure a wad and wail into it. I don't want to cry this much, I can't believe I'm crying this much, but it's all coming out, everything, Cal and Ralph and his mother and the goddamn medium with her horrifying prediction, her largely unhelpful advice. This is misery rage. Language has failed the power of my misery and my shoulders are bouncing from it and Ellen is rubbing between them, hoping that a bug like me can be fixed. And it's helping, the way she's touching me, the way it works, each breath digging deeper into my lungs so I'm able to calm down a little.

"It's okay," I manage to say, able finally to sniff everything back. "It's fine."

"Now." She removes her hand mechanically, touch-industry professional that she is, like a masseuse who's just finished administering a hand job. "I need you to take the rest of the day off."

"No, no," I sniff. "No, I'm okay." I straighten up, things are calming down inside me, my heart finding its right spot again, leaning into its familiar rhythm.

"I must insist. Janet's coming by soon. I think it's best if you're not here."

"Oh."

"I'm sorry."

"I don't want to go home."

"You can come back tomorrow, okay? It's just for today. Just while Janet's going to be here."

Big Beauty stands up, indicating that I should stand up too.

"No, you don't understand," I say, and she doesn't understand. I look into her eyes. I can't tell her the truth, I can't tell her why I don't want to go home.

"What is it?" She's being so kind, just like Carol was so kind, just like everyone is so kind to me even though I don't deserve it, even though I pry jewelry from dead fingers like some greedy pirate. No one knows that about me, no one knows who I really am, or who Ralph really is, or what we're dealing with at home: a ghost, a demon, farming darkness inside us, neither of us long for this world.

I shake my head. "Nothing, it's nothing. I'm sorry, I'll go."

Big Beauty gives my arm a squeeze before I turn around and leave, shut her door behind me.

Just go home, Abby. Just go home, just go home, be a good wife, feed him, feed him good things from The Book and be a good wife and everything will be okay. You've endured the suffering of a mystic, you know a thing or two beyond this world. The medium knew it. She trusted you with the real advice she doesn't give to just anyone. Feed him, Abby, feed him. Be a good, devoted wife and feed him.

You smashed the window in your bedroom, smashed it with one of those toy rotary phones. It made a dinging sound when you did it. Ding ding ding! Glass showered the patio. The rotary phone came apart in your hand.

What if Mrs. Bondy had been my mother instead? What might I have inherited from her? Good things. Maybe I would have wanted to *be* like her. Instead of how it is with my mother, where everything I do is to try to *not* be like her, which is basically the same as becoming her in a way, how a shadow of your hand is both your hand and its opposite.

Ding ding ding! Shards of glass in your little arm. Shark teeth. I had to pull them out one by one with a set of tweezers and you didn't make a sound, you didn't even wince, just stared at them as they came out, dropping in the bowl, ding ding ding!

Andre, her first boyfriend after my dad left and the only one I ever liked. He was tall, thin arms and legs and a low, heavy potbelly, round as his head. A gentle buoy of a man with big blue eyes, gray in his hair and beard. And he believed in God. He went to church every Sunday and requested that we say grace before dinner. He had a soft voice and didn't eat meat. He fried tofu and pureed chickpeas and ate peanut butter sandwiches between meals. Mom wasn't religious but she seemed to like the structure of it, the way he could teach her, fill her head with Jesus and Mary and sin and mercy, and he'd listen to her when she talked about her life, all the people who'd hurt her and wronged her and treated her like she didn't matter, shaking his head, clucking quietly, squeezing her hand through the hard parts.

I liked the church. It was clean and everyone looked nice, trying to attract God's special attention. It made me feel jealous when I saw someone with finer clothes than me, a better shot at being noticed by God just because they could afford a better dress. I wanted so badly to be the one God noticed, sitting there in the pews, the way that Ralph would spot me sitting and looking nice at that bar twenty years later.

It'd been such a relief to learn that there was more out there, God and prayers and miracles. And all I had to do was believe in it; believe in this world I couldn't see. Believe in a hidden logic to the universe, an authority that unifies, that gives you the power to affect things: change your luck, change your destiny, because you're devoted to a bigger purpose, a nebulous, sticky energy that exists between what you can see. Like the bacteria that writhes on surfaces in commercials, the confetti critters that one swipe of Lysol kills 99.99999999 percent of.

Germs are the god of the woman in the Lysol commercial, the woman in the Purell commercial, the woman in the Tylenol cold-and-sinus commercial burdened with a whole family of noses rubbed to bubble gum.

Gut flora is the god of the yogurt type. A reef of fantastic organisms, which sway and dance, gyrate for their probiotic offerings. Reward the yogurt type's healthy choices with smooth skin and hearty nails, insides gleaming clean as new copper pipe.

The morning after Andre left, shafts of light break through window grime, sear a pattern onto her skin, then the light shafts are the same color as her skin, are her skin, and she's connected to the light, to the window grime, to the filth, which she is because this is her house, she's the adult, she's the one responsible for cleaning the grime or teaching how the grime should be cleaned, stocking the cupboards with the right germ-killing cleaning supplies. Levels of fluorescence in the dark cupboard under the sink: green and blue and yellow bottles. Rectangles for scrubbing, soft on the top, coarse on the bottom, like her pubes in the tub, softened by the soapy water, moving gently like seagrass to the rhythm of her crying.

Another man has come and gone, and just like my father before, and all the men who'd come after, he'd been *the one*, she was sure, but she fucked it up again, just fucked it up, and now she's back to being nothing. Nobody. Worthless because nobody loved her. *Ahem.* I know you do, Abby. I know you love me. But it's different, one day you'll see, when you're older, you'll see. There's just no greater feeling in the world than being loved by a man. By someone sensible. Someone who matters. It makes you feel legitimate in a way. You have to be real for a man to love you, you know? Does that make sense? Pass me my smokes, sweetie, thank you. And the lighter. Click. Glow. Burn. Bath steam and cigarette smoke wrestle in the air. She ashes into a plastic cylinder, saved from some long-ago bottle of mousse. Lifts the raw poultry of her freshly shaved leg over the side of the tub and exhales smoke from every hole. Couchy Motherthing calls, *Abby Aaaaaaaaaaaaaaaabby Abbyyyyyyyyyyy, now, get away from her, get away from her right now, come on downstairs right this second, come to me right now. Your shows are starting.*

And I should listen to Couchy Motherthing because she's good and she takes care of me, but I don't. Instead I go to my room, dig the toy phone from my closet, and smash my grimy window—my window, her grime—to smithereens.

I hear her panic at the sound, launch herself soaking from the tub so the water, which had tried and failed to keep her, splashes all over the floor. In a second she's standing at my bedroom door, barely covered by a hastily snatched towel, dripping water into a pool accumulating around her feet. I'm making my own pool, fed by the rivulets of blood each chunk of glass has claimed in my arm. Light catches the half-buried shards as it might have caught the scales of a fish undulating just beneath the surface of the water, whole body one big muscle, like a tongue, bones so fine they can be crushed and eaten, said Mother, when we got all those free cans of salmon from Andre's church.

"I want to keep going to church," I say to her, dripping my blood.

She nods. "Maybe. Another church."

"Andre's church."

She rolls her eyes, tightens the towel around her chest. Disappears, then reappears with tweezers and a sterile bandage that I'm shocked exists in this house.

"Where did this come from?"

She doesn't answer. I wait for her to yell at me. To ask what possessed me to do such a thing, but she doesn't. It's better for her, I realize, to pretend I'm just fine. She will never react. She will never yell at me. She sits on the bed, pats her lap, where I'm to surrender my arm, and she carefully plucks each glittering fish scale, cleans the blood with her own towel, wraps me up tight in the bandage. When she's done, she returns to her bath and I go to Couchy Motherthing, who isn't mad that I disobeyed her. She's just happy I'm okay, because that's all good mothers really care about, no matter what, just that you're okay.

And now *I'm* the filth, the *grime,* in Laura's house. Just like she used to be. Just like my mother had been in our house.

And Ralph is my god.

If God gives you meaning, if God makes you good, if God makes you real and worthy and powerful, then that's my Ralph. Ralph made my suffering better, healthy and righteous. He made my suffering want only good things: make the pain stop and I'll be the best wife in the world, make the pain stop and I will feed him only good things from The Book. I'll clean every mess, I'll be with him when his mother is too ill to take care of herself. I'll be the best daughter-in-law too, *A Good Woman,* I will make her love me, make her love me and the pain will stop, get a real, live Motherthing, not the mother-type thing I grew in and out of.

And this is how it should be. To everyone, a personal god. I inscribe Ralph with goodness and he inscribes me with goodness and we have meaning now without the oppressive horrors of something you have to share with everyone. Like trying to order a pizza for 1.2 billion people. We are each other's personal pan pizza from Pizza Hut. Made for each other.

"I *am* devoted," I whisper, the words bubbling up from nothing, then clasp both hands over my mouth because someone's coming toward Big Beauty's office.

I'll say goodbye to Mrs. Bondy and then I'll leave, I'll just leave, I'll plant myself on the couch next to Ralph, and maybe if I'm as thick with misery as he is for once, for once I won't care that he is.

Mrs. Bondy is sleeping silently, chest rising and falling, and I place my hand on it because it makes me feel good that her lungs are still plugging away, taking the same share of air they always have, politely, quietly, but starting to feel as though they aren't entitled to it anymore.

A crumpled tissue, the nail file, a tiny galaxy of clippings and dust, are still on her nightstand. The nail polish is gone though. The nail polish I'd handed to Janet, *I can finish that,* she'd said, *that's a nice color, Mom, do you like this color?* Screaming into her face like she can't hear, like she's too dumb to understand. That almost-black color that used to belong to Ralph's mother, gone. I look under Mrs. Bondy's bed, in her nightstand drawer, scour the floor, her vanity. Gone. Stolen. Buried in Janet's coat pocket, ferreted out to her car, and now God knows where, her house maybe, in her cupboard, welcomed quietly by her own familiar collection of nail polishes, greetings, welcome, this is where you live now, this is where you'll slowly separate, pray to be shaken back to original homogenous splendor when she opens the door, washes us in light!

What if she has the color on her nails today when she shows up? I bubble again with blinding-hot, spine-severing cumshit-kill. I close my eyes, watch the light that'd been burned into my eyelids flicker, then disappear. I put the nail file in my pocket, toss the used tissue into Mrs. Bondy's trash, then lay a hand on her forehead, gently, softly, so she'll never feel it.

"Goodbye, my baby." I lean over and I kiss her on the cheek. She doesn't move, just breathes in and out and in and out.

Outside, I squint against winter's sunless moon-bright. Instead of heading immediately to the subway, which is what I usually do, I scuttle to the side of the building, lean forward, hands pressed against the cold bricks, and watch the front door, ducking low behind one of the bare shrubs whenever someone passes through. I focus on my breathing, in and out and in and out like Mrs. Bondy, but not like Mrs. Bondy, because these are my rude, greedy, entitled lungs, and this is my breathing, and these are my hands pressed against the building's cold brick. Knees bent, ready to drop low behind the bare shrub if anyone comes, and the shrub's bitter, organic bite is in my nose and I'm taking it in, here, crouching here next to the building, greedy breathing in and out and in and out and in and out.

The shrub looks like the bare, brain-shaped bush that now marks an empty hole. It looks like the branches that fill my lungs, buds that expand and contract, turn oxygen into poison and expel it as quickly as possible from the good old body. Always looking out for you till it gets bored and stops, lets a cancer sneak into your throat that will keep you silent, morph you into a nobody, indistinct and drooling in head-to-toe Eileen Fisher and eventually nothing at all, tossed to the sexual assaulters and the bedbugs at Kingsmere.

"Abby?"

"Carol!" I yelp, grab my chest and spin around. "What are you doing here?"

"Me? What are *you* doing?" She's picking her way through the skeletal shrubs toward me, supporting her precious, pregnant body with the side of the building.

"Nothing, I, I just needed to take a little walk."

"You forgot your purse." She hands it to me, then holds her

coat together with both hands. The knife handle is sticking out from the top.

"Thanks." I grab the purse, shove the knife back in, and tuck the purse under my arm in one motion. I eye Carol suspiciously without meaning to. There's a long quiet while a strong wind thrashes our hair.

"What happened with Big Beauty?"

"Janet Bondy complained. Big Beauty sent me home."

"No!" Carol slaps the side of the building with her supporting hand. "Goddammit, I'm sorry, Abby. You take great care of Mrs. Bondy, of all the residents, and we all know it, okay?"

"Thanks, Carol." I smile.

Carol smiles back but it quickly fades. She pulls her hand off the wall, too cold, and wrings the other with it. "Abby, are you okay?"

"I'm just taking a walk," I say, even though that's not exactly what she's asked. "I'm just taking a little walk because Big Beauty gave me some bad news, and I need a walk before I head home."

Carol clears her throat, wrings her hand more, stares at me like she knows that I'm thinking about stabbing her in the stomach.

"What is it?"

She glances at my purse. "I thought you were kidding about the knife."

"Oh, that." I laugh, three unsettling *ha*s like a person whose only ever read about laughing in a book. I pull it out of my purse.

Carol flinches.

"Christ, Carol." I can't help but find it incredibly annoying, even though I was literally *just* thinking of stabbing her in the stomach, but she doesn't know that, for God's sake. Unless she does. Because the universe is alive with things you can't see, like the menacing vibrations of a violent woman for example, oozing like a stench, triggering alarm in the sensitive olfactory system of a pregnant woman. "It's from when I brought the salmon!" I lie. "I kept forgetting to bring it home."

"Oh!" She sounds so relieved, too relieved, an offensive amount of relief, considering that having brought in a generous-size sharing dish is a perfectly reasonable excuse for having a knife in my purse, one that she has no good reason not to believe. Maybe if she brought more sharing dishes into work she'd understand why sometimes it's better to bring your own knife instead of relying on the nearly useless drawer of misfit utensils at work.

We both stand there, out of things to say. It occurs to me that she's been sent out here to get rid of me: someone spotted me on their way into the building, *There's a crazy bitch in the shrubs,* and they told Linda at reception and Linda wiped bagel neatly from her mouth, picked up the phone to page Big Beauty just as Carol walked by and asked what was up and Linda told her and Carol, who knew I'd seen Big Beauty this morning, who knew I'd had a problem with Janet Bondy the day before, she had a hunch it might be me lurking in the shrubs, because I am a crazy fucking bitch who asks her how often she shits and lugs a whole jellied salmon into the office. And at that point maybe she'd even seen the knife in my purse. So she said, "Don't call Big Beauty, let me handle this." And she came out and she found me here and she doesn't want to leave until I do. And that story is so plausible that it's very definitely true. Thank you, Carol, you good, sweet person, I don't deserve you.

"You're wonderful, Carol."

Carol laughs, confused. "Well, thanks, Abby. You're wonderful too." She reaches out and squeezes my arm, an I'm-here-for-you gesture, something she's downloaded into her circuits. A must-have for women who identify as *supportive, encouraging, compassionate, kind, gentle, inspiring.* I appreciate it, I do, but I could never take her up on any of those adjectives right now, impossible to open up, because a yogurt type could never believe in an undead mother-in-law demon haunting basements and bathrooms and backyards. They're not capable. Yogurt types would never steal the ring off a corpse, not ever, easily resisting the cackling impulse, probably never even tuning in to it at all.

I look behind my shoulder, just for a minute, and spot Janet's car, finally here, but no Janet inside it. Which means I'd missed the thing I'd been waiting for, and I feel very angry with Carol even though she'd had no idea and was just trying to help and literally one single second ago I loved her more than anything.

"Fuck."

"What is it?"

"Nothing, nothing. Okay, you can go inside now. I'm going home."

Carol exhales, relief I'm fairly certain. "Yeah. Just relax. Tell Ralph he's gotta make the jellied salmon tonight!"

I nod. "Bye, Carol." I begin to walk toward the subway.

"Bye, sweetie, I'll see you soon!" She turns around and leaves too, back around the building toward the back door.

I stop at Janet's smudged car, peer into it again just to

see—same files in the back, a few pieces of mail. I note her address without really meaning to, a neighborhood I know.

And there's a welcome package. Kingsmere. She's here to officially evict Mrs. Bondy from the Northern Star. A box of tissues from Mrs. Bondy's room and a scatter of single-serving saltine packets, which she absolutely stole from the cafeteria. My nail polish. My fucking nail polish, on its side, settled into the curve of the upholstery. Entitled to everything, just because she's her, all of these objects, plus her mother's last remaining comforts in life.

I'm scared that everyone is watching me from the windows; that Janet's even wheeled Mrs. Bondy over to see how crazy I am, *Look at her, Mom*, standing in the parking lot, staring into Janet's car, *Look at how she's obsessed with us*.

I scurry to the subway as fast as I can, on the platform rubbing my legs together impatiently, knees starting to hurt when the train finally whips into the station, dings open. I get on and close my eyes till I hear my stop announced.

28

MY MOTHER HAS AN INSTINCT when it comes to men: she can be exactly who they want her to be at first and for a while, a long while, without them telling her, without her even knowing them, it's something she can sense in the same way a baby sea turtle knows which way the ocean is; a drive, a will, because when she's with someone, she's born again.

It goes fast. They say *I love you* quickly, within a couple of weeks, and often they move in. By the time that happens she'll have scrubbed the house of her grime, filled the cupboards with food, made it seem like this is how she lives all the time. But after a while it's hard for her to be someone else. Or maybe she just starts to crave the pattern of it again: the meeting, the quick *I love you*s, the dramatic demise.

Instead of breaking up with the men she begins to resent them for making her someone else, for forcing her to change. *Why do we always do what you want to do? I'm a person too, you know, you're so selfish, you're so mean.* They're confused because she's confusing. They're hurt because they really loved her. They act out because that's what confused and hurt things do. Some cheat, some hit her. One of them broke our television, and I shrieked and wailed like he'd murdered Couchy Motherthing.

DANI: *[Enters the living room, beaming.]* I just had a brilliant idea, Doug. Why don't you take Abby into work with you?

[Abby is sitting on Couchy Motherthing. She's flipping through one of the gossip magazines addressed to the previous tenant, a monthly gift Abby treasured, not just for its bounty of bright, glossy photographs, but also because at any point they could suddenly stop showing up. She drops it into her lap, irritated, exasperated. Despite her mother's performance of having just been struck with a brilliant idea, they've had this conversation already.]

ABBY: Mom, *please,* I already told you I don't *want* to go.

DANI: *[Completely undeterred.]* Doug, take her in. *[Walking toward Doug, who's sitting at the table in the adjoining kitchen, smoking a cigarette, scanning the classifieds for promising used cars to flip, a side hustle he could finally undertake now that he was dating a woman with a garage.]* It's Take Your Daughter to Work Day. Why don't you want to take her in?

DOUG: She doesn't wanna go, Dani.

ABBY: And I'm not his daughter, Mom, come on. I barely know him.

DANI: *[Obviously hurt. She has the uncanny ability to make herself physically smaller when she wants to.]* I see.

Of course I end up in Doug's truck, where it's hot and smells like cigarettes. A cold coffee in the center console, butts jerking back and forth as the car moves. This boyfriend works as a glazier and there's nothing for me to do there, so he asks his boss if I can sit in the office and play with the typewriter. His boss wears a short-sleeved button-up shirt with an oversize collar, stiff as a wimple, whiskered buttons pulled tight down his center, glimpses of hairy bloat beneath. His hair, plowed every which way to cover his scalp, is wet as a newborn's, and he looks confused as he points me toward the typewriter.

After half an hour or so he brings me a glass of water and a couple of hard oatmeal cookies on a thin take-out napkin. He asks if I'm dying of boredom, if the air-conditioning is too aggressive, if the lights are too bright. He tells me his mother is so sensitive to light that she has to wear two sets of sunglasses, and at lunch he offers me half his sandwich. This girl doesn't have anything, he thinks. That deadbeat hasn't brought her any lunch. And he hasn't. He went out and got Burger King, I could see it from the window, he got Burger King only for himself.

On the typewriter, my fingers marching: *fuck, bitch, cum, whore, piss, ass, asshole, anal anal anal cock, fuck, fuck, fuck, fucking, fucker, shit, shit, shithead, shitbag, shitface, shitter, cunt, whore, she's a whore, a whore a whore a whore a whore's daughter, sad whore's daughter, daddy, who cares, daddy, who cares, someone who hurt her, hurt HER so badly. Hurt HER so BADLY. We're never allowed to talk about him. Hurt her so badly, so badly, so badly, please. Please stay. What do you want? What can I do? I'll give you anything, anything, anything you want, you want her too? You can have her. You can have us both. You can have us both. You can have us both. You can have us both. You can have us both. You can have us both. You can have us both.*

That same guy who broke the TV and took me into work and ate his Whopper right in front of me: it sounded like wood striking wood. So loud maybe the house cracked in half. Except it was actually the sound of his skull against the charred bottom of a cheap metal pan, her standing behind him, still holding it, eyes wide, too much white around them. He blinked, his mouth moved, a silent triangle of blood spilled out, grew longer, longer, till the tip broke off and landed with a splat on the floor.

W-what . . . But he could barely get the word out. He turned around, took in the shape of her, arm up, pan in her clenched fist, pulsing, like some idling video game character, visibly inflating and deflating. A radio ad chattered static in the background, water hissed into the sink. He wiped his mouth with the back of his hand. *My hucking tongue,* he said. *I bit my hucking tongue in half, you hucking, you're hucking crazy.* He took a step and his knees hit the ground. Head down, arms down, she got closer.

DANI: *[Growling.]* Get out.

DOUG: In front of Abby, you—

DANI: *[Louder.]* Get out.

DOUG: *[Blinking, trying unsuccessfully to firm up his eyesight.]* You could have hucking killed me. Abby, pass me that cloth, all right? And some ice—

DANI: *[Raising the pan again.]* Don't you talk to her, get *out*.

He lumbered out the door, a trail of blood on the carpet, and he never came back. She sat me down and told me he'd tried to hurt her, explained the whole scene in great, imaginary detail.

But I knew, because I'd heard it all, that this one hadn't tried to hurt her. This one had tried to leave before she was ready for it. *You can have us both,* she'd said, meaning me, meaning he could have me too, fuck me too, and her, the both of us whenever he wanted if he'd just promise to stay.

On the rare occasions I think about what she said, I laugh—*You can have us both*—not because it's funny but because I don't know what else to do, like learning after you've walked a tightrope that the safety harness was never attached. You've gotta laugh! You've just gotta laugh.

So I laugh. And I press both my hands against my face and silent scream behind them.

29

I OPEN THE FRONT DOOR of the house and an impolite wind elbows past me. It stirs up a family of dust bunnies in the entryway, eddying their way into corners and under the side table. The last time I cleaned anything in here was the night Laura died, scrubbing footprints from the floor, tearing up carpet, burying her ring in the backyard.

Now it's filthy again.

This is what the house looked like when Laura got low, so low, the night we moved in to be with her, to help her. Ralph and I spent the whole weekend cleaning up while Laura sobbed and apologized, followed us around berating herself for being disgusting. *You're not disgusting, Mom, you just need some help, that's why we're here, this is what family's for, you've gotta stop, you've gotta relax, go sit down, make a cup of tea, Abby could you make Mom a cup of tea?*

I know this grime well, the grime of the tormented. Spreading without stopping into the deepest, darkest corners of every room. How could the house have gotten like this with me in it? How could I not have noticed?

I trace the infestation to its source. The living room, ground zero, where Ralph is surrounded by papers, ripped-open mail and flyers, blankets and pillows; towers of plates and forks and knives, barnacled with food. Stacks of nickels and dimes and quarters. Change everywhere in fact. Ralph in the center, warm glowing nucleus of this cell of filth.

He's watching the nighttime murder shows, which tend to be about gang crimes, men being murdered with guns for important business reasons, kill shots if all goes to plan, right through the head or heart. During the day these shows are mostly about women being murdered, because women are usually who're watching: young moms like I'm going to be, bound to house and newborn, scared of everything already what with this precious, delicate new thing to love. And look at this world you brought her into. Buy the antibacterial wipes and save your family. Make the prepackaged pesto and save your family. Women on daytime murder shows are always strangled or stabbed or chopped up for no reason at all, except that they're women, I guess, and to some men that means they deserve it. Women are lucky to get shot, really. I'd rather be shot than strangled. Thank you, Son of Sam, you were uncharacteristically good to us.

"Ralph, it's a pigsty in here."

"What's that?" He tears himself from the murder show, the ectoplasm that'd forged between his eyes and the TV broken and swaying in the air like a cobweb.

"It's filthy in here. We have to clean."

Ralph surveys the room, blinks a few times. "Christ. It's like when we first got here, isn't it." He drops his head, ashamed, maybe waiting for me to disagree, *No, it's not that bad, Ralph, you're not that bad,* like he would do for his mother, but I can't because it is that bad. He turns his head to look at me, neck long and straight as a baby bird's in his nest of blankets and garbage.

Birds in the city use garbage for their nests. I saw a nest once with an Oh Henry! wrapper braided throughout, and I wondered if maybe every time those baby birds saw an Oh Henry! wrapper they'd think of home, think of their mother, think of their safest, warmest time in life, when everything you need comes from one soft, dependable body.

"Sorry," he says, then turns his head back to the TV, where a man in an orange jumpsuit talks about the way a little bit of blood tastes, from your finger for example, when you nick it with a knife, compared with how a lot of blood tastes, when you slice open a person's throat and clamp your mouth to the wound.

When a baby is crying, you feed it, let it nurse, suckle, exercise its first and most powerful survival instinct, not just for nourishment, but for comfort as well.

And what becomes of that instinct which connects comfort with food? Is the instinct distorted by the food itself? Yogurts and jellied salmon more signifier than sustenance? Or is the instinct destroyed by harmful additives and preservatives and sugars and fats that hook you, not by the good and wholesome satisfaction of exercising your most profound need, but by the same nefarious means as drugs?

I see it now, the contours of a plan, a perfect food or, rather, a meal perfectly executed, which will revive that long-buried instinct in Ralph, to be alive, despite the shock of it. To stay alive, despite the pain of it. A food, a flavor, offered once by his Motherthing to make suddenly *being* alive all right. I can revive that instinct. I can replicate that flavor.

I just have to grab a few things first.

30

Scene: A large front porch made of natural stone. The withered scarecrow of some unknown bush frozen stiff in a terra-cotta pot next to the front door. It's a nice street in a nice neighborhood, where a layer of snow makes the tidy, cottage-like homes seem to glow with warmth. Abby is standing on the porch. She's filled with electricity but also with nothing at all. She is beams of light barely contained by the skin that disguises her as a normal human woman when Janet opens the door.

ABBY: Hello, Janet.

JANET: *[Letting the word hang like drool from her mouth.]* Hiiiiiii. *[She wants Abby to know that this isn't normal, that she shouldn't be standing on her porch right now.]*

ABBY: I'm so sorry to bother you. May I come in? This won't take long.

[Janet conspicuously observes Abby's bare face and unwashed hair; her black leggings and long T-shirt and squeaking wet sneakers, lingering for some time on the soft-shell cooler bag in her hand.]

ABBY: *[Straightening her spine, a reaction to Janet's judgment and significantly more polished appearance, superior in a long-sleeved dress, with a deep, asymmetrical neckline, shimmering in jewelry and some lavish powder.]* I know we got off to a bad start, but there's something very important I'd like to discuss with you. About your mother. Please?

JANET: About my *mother*, well, I suppose I'll look like an asshole if I say no then, right?

[Abby shrugs, smiles, and Janet steps out of the way, holds her arm out to guide Abby very directly to the living room, where she's stalled by the sight of Janet's couch, clean and new and the color of French vanilla ice cream. There are even little flecks of brown woven into the fabric. Abby can smell it. Big, colorful throw pillows, karate chopped in the center the way that women of a certain age like it. It's nicer in here than she'd been expecting, Janet living the kind of fantasy life that lures women into the world of multilevel marketing schemes. A crystal bowl on her coffee table holds six decorative wicker balls. In the medium's attic this bowl might have seemed ominous, the number significant, each a cursed soul. Here it's a harmless tchotchke because Janet hasn't endured the suffering of a mystic.

Abby sinks into the couch with her bag in her lap and drops the cooler next to her feet. She notices a large, tattered cushion in front of a brick fireplace, a sticky rawhide bone.]

ABBY: Where's your poodle?

JANET: *[Sitting in a matching chair facing the couch.]* How do you know about Louise?

[Though Abby probably shouldn't be, she is taken aback by the hostility in Janet's voice, this woman, Mrs. Bondy's daughter, who might have been Abby's sister in another life.]

ABBY: Oh, I'm sorry. Your mother told me.

JANET: *[Leaning back in her chair.]* She's told you a lot I guess.

[She's jealous, thinks Abby. Just jealous. Because Abby has all of Mother's love. Smarter, younger, prettier, superior to this genetic practice run who came before her. She was there for us, Janet, don't you know that now it's our turn to be there for her? We're the mothers now. She's the baby.]

ABBY: She has. She's a really wonderful woman, Janet, I can honestly say I've never enjoyed a resident more.

JANET: *[Forward again, elbows on her knees. She laughs.]* Right.

[Abby can see down Janet's fancy dress, her bra is beige, thick, positively orthopedic.]

ABBY: What's funny about that?

JANET: I'm sorry, what was your name again?

ABBY: Abigail. Abby.

[I can see your bra, stupid, I see that you're weak in your ultrasoft Eileen Fisher support-wear, because they don't even call them bras at that point. They're scaffolding, structural, hard at work.]

JANET: Abigail, why don't you tell me exactly why you're here.

ABBY: Well, I understand you've decided to move your mother to another facility, and—

JANET: Who told you that?

ABBY: No one, exactly. Word gets around.

JANET: It wasn't supposed to have gotten around to you. You're not to have any more to do with my mother's—what do you call it?—*care strategy*. The fact that you're here at all is honestly very strange. I'm going to tell your boss about it, you realize that, I'm going to pick up the phone and call Ellen first thing tomorrow morning.

ABBY: I really wish you wouldn't, Janet. I'm just trying to do the right thing here. Your mother is a good woman, she doesn't deserve to be uprooted this way, especially not by her own daughter, who she worships by the way. She absolutely lit up when you walked into her room. *[A pain-*

ful admission, but true, Abby gulps.] I'd never seen her that way before.

JANET: Listen, you don't know her. By the time you met her she couldn't even speak.

ABBY: But she can speak! She—

JANET: Not really. A few words here and there. And, honestly, everyone who *does* know her, who *actually* knows her, is pretty thankful for that. She isn't *a good woman,* Abigail, I know it's easy to project whatever you want onto that feeble old frame, but the truth is, my mother is a cold, calculating crook. It's not her money she's blowing in there. Not that it's any of your business. It's mine, from my father, her *ex*-husband. Divorced almost twenty years now, and she got her fair share then, let me tell you. Now, after a very difficult year in litigation, I've finally got what's mine, and she's going to the type of facility that *she* can afford.

ABBY: *[Her brain knocked from its orbit, Abby searches the table for something to focus on.]* That's not true.

JANET: What do you mean it's not true?

ABBY: She's not a bad mother.

JANET: Oh, well, that's a relief. I guess I should let my therapist know.

ABBY: You're wrong about her, Janet. She did the best she could, she—

JANET: Dear God, she's really gotten into your head. I get it. I feel bad for you, Abigail, I really do. I know what it's like to be taken on one of her rides.

ABBY: If she's so awful, if you hate her so much, why are you kind to her when you visit?

JANET: Am I kind to her?

ABBY: Well, you certainly seem to care about her comfort.

JANET: That's because I'm paying for it. *Was* paying for it. *[Smiling.] Now* I don't care.

ABBY: I don't understand. *[Whispering, more to herself than Janet.]* Why do *you* get to punish a perfectly good mother, when there are lots of mothers out there, awful mothers, who get to live unpunished, *die* unpunished, I don't—

JANET: *[A flash of confused pity softening her face.]* Abigail. Abby. You don't *know* her, all right?

[Abby sees herself sitting on the edge of Mrs. Bondy's bed, chatting the way they do, both hands cupped beneath the old woman's open palm, Abby pressing her thumbs along the most troublesome creases. The skin over Mrs. Bondy's flesh moves so easily, like a sheet

*animated by a ghost. Maybe Abby's always been able to see ghosts,
in a way, a person's true spirit. Mrs. Bondy wasn't a bad mother,
Abby knew that with absolute certainty, despite Janet's attempt to
twist Abby's perception, press it between a pair of cold glass slides,
slip it flattened and deformed beneath the cruel lens of a micro-
scope, which, everyone knew, was incapable of revealing truth the
way a long-suffering mystic could.]*

ABBY: I do know her. *[Quietly.]* I know her.

JANET: *[Voice softer, warmed by sympathy. Maybe even recog-
nition.]* You should stay away from her.

*[Abby realizes that Janet thinks they're the same now, that they
have something in common, that Mrs. Bondy was somehow just as
awful as Abby's own mother, Janet and Abby both girl-monsters,
abandoned in the world, grotesque and unlovable, but that's not
true, Janet, I'm loved beyond my wildest dreams, loved by the
greatest man in the world, whose life I'm going to save tonight.]*

ABBY: We're not the same.

JANET: *[Laughs.]* I never said we were!

ABBY: Your mother *is* a good woman. *[And she should have
been* my *mother. You're the one who should have endured the
suffering of a mystic, not me, Abby squeezing her fists, hands
aching.]* I won't let you kill her.

JANET: *Kill* her?

ABBY: Moving her to a place like Kingsmere will kill her, I promise you it will.

JANET: How do you know I'm sending her to Kingsmere? I didn't even tell your boss that.

ABBY: Oh I, um— *[Abby's guts roil suddenly, a frenzied cauldron, aching for the final ingredient that would make it a spell. She knots her lips tight around the roiling, a single bubble sneaking past her gag reflex, triggering almost overwhelming nausea.]* I, well, I saw the documents in the back seat of your car.

JANET: You snooped through my car? *[She isn't angry. She's impressed, not at Abby's initiative, but rather her genuine strangeness.]*

ABBY: I just noticed them. *[Shifting so that the cauldron, grasping for her esophagus, loses a bit of ground.]*

JANET: How did you know which car was mine?

ABBY: Your dog, Linda, I saw her back there and went over to say hello. You never told me where she is.

JANET: Her name's Louise. She's with her father. My ex.

[Abby remembers waving at Janet down there, waving at you with the rest of the children of divorce, screaming along that nasty, lonely curve. Grotesque and unlovable because that's who you are, Janet,

not because of anything poor Mrs. Bondy did. You are who you are, just like Ralph is who he is, the Perfect Good, despite Laura, and I his disciple, so lucky to have found him, to have been saved from the unsavories, from my own mother, who might have held the bedroom door shut with her back, grinning, grateful, thanking God that Todd or Doug or Randy would stay and have us both.]

ABBY: Right, sorry.

JANET: That's fine. Are we done here, Abby? I've got some things to—

ABBY: Wait, I just— *[Too loud, not really knowing what to say but knowing she can't leave, nothing resolved, Mrs. Bondy still destined for certain doom.]* If you could find it in your heart to reconsider, I—you have no idea what she means to me, you really don't, taking care of her has been, she's been like a mother to me, she really has, and I'm sorry you don't think she got it right with you, but she's getting it right with me, and I can't lose her. I can't. And she can't survive a move, I know that. Growing old, Janet, people just don't understand how difficult it really is, your body snatching control from your brain, taking over completely, dragging you kicking and screaming toward death. It's a sort of horrible slow-motion autopilot, and there's nothing you can do about it. Imagine—imagine jumping off a building and then time all but stops, and you're falling so slowly, regretting having jumped, wishing you could just be back on the ledge, miserable with everyone else, but you can't, it's over, you have to come to terms with this part while it's happening, and it's so hard, the physical pain, the indignities, it's just so hard, no one really knows, not yet, and that's what I do, you understand? That's what I do for your mother, for everyone at the Northern Star, I help them let go, let their autopilot take over, and your mother, she's almost there, things could be so peaceful for her now if she could just stay, stay with me at the Northern Star and let me take her all the way.

[Janet is quiet for a moment, scanning Abby's face, maybe even, Abby hopes, considering what she's said. There's so little time left, Janet has to see that surely it would be more costly, time-and-energy-wise, to move her mother at this point. And Abby would talk to Big Beauty, they'd work something out, cut some costs where it didn't really matter. Maybe they'd been born to the wrong mothers, but Abby could at least right this wrong, she could at least be with her real mother when it mattered.]

JANET: What would you do if it were your mother, Abby?

ABBY: What do you mean?

JANET: What would you do to the woman who raised *you*? Would you show her every mercy? Bankroll her comfort? Did she do the same for you? *Would* she do the same for you?

ABBY: I—

JANET: Maybe you're a better person than I am. Maybe if she'd been your mother, you would have taken care of her. But she wasn't so lucky. She ended up with me, all right?

And I can't let go of the things she did to me. And this is what I'm doing about it.

ABBY: Please Janet, please, I— *[Definitely going to vomit, the bubbles boiling hot are licking the top of her stomach, threatening to work their way up.]* We could help you cut costs somehow, I could talk to Ellen about discontinuing the cable, the salon services, the snack cart between meals, I—

JANET: No.

[The cauldron whips, the bubbles gaining again, Abby grips her stomach with both hands and Janet clocks Abby's physical suffering with a notched eyebrow.]

ABBY: Just, hear me out, I—

JANET: No, Abigail.

ABBY: But Kingsmere is a—

JANET: It's fine.

ABBY: It's not! *[Vomit in her chest, stubborn as tears.]* I'm telling you it's not. Trust me. It'll—it'll break your heart—*[she burps, vomit slow, hot, determined]*—to see her in there—sorry—you'll regret this, I promise you, you'll regret this. Please don't send her there.

JANET: What did she do to you?

ABBY: *[Startled, confused.]* Who?

JANET: Your mother. What did she do to you?

ABBY: *[You can have us both, you can have us both, you can have us both, you can have us both, you can have us both, you can have us both.]* I—

JANET: Think about it. You're thinking about it, I know you are. Now, I hope no one ever stands in the way of you getting your revenge, all right? Or your peace, or whatever it is you need to move forward with your life. *[Hands on her thighs, Janet rocks herself up, steps toward Abby, attempts to herd her back toward the door.]* Now, get out of my house.

[Abby feels it, the cumshitkill making everything sizzle red and endless. She reaches into her bag and feels the knife. Squeezes the handle for support. Squeezes it so tight that her forearm swells. Coming and shitting and puking and stabbing at the same time, beams of fluid, she's a blasting star.]

ABBY: *[Refusing to stand, her arm buried to the elbow in her bag.]* Janet you can't move your mother.

JANET: Please get up.

ABBY: I won't let you.

JANET: Won't *let* me? Stand up, Abigail, get the fuck out.

[As Abby stands up, she pulls the knife out of her bag, lets the cumshitkill fling her arm up, bury the knife to the handle in the softness between Janet's chin and neck. Blood spills out, coats Abby's fist like a candy apple, and a waterfall of yellow, simmering bile rolls over Abby's chin too, finally, hits her shirt, splatters on her sneakers and the floor and a bit on Janet's pristine French vanilla couch. Janet's eyes so wide, shocked, yes, yes, you're dying, you're going to die, killed, you, it actually happened to you! But you're no victim, Janet.]

ABBY: *[Inches from Janet's face, hissing.]* I'll tell you what I'd do, I'll show you what I'd fucking do to her. *[Twisting the knife so Janet's jaw loosens a bit, her lips part, Abby in control of this minor movement. She twists the knife back and forth, back and forth, so Janet's jaw moves up and down, up and down like a ventriloquist's dummy's.]* You can have us both. *[Twisting the knife so it looks like Janet is speaking.]* You can have us both. You can have us both. You can have us both.

[The shock on Janet's face ebbs to suffering. She's able to pry her lips back slowly, trying to speak, but instead of words, blood spills between her teeth, splats of blood and vomit merging on the floor between Abby and Janet, Janet's outline draining like a toilet tank and soon she'll be empty. Conquered. Defeated. She swats, arms limp, polished nails grazing Abby's shirt. Janet's wearing the nail polish she stole from her mother's room. Abby lets go of the knife. Steps back. Yanks a clean section of her shirt, wipes the bile from her chin. Janet's eyes flutter and she crumples to the floor like a jabbering marionette, jewelry jangling, whoosh of perfume. Look what I've done, thinks Abby. I've saved Mrs. Bondy, my baby, our

mother, I've saved her life. She's going to be able to stay at the Northern Star now, spend the rest of her days with me, happy and healthy, doing what babies always do—turn the women who care for them into mothers.

It would be much easier to kill someone and just leave them at their house where they belong anyway, rather than try to get rid of a body from your own house. Okay, now I'm starting to think you're a murderer.

Abby doubles over with laughter, it's absolutely hysterically funny now, because, look, she thinks, I am *a murderer! Look at me! Murdering the bad people, a bad person who tried to be a murderer first. A person who deserves it because some people do. They just do, some people deserve to die, some people make the world a worse place to live and that's just not fair to everyone else. People who would dump their mothers into a hellhole, knowing that they'll endure torture, knowing that they might not survive, just for some extra money at the end of it all. People who don't appreciate the good mothers they have, the fucking liar, lying about my baby. You're the problem, Janet, not my baby. You're the one who made things bad. Which Abby would never have done. If Mrs. Bondy had been Abby's mother, things would have been so wonderful, learning how to file her nails properly, how to be a real person. Janet, you wasted it, you fool, you didn't know how to appreciate a good mother, but someone like Abby could have, Abby, who never hurt her own mother, even though she actually fucking deserved it.* You can have us both, *should have stabbed her then, right then, instead of waiting her whole life, destroying herself with unsavories, groping her way through the painful darkness till she found her sweet Ralph, whose light bent and multiplied in her mystical gems. Ralph made her a good woman. Ralph made her a savior.*

Still life in Janet's eyes, but it's more like the bare instinct a fish has to simply resist death. Jellied salmon. Abby bends over Janet's body, pulls her head back, and just like it says in Secrets of a Famous Chef *she locates the jugular vein, opens it. Locates the carotid arteries and opens them too. Deep red curtains fall and gather in a warm pool around Janet.* Animals must be bled as soon as possible. It is important that all major blood vessels are severed. If only one carotid artery is cut, the animal may take over a minute to die. *A Good Woman butchers her meat properly, without cruelty. A Good Woman takes only what she needs for Chicken à la King and nothing more. Two or three pounds, maybe. Not much. The best of her will come from the middle says The Book, thighs and rump. A Good Woman has to make sure she doesn't contaminate the meat either. A Good Woman avoids the gallbladder, intestines, things that leak poison when ruptured.*

Abby finds ice packs in the kitchen, as well as a book, dog-eared and open on the breakfast table next to a half cup of cold coffee: Codependent No More: How to Stop Controlling Others and Care for Yourself. *A Good Woman recognizes that you can be good and bad at once. A Good Woman can acknowledge your humanity while recognizing the fact that you also need to die. That's why it's hard to be A Good Woman. That's why we're not all good women, are we, Janet?*

Moving on quickly, she grabs towels, another knife. Generally speaking, the older the animal, the darker the meat. *Right again, Book. When Abby digs the knife into Janet's thigh, walks it up off the bone with her fingers, the meat is dark, purple, sinewy. Abby wraps a dripping cut in one of the towels, places it in the ice-lined cooler. She then works Janet up and rolls her over, like a client at the Northern Star. Etches her rump from the bone, leaves a gaping crater behind. Janet's face isn't really a face anymore. It's unspooled flesh, squished open mouth turning blue. Not a Janet anymore, but a Janet Thing.*

Abby gets to work cleaning the house with the environmentally friendly cleaning supplies from her bag, the same she'd used to sop up so much Laura. She sees the squiggling germs everywhere, what exists in between, the way the Good Women in commercials do. She sprays them down, wipes them away screaming, leaves a sparkling surface behind. Balls up the bloody towels, squishes them into the cooler's side pockets, safely separated from the meat. The meat. Leaves Janet lying exactly like a great polar bear rug, arms out at her sides, legs spread, picked at like the last few days of the jellied salmon in the fridge. Abby leaves the door unlocked behind her. She was never really there.]

31

I RINSE THE MEAT under the sink, pat it dry. I don't know if it's still fashionable to rinse meat, but all The Book's recipes demand it, so I do. I flip to the very last recipe in the meat section: Chicken à la King.

Sauté in butter the following: 1 cup chopped mushrooms, 1/4 cup pimento, add a pound of diced chicken thigh, and heat until hot and cooked through. Turkey thigh may also be used, or any other dark meat.

I pull Laura's heavy cast-iron pan from the drawer, set it on the stove, and crank the gas. I dice the meat while the pan gets hot, then feed it a fat pat of butter, which it melts, mercilessly, but it wants more, so I dump in the meat cubes, which scream against the heat, like thousands of earsplitting lice, red and wet, really such a nice color at first, the way wet things are always a nice color: wet skin, wet paint, wet grass, wet road. Wet gets itself on you if you touch it, travels and breeds, alive and dangerous. Dry is dead and looks that way.

I use Laura's knife to chop a busy detritus of mushrooms and roasted red peppers (Ralph prefers it to pimento) and dump that in too. He also likes me to add some green pepper, but we don't have any, and serve the dish over fried potatoes, which we do have, an unorthodox substitution, but it works. As I peel the potatoes, some flaps of skin slap the sink and stick like tile. I scoop them out, throw them away, chop up the potatoes, and put a big pot of salted water on, start it boiling. Once they're soft, I'll fry them till they're crispy. But first, back to the main dish.

Heat 1 pint of cream and add it to the chicken mixture, shake the pan, but do not stir nor allow to boil.

I heat the cream, swirl it in the pan, watch it warm and thicken till it coats the sides, then dump it over the meat. When it is very hot, I *carefully mix the beaten yolks of three eggs, add them to the chicken mixture. Sprinkle with paprika to taste.*

I drain the potatoes, fry them in chopped onion and butter and salt and pepper. They brown quickly, smelling good. *Serve in patty shells,* says The Book, or in our case over fried potatoes, and voilà! Laura, look at me, the Queen of Good Protein. Cooking up some good protein for Ralph right now, to activate his survival instincts with this good and special plan. Watch, Laura, watch me.

"Watch me," I say out loud, and almost catch a glimpse of her, I'm sure of it, the corner of her blue dress disappearing from the doorway, the knock of her ring against the wall, the ring, the ring. Back where it belongs and soon Laura, back where she belongs.

I ladle a perfect-looking portion over potatoes, then head into the living room and hand the bowl to Ralph. I've made myself a bowl too because it only seems right. This isn't something that Ralph should have to do alone. Devotion. Commitment. *A Good Woman.* The very best.

He accepts it, sets it down on the table without even looking at it, without even asking what it is. He's absorbed by the television, another murder show starting, this one about two elderly women who were killed in their homes in California, someone snuck through the window, beat them both with a hammer. It's a classic as far as serial killers go, I recognize his face: greasy black hair, hollow cheeks, a symbol carved into the palm of his hand.

Ralph's not going to eat his food. He's going to let it cool, congeal, then apologize to me again for not being hungry, my plan thwarted before it can even begin.

"Ralph. Look at what I made, would ya?"

He glances at the bowl I've handed him, hoists the meat molecules up through his nose. They start to work on him, I can see, the way he softens; he's moved too by the gesture, whispers, "Chicken à la king," as he exhales.

"Your favorite."

On TV the women's neighbor describes the man-shaped shadow she saw, inching out their back door, swallowed by the concentrated dark of a woodsy deposit that ran behind their houses.

There's a picture of the elderly women together when they were alive, and I think about my baby, Mrs. Bondy, soft skin and bright eyes. I wonder if she's sleeping and I wonder if she ever made chicken à la king for her ungrateful beast of a daughter. I bet she did. I bet she didn't just drop a box of cereal in front of Janet's face every morning, then go back up to bed, looking like she'd spent half the night being dragged through the bushes by the Night Stalker. Bloated, rubbed, reeking of crotch and beer and sweat and cigarettes. Maybe my mother is dead too. I wouldn't know. I wouldn't even know anyone who *would* know. It's been better that way, but also very hard.

I hold my breath as Ralph reaches for the bowl, spears a craze of potato and meat with his fork, raises it to his mouth, and takes the first bite I've seen since that night at Aunt Tony's. Chewing. Chewing. I follow the masticated bulge down his throat, into his chest, stomach, like it's a carnival game, tumbling in his stomach acids till it becomes a terrible prize.

"How is it?"

"It's great. That's chicken?"

"Yep."

"It's good."

My turn. I stab a cube, drag it through sauce, put it in my mouth. It tastes exactly how it should—chicken in a cream sauce. Maybe just a little bit off, not quite like chicken, maybe alive just a couple of hours ago, maybe a horrible human being about to commit a horrible deed before she was stopped by me and forced to use her worthless, wicked life to save one of the greatest men in the entire world. In that way you do suspect that there might be something more to this meat, because in that way it's more delicious than any other meat I've ever had in my life. I fill my fork with more of this good meat. Ralph is right about the roasted red pepper instead of pimento, it really is tastier.

Ralph breathes in deep through his nose as he eats, pulling up huge sheets of meat smell with every bite. Chewing, swallowing, stoking to a flicker, then a steady beam, the vital light he'd been separated from for so long. Still chewing, breathing loudly, brightly, he says, "Can you imagine?"

My fist tingles, the warm press of Janet's soft underchin

throbbing against it, her eyes wide, arms flailing, slapping limp then limper at my arm. "Imagine what?"

He nods at the TV, the murderer behind a plexiglass window. "Being this guy."

I lean forward, elbows on my knees. "I used to imagine what it would be like to kill my mother and her boyfriend. Going to school the next day, how detached I'd feel from everyone. My mother and Randy or Doug or Todd dead in the house and everything outside completely different now, all the people you know, they don't know that you've killed people, that you've done the most insane thing a person can do. It's like you're glowing, phosphorescent, and everyone else is mud."

"Mud." Ralph nods.

Big Beauty with her perfect folders, Carol with her baby, Linda with her braid and her neat little bagels. "Yeah, everyone smoothed together till their colors and shapes surrender. Become matter. *Brown* matter." I raise an eyebrow at him.

"You're"—he smiles. *Smiles*—"thinking about diarrhea, aren't you."

"Always." I smile back, my cheeks crack like something brand-new, unused, like I'm a fresh clone. It feels brand-new too. Like maybe I've never smiled quite like this before—a confident mystic, brimming with non-Kay jewels of knowledge, power, carrying out a plan that is *working*. It's *fucking working*. I inch closer to him, our thighs touching, and he lets it happen, he doesn't move or get up or ask me why I'm making things harder for him. He just lets our thighs touch like they used to. Another deep sniff of dinner, held glowing in his lungs for a moment this time before release.

And then we're both drawn back to the television, an interview with the murderer in prison. His back is curved, his arms bent, elbows touching, chewing at his cheeks like he was trying to keep his face on. It pains him to make eye contact with the interviewer, wincing every time. Ralph is watching intensely, chewing slowly. The tiniest morsel of fried potato clinging to the corner of his mouth falls finally, back to his bowl, rejoining, reintegrating, and maybe no one knew what it'd been through, so close to the mouth, clinging for dear life, like the murderer I imagine: rejoining society again every day, continuing to go to work and living a real life like a real human despite having committed the most inhuman act imaginable.

"Do you think some people deserve to die, Ralphie?"

"Like this guy? A murderer?"

"Yeah, do you think a murderer deserves to die?"

"I really don't know. I guess I don't think anyone deserves to die." He doesn't really mean that, he's just saying a Ralph thing. Ralph *would* say he doesn't think anyone deserves to die, but in his deepest, truest filth he knows that some people do.

"Want more?" I nod at his empty bowl. He does. And I do too. I refill our bowls, two more full helpings. With that we finish off almost the entire pan, both of us inflated with so much meat that we're made dumb by it, barely functioning, bodies too preoccupied with digestion.

"Ugh, God." I roll over to face him on the couch, meat breath scrubbed into every pore and cranny of my mouth. It's good to be this full. Giddy full. Like being drunk. Ralph sits with his head over the back of the seat, eyes closed, legs out, a hand resting over his stomach. I wish I could sculpt him this way, this perfect, painful overindulgence. This moment in which I'm certain that the plan is working, that I'm saving him.

I manage to hoist myself up off the couch, stack our plates and knives and forks and bring them into the kitchen, where I rinse everything in the sink, thoroughly, A Good Woman, and file them away into the dishwasher. I scrub my pan clean, dry it with a towel, then my knife, which I stroke slowly under hot water and put back in the empty knife drawer. I remember the knives I've frozen and pull them from the freezer to thaw on the counter, so confident I am in my plan.

I step back into the living room, hands on my hips. "All right, Ralph. I'm hitting the sack."

He rocks himself up off the couch like how an egg would move if it could. "Me too." He follows me upstairs.

In the bathroom there's grime in the corners, dust and fallen hair and skin cells and generalized, indeterminate stickiness. Surfaces streaked thickly with soap, lotion, toothpaste maybe. A fat, healthy roll of toilet paper sits on top of an emaciated one abandoned on the roller, like a bone picked clean. Another room tormented by Ralph's filth. But it's fine for now. We can deal with all of this later. If I can accept minor disrespects from certain clients at work, I should certainly be able to accept them from my husband, who I love with every throbbing cell in my body.

I hear him milling around in his mother's room, waiting to use the bathroom. When I leave, I holler, "All finished!" and head into our room, into our bed, alone, as I have almost every night since she died. Actually my nightstand is filthy too. Three glasses of half-finished water, an extra phone charger, unraveled and snaking through piles of change, a bottle of Vicks VapoRub, two pencils, and a shimmer of broken cellophane. A mountain of tear- and snot-filled tissues, some fallen to the floor, mingling with dirty clothes and towels that'd dried where they'd landed, stiff and smelling of mildew.

I'm not sure when this happened. When our room started looking this way and smelling this way. A chair in the corner is completely concealed by heaps: clothes, bags, a set of now-stale sheets that I've been meaning to put on the bed for days? Weeks? I'm not sure anymore.

Now I wait. Imagine how the meat is working on them, him and Laura together, digesting, Laura absorbing the sense that he's satisfied, happy, well taken care of, losing his frequency, forgetting about him, about why she needs to be here, looks down at her ring, what was it about the ring, why am I still here when I've got my ring and all is right with this world?

A heaping plate of seconds, and letting our thighs touch the way he did, no recoiling or screaming at me to leave him alone. Talking and talking, about the TV show, connecting with the thrill of murder, *can you imagine?*

Then he knocks, all according to plan, opens the door slightly, his head sprouting from the crack.

"Hi, can I come in?"

I nod and he steps inside. He's changed into fresh pajamas, brushed and scrubbed, the hair around his face coiled wet.

"Hi." I draw my knees to my chest beneath the blanket, making room for him at the foot of the bed.

He smiles when he sits. "Thanks for dinner. I needed that."

"I know." I clench my fist, resist the urge to reach for his hand, not yet, not yet, wait for it, wait for the plan. I press my teeth against one of my knees and close my eyes. It's going to work. I know it's going to work. Because I am chosen. Chosen to endure the prolonged and immeasurable suffering of a mystic so that I could meet Ralph, bring him to the apex of his sublime love without obliterating. The world needs Ralph, free from darkness, finally, the Perfect Good.

"I want to say"—he reaches out, touches my chin with his forefinger so I open my eyes and look up at him—"I want to say that I'm sorry." He scoots forward. "I'm just, I'm really fucking sorry, Abby. I'm fucked-up and I've been a dick about it, but I'm not going to be a dick anymore, all right? I'm going to do something about this. I'm going to fix it."

Tears fill his eyes and mine, and they slide down our cheeks, pat our chests, damp prints that chill quickly, pressed cold between us when I throw my arms around him and squeeze so tight we can barely breathe, part of the plan, this squeeze another step in the ritual that will restore my Ralph. And restore me too, I now realize, my *something*, quaking like a cracked seed, sprout unfurling unexpectedly.

He pushes back. "I'm not, I'm not quite ready to . . ." But then his face changes, fills with my magic, he pushes me down on the bed and crawls on top of me and I hold my breath, heart thudding, please, Ralphie, *please please please stay with the magic, stay with me, on top of me, kiss me, Ralphie, kiss me kiss me kiss me,* and he does, cautiously, not sure yet what's happening, why he's kissing me now, unaware of what's working inside him, reacting to his stomach acids, filling him with a powerful, magical steam, and I am motionless, recalling the first time he felt my temperature with his palm, how I went still as a moth because I didn't want to ruin anything. I don't want to ruin anything now, I stay exactly as I am, letting the magic control his mouth. So still, barely breathing, I imagine I'm the protagonist of some ludicrous, high-concept porno where a homicide detective (me) somehow has to go undercover as a sex doll and Ralph is my mark. It's called something really obvious so people know exactly what to expect, like *Officer Fuckdoll,* or something to that effect, but the twist is that *The Fuck Doll Detective* (another good porno title) might actually be *The Murderer* (a terrible porno title).

Ralph's kisses soften, expand. He pulls my shirt up over my head and tosses it onto the floor. It's working, the plan is working, the magic growing stronger, I can smell it oozing from his mouth and mine, working, working, more alive than he's been since Laura died, and we're about to fuck again, maybe, if I don't ruin it, we're going to fuck right now, his living dick will be hard as a rock and inside me, gliding in and out till our nerve endings explode and melt and die and come back to life.

Just when I think I'm safe to move, put my hands on his neck, move them down to unbutton his pajama shirt, he pulls his face back, watches me, I hesitate for a split second before slipping his buttons from their holes, one after the other, pull his shirt down over his arms, let him free himself entirely while I unhook my bra and toss it over the side of the bed. He buries his face in my breasts, breathing deeply, "Abby," he whispers, then moves his mouth around my nipple, sucking and sucking, goodness radiating out from where he sucks like a drop of blood coming apart in a glass of water, sucking, sucking, my baby, I love you, "I love you," I say, and I stroke his head, look down into his eyes, I work my underwear down, fling them from my leg.

He pulls back again, looks me up and down, his wife, a powerful familiar for whom no act or deed is too depraved. Her love fierce and boundless. Unconditional. Devoted. I smile, and according to the plan he should do the same, but instead, his mouth oozes over either side of his clenched chin. He's going to cry. He's crying.

"No," I whisper as he lays his head down on my chest again and exhales. "No, Ralph."

"Abby," he says again, sadly this time.

"No, Ralph, no, no, no, no, no, don't stop." I grab him by either side of his face, try to pull it gently toward mine, but he holds it where it is, pressed against me. I can't be more naked, can I? Not unless I flay my skin, peel it back, every inch of me pink and sticky as my vagina. What I've got now isn't enough. If I can't touch him, it's not enough. I can only lie here and pray, pray to Ralph, that the plan will work. Just lie here and wait for my good Ralph to be healed and my Cal to be delivered to me.

"I don't deserve you," he whispers. "I almost—I almost killed you too." His face is sodden, salty, warm against my chest when he presses it down, sprays wet as he breathes deeply in and out. And I like it. Just like I'll like it one day when Cal comes running to me, perfectly fine, but crying all the same, from some shock or indignity that she'll understand eventually and deal with on her own one day, but until then she needs me. I'll love the smear of her precious anguish all over my neck, dampening my shirt, because I'll know that she's okay, that she's wrong about the magnitude of whatever's upset her, just as I know that Ralph is wrong about this. About me. He didn't even come close to killing me. Could never have killed me. Because I'm already dead, I realize that now. I'm the dead one, Ralph, do you see now? *You can have us both, you can have us both.* Empty. Indestructible. And finally I understand that *this* is who I am, my something is *nothing*. Infinite nothing. Absolute power. Never hurt. Never ruined.

My something, finally realized, bursts open now, overrun with ravenous dendrites, its size breathtaking, its strength divine, my eyes flutter, roll back into my head, neck limp, arms limp, fallen out on the bed like I'm really dead, a real dead person, who I am, this is who I *am*. And Ralph guided me here, just as I knew he would, built a path back to me, *me*. A memory from before I drifted away from myself, of my mother coming into my room, how I'd pretend to be asleep and she'd honor it, wouldn't scream or cry or wake me up to tell me something awful. She respected the holiness of a sleeping person. So I'd pretend to be asleep all the time, just quiet with my eyes closed, alive in a dark world. A genius at regulating my breathing in out, in out, in out gently and so uniformly that eventually I barely needed any air at all. My dendrites electrified. *Fuck me, Ralph,* fuck me like all those corpse-fucking weirdos on daytime TV. Kill a monster and save your husband, cook its flesh and save your husband, pretend to be a corpse and save your husband. Be more than naked. More than wet for him. Be dead! He deserves it! A night with Corpscilla, cold and blue and beautiful, dragged from a river where she swayed, lovely as a sea anemone. A potion that puts you to sleep temporarily so your husband can pretend like he's fucking a dead woman, *perfect for anniversaries, birthdays, Valentine's Day, Saturday mornings when Cal's at gymnastics. Side effects include sudden death, so please check her pulse before you initiate fucking.*

"What are you doing?" he asks.

I don't move, I lie there empty as Officer Fuckdoll. He pulls my head up, looks into my slack face, tongue hanging out like an unrolled rug.

"Abby, what are you doing?"

"I want it like this," I whisper. "Please."

And Ralph is so good, always so good, he understands, finally, that he can't hurt me; that my nothing *is* my *something*. Indifferent flesh. A canvas for his will. Transformed by it into something beautiful, something real and *seen*. This is what I want, more than anything ever, to be fucked like this, as my true self, and he's always wanted me to want something this badly: *Do you like that? What do you want me to do? Is this good for you? Yes! This! Yes!* Even if it wasn't good, because what do I know? But I know now. And he knows now, he can tell, that I'm really and truly *liking* this, *wanting* like I never could before but now I can because I'm dead and all I *want* is to be dead and seen that way and fucked that way, liberated of myself, of my body, and becoming *thing*, some*thing*.

My no*thing* is a vacuum, sucks Ralph's dick right in, and he's thrusting so hard, groaning, gripping my shoulder with one hand, thumb pressed into my throat's hollow, slams me down on him harder and harder while I flail empty as a wind sock, every bit of tension pulled into my center, held there like a pack of froth-furious dogs on leashes, be a good wife, the best wife, A Good Woman, feeding him the most special dinner, giving him what he wants, and look at us, sick together, canvas and artist, fucking like I'm dead, eating that good meat, Ralph will love me more than ever now because look at me, I'm my real and actual self, my *authentic self*, the yogurt types would say, and look at what my *authentic* self has done to save him, to save *us*. Ralph my savior, but me *our* savior.

I am *our* savior.

A droplet of light lands suddenly behind my eyelids.

Quivering brighter, brighter, such a deafening density of packed light it feels like a portal, another world moaning open before me.

Come to me. Come, my sweet one. Come to the light.

The medium had been speaking to Laura when she said that. Magic words.

Come to me. Come, my sweet one. Come to the light.

Come to me. Come, my sweet one. Come to the light.

And it's Cal.

I see her.

Cal, Cal, Cal, Cal, Cal. Yes, yes, yes, yes, yes, yes, yes.

Tears warm the seal of my eyelids. My smile spreads past its borders, toward my ears, beyond my face, taking flight.

Cal, tonight, my baby, no question, she's *here,* she's here, she's here, she's here! And Ralph, my baby, returned to me finally. And me, I realize, a baby, coming to life tonight too.

Come to life.

Breaks the otherworldly stillness I'd brought to my sagging lips and tongue.

I lap at the drool I'd worked up from somewhere inside, spilling out, pressed fat and glistening on my cheek, lift my hand, wipe it with the bend of my wrist.

I palm a spread of Ralph's slick back with one hand, use the other to drag up into his hair and squeeze and pull back his head, lick the sweat from his neck. He's picking up steam, this is it, my plan, *my* plan: more powerful than I'd even realized, all of us, my whole family, coming to life at once.

I open my eyes, bring them back to center, peer over the mountain of Ralph's warm shoulder and I see her, finally. In the deep dark of the hallway, through the open bedroom door, Laura is standing there, staring straight at us, head low, mounted on her frame, hair in gnarled sections of hard jerky, bisecting her sneer. But she's faint, crackling more out than in. I direct all my new life to my eyes, focus on her, and she crackles louder, whorls of distortion growing, rubbing out her face, her hands. She feels it, but she's not resisting, allowing herself to be scrubbed from this realm. A stain lifted. Fainter now. And fainter still, no match for my powerful cleansing stare. Lifted, lifting, until she's completely gone, and Ralph comes like he's stuck his dick in an electrical socket.

He rolls off and his semen weeps from me like a popped blister. "Oh, shit," I say, because that's Cal oozing out, my baby yowling on a wave of semen seeping into the sheets. I grab a wad of tissues from next to the bed, scoop most of Ralph's stuff back into me. Hold it there, *Welcome, Cal,* while the rest pools jiggly in the center of the tissue wad, like some extremely upsetting Danish.

Ralph kisses me on the cheek and gets up, still naked, walks to the bathroom, and turns on the sink. He's cleaning himself up but I won't. I'm going to steep in this residue, our fluids, my favorite smell in the whole world. I close my eyes, breathe the smell in so deeply and effectively that it disappears inside me, coming out of me and back inside me, in and out and in and out and around and around and around and I'm almost asleep when I hear Ralph retch.

I get up, also naked, find him kneeling in front of the toilet, wedges of muscle along his back ratcheting with every backward yank of his digestive tract. I don't ask if he's okay because I know he is, the final step of the plan, the magic exorcising itself from his system.

The way he holds the bowl reminds me of the girl on the raisin box, golden hair in sumptuous buttercream masses over her shoulders, held off her pink face by a radiant red bonnet. In her arms a basket of ORGANICA, not shit this time, but some overflowing, uncontrollable cancer of fruit or vegetables or flowers, grown from the ground and ready for a yogurt type like Carol to fill her fridge with. Expensive, natural products that prove that you love yourself, that you're a healthy, happy person with clean, flushed interiors. Though Ralph held the toilet bowl with that same lust for life, it was filled instead with the acrid glut of a spent enchantment: half-digested Janet à la king and the remnants of his mother's influence. Ralph is sweating, spent, lying empty on the cool bathroom floor. I lean over, look into the bowl, and spit into our bubbling black victory.

32

[Scene: Ralph's well-preserved childhood bedroom. Bright morning light sears the bed, where Abby is stirring, smiling before she even opens her eyes, feeling the warmth of the wide-open curtains, hearing the sound of Ralph in the kitchen downstairs, plates clanking, dishwasher latched and humming and forks and knives on their feet, rattle-dancing in their cages.

He's awake. He's cleaning. He's cured. She rolls around the bed, wrapping herself up in sheet and blanket, stretches all the way awake, then stands up, yanks off the bedding, tosses it in the hallway. Pulls Laura's bedding off too and adds it to the pile. Fresh sheets and blankets and pillowcases, all the curtains wide open and the sun pouring in thick and sweet as honey. Imagine a hot tub, an artificial womb for your very own backyard, filled with honey, better than shit, devoured by the overwhelming, all-consuming stick of it. Honey is better than shit and maybe that's the lesson in all of this.

Or maybe the lesson is that honey and shit are the same, rich fluids, and what matters is the person devoured by them, like how Abby can lie and it's good, but when Laura lied, it was bad; Abby's world sweet and nourishing to Ralph, Laura's world bitter and toxic. Abby's plan had made Ralph well again, a perfect recipe of her loving design, restoring his mind, bringing him back to life, and now willing his happy, healthy Cal into being, most definitely here now, no question, the precious logic of her brand-new cells organizing undeniably in Abby's honeyed womb. Hello, Cal, I can feel you. I can feel you there. A mother. Finally.

Her first duty as a new mother would be a good, productive Sunday. They'll clean everything up, then maybe go for a walk, get dinner somewhere, snuggle up at the end of the night and watch a movie. Abby will fall asleep because she always does, then later, after Ralph's pulled her up from the couch by both arms, herded her up the steps and into bed, he'll tell her what happened in the rest of the movie like a bedtime story.

With all the sheets and blankets in her arms, piled high, she uses her feet to feel her way down the stairs, along the hallway, through the kitchen, where Ralph is puttering.

She opens the basement door, deposits the sheets in front of the washing machine, which she's surprised to find already hard at work. The keyboard is gone, folded up in a closet somewhere. He's pulled the pillows from the windows, sunshine streaming in, dust scrambling to look busy.]

ABBY: *[Making her way back up the basement steps.]* Hello!

RALPH: *[At the sink, rinsing the suds from a pot, laying it upside down on a tea towel to dry.]* Morning!

ABBY: *[She wraps her arms around his waist, pulls him toward her for a long, comfortable kiss.]* You're feeling better.

RALPH: I am feeling better. *[Reaching for the coffeepot.]* Want some?

[Abby grabs a mug and Ralph fills it up and they sit at the kitchen table, leaned over either side of a month-old crossword like they used to on Sunday mornings. Ralph has already filled in some of the top corner, a few of the usual short, vowel-heavy suspects, épée, era, ire. A wet splotch lands on the page, fills with the slow swirl of blue ink, then another. Ralph is crying.]

ABBY: Oh no, Ralph, no, please, please, you're better now, aren't you? I thought this was over.

RALPH: *[Face soaked in tears.]* Abby, I love you. I—

[A knock on the door. He bites his bottom lip, stands up, makes his way to the front room, and Abby follows him.]

ABBY: Ralph, no.

[He turns to her: pained, confused. With the split-second totality of a car accident, she knows exactly who it is, exactly what's happened, and what she's going to see. He found something this morning, something she'd overlooked, the cooler bag full of blood, a hunk of flesh in the garbage that he found and pulled out and examined, not chicken, obviously not chicken. And she can't blame him really, can she? She can't blame him for doing what he does. Because he's

her Ralphie, he's her god, he's not psychotic anymore and he's not going to leave her, but he is going to turn her in because that's who he is. What she herself restored: the Perfect Good, Ralph the Perfect Good, with the strongest sense of justice, of what's right and wrong and fair and noble. He'll tell them it was all for him, that he's responsible, how it was his psychosis that created the whole disaster. You can have us both, he'll say, a genuine offer, but they won't take it. Just like Randy or Doug or Todd didn't take it. Because Abby, she's the murderer. She's the cannibal. She's the bad one. And Ralph is the one who saves her.

Except when Abby opens the door, it's not the cops. It's Irena, Cud sitting hunched and splay legged at her feet. She tells Abby to hold out her hand, so she does, too tight though, like she's feeding a horse. Irena cups hers underneath Abby's, softens it into the right shape to accept whatever's coming, and Abby feels it, light and small, it bounces a bit, has to settle before it lands.]

IRENA: Cud found it.

[Abby opens her eyes and the old woman's opal eye is staring up at her. She screams and drops it to the ground, where it clanks across the floor, settles a few feet away.

She drops to a squat, level now with Cud's exposed button of a penis, hands over her ears as Ralph bends over, pinches the eye from the ground.]

IRENA: *[Laying a hand on Abby's back.]* Honey, what's wrong?

[Ralph steps forward, Laura's ring between his forefinger and thumb.]

RALPH: *[A mixture of confusion and relief.]* Where did you find this?

IRENA: It was in Cud's bed. No clue where he got it. Maybe snatched it one day when your mother took it off to repot flowers. It's a bit muddy. *[To Abby.]* What did *you* think it was?

ABBY: *[Standing up.]* Honestly I . . . thought it was an eyeball.

IRENA: *[Smiling.]* That's a good omen, seeing an eyeball. Means someone's looking out for you two. *[Turning around, making her way down the steps with Cud at her heels.]* You'll be all right!

[Abby marvels at the bounce of Cud's hindquarters down the porch steps. You fucking rascal. He'd gotten into their yard before, a burrow beneath their shared fence that Irena tried to keep blocked with loose dirt. And a few times through the alley after Laura, arms full with some garish centerpiece, couldn't quite kick the gate hard enough to relatch. Hadn't that happened the day Ralph found his keyboard? The gate yawning open, arousing Ralph's gloomy eye, and Cud's idiotic curiosity. Once Irena and Cud are gone, Abby closes the door. Ralph is still holding the ring, shocked, smiling; he etches a bit of dirt from one of the prongs with his thumbnail. The ring is Abby's reward, she knows, for defeating the demon. For

saving Ralph. Laura a more honorable foe than Abby had given her credit for.

And Ralph so happy, his mother's ring recovered, and his most devoted wife by his side.]

ABBY: *[Stepping toward him, holding her hand out for the ring.]* I thought you'd called the cops.

RALPH: Why? *[He flips her hand, moves the ring up her finger.]*

ABBY: I don't know, I don't—well, what were you going to say then, before Irena came?

RALPH: I was going to say we should make a baby together.

ABBY: *[A hand on her stomach, the spot where Cal was most definitely rooting this time.]* Too late.

ACKNOWLEDGMENTS

Thank you to Rach Crawford and the team at Wolf Literary. Rach, I can't thank you enough. You're a class act, and I'm so lucky to work with you.

Thank you to Caitlin Landuyt and the team at Vintage/Anchor. Caitlin, the way you understood this book, and me, felt like magic—written in the stars, even! Thank you for being the absolute best.

Thank you to Jordan Ginsberg and the team at Strange Light. Jordan, you went out of your way to give me a home in Canada—and what a home! I'm so proud to be a part of it. Thank you, pal.

Thank you to Meaghan McIsaac. Megs, what would I do without you?

Thank you to my precious shrimps for making me a better writer.

And thank you to Paul for absolutely everything. Every single thing. None of this is possible without you. You are my FD. You are my AOQ. And you're right, I should make the coffee more. Thank you, thank you, thank you, thank you, thank you, thank you, thank you . . .